ESSENTIAL MAPS
for the LOST

Essential Maps for the Lost

DEB CALETTI

Simon Pulse

NEW YORK LONDON TORONTO SYDNEY NEW DELHI

SIMON PULSE

An imprint of Simon & Schuster Children's Publishing Division

1230 Avenue of the Americas, New York, New York 10020

First Simon Pulse hardcover edition April 2016

Text copyright © 2016 by Deb Caletti

Jacket photograph copyright © 2016 by Cultura/Masterfile

For information about special discounts for bulk purchases, please contact Simon & Schuster Special Sales at 1-866-506-1949 or business@simonandschuster.com.

The Simon & Schuster Speakers Bureau can bring authors to your live event. For more information or to book an event contact the Simon & Schuster Speakers Bureau at 1-866-248-3049 or visit our website at www.simonspeakers.com.

Jacket designed by Jessica Handelman

Interior designed by Steve Scott

The text of this book was set in Adobe Caslon Pro.

Manufactured in the United States of America

2 4 6 8 10 9 7 5 3 1

This book has been cataloged with the Library of Congress.

ISBN 978-1-4814-1516-3 (hc)

ISBN 978-1-4814-1519-4 (eBook)

For Sam and Nick

Come now, children. . . . You must tell me
all about your adventure. All, all, all about it.
What you thought and what you said, and
how you managed to carry off the whole,
crazy caper.

—E. L. Konigsburg,
From the Mixed-up Files of Mrs. Basil E. Frankweiler

You got a fast car
I want a ticket to anywhere
Maybe we make a deal
Maybe together we can get somewhere. . . .

—Tracy Chapman,
"Fast Car"

ESSENTIAL MAPS
for the LOST

Chapter One

Here's the biggest truth right up front: The way Mads and Billy Youngwolf Floyd met was horrible, hideous. Anyone will agree. You will, too. You'll think it's awful. And then maybe beautiful, which is precisely the point. When the story gets sad and terrible, when there are too many mistakes to count, hang on for the beautiful parts. Wait for them. Have some faith they'll arrive. This is also precisely the point: the hanging on. The waiting, the faith.

Now.

This story starts the same way every morning does, during the spring when Mads meets Billy Youngwolf Floyd. She gets into her swimsuit. She rolls her towel into her bag, sneaks downstairs, careful not to wake up Aunt Claire or Uncle Thomas or Harrison. She edges out the front door, making sure Jinx, their cat, doesn't slip past her on the way out. She starts up Thomas's old truck and heads to the reedy bank of the park by Lake Union.

It is early. So early, only weary insomniacs and people catching airplanes are up. Mads was on the swim team at Apple Valley High; for four years they had practice in the steamy old community pool from five thirty to six thirty a.m., and so this is the routine her body still follows. She loved that hour—it had the peace only habits and rituals can give. There was the snap of goggles and the clean burn of chlorine in the air and toes bent over the edge before the plunge. But now the steamy old community pool is gone from her life for good, and so are all the disciplines that keep you from thinking too much. Swim team, orchestra, AP calculus study group—every one of them is finished since she's graduated, a quarter early, too. Her poor cello seems like the high school boyfriend she was supposed to outgrow but who she still kind of likes.

Look. Here she is, already at the end of the dock, trying to get her courage up. The waters of the lake are much colder than the community pool. The spring Seattle morning is all hues of gray. The sky needs to figure out whether it's in the mood to turn blue or not, like some people Mads knows who will remain nameless. It smells good by the water, that deep kind of murky, and she inhales a few delicious hits of *beneath*.

A row of ducks paddle by. "Good morning, ladies," she says to them. They appear to have serious business. She waits for them to pass because she's a nice person. Then she kneels on the dock, tests the water with her hand. Brr. The waves are choppy and industrious, but not too crazy to swim in. In spite of the gray and the chop, the water is inviting. But it's keeping secrets, for sure.

She dives in.

The cold takes her breath away. Now comes the payoff, though. Not the dramatic rush of water past her head and body, not the shock of immersion, but the thing she swims for, the thing that arrives after the drama and the shock—the calm. The blissful burble of being underwater, being *away*, the moment of otherworldly quiet just before her head rises for air, before the slash of her own strong arms and scissoring legs. Under there, the needs of other people do not press, and the sorrow that's been her most constant companion floats away. Back home, in the water of the community pool, even on the days Coach King's whistle shrieked and her friends shouted above the surface, her own liquid element was like a sweet dream. She could forget those college applications she'd filled out but never sent, and the face of her mother, Catherine Murray, on all those real estate signs, and, too, the way her mother always wept after Mads's father would call from Amsterdam, or else, became furious enough to hide from, like the time she took the kitchen scissors to the family photographs. Swimming is sort of like running away, and Madison Murray has wanted to run away since the first real chance she had, when she was three and got lost on purpose in the Wenatchee Safeway.

And here, in a lake in Seattle, five hours from home, where there is only a kayaker off in the distance and a seaplane taking off against the sky, she is exquisitely elsewhere. She is a fish; she is a mermaid. She lives in a coral castle and wears a seaweed crown. The ticking clock bringing that awful deadline is gone,

gone, carried off on a ripple. Somewhere up there is Harrison's spying, and her own deep sadness, and her profound desire to kidnap baby Ivy. Down here is some centered soul-version of the real her, the one she's not in real life.

Of course, Madison Murray won't feel the same way about any of it, even the water—especially the water—after that day. In some ways, it's a shame. It's a shame, the way you always have to lose stuff to get other stuff.

She swims out until she is parallel with the tall, abandoned smokestacks of Gas Works Park at the other end of the lake. She treads water for a while, floats around on her back and watches the sky, nothing she could ever do when Coach King paced poolside in his blue tracksuit. She has plenty of time. She's in no real hurry. She has come to Seattle to take Otto Hermann's real estate licensing course at the community college, which doesn't start until nine. It goes until noon, and then comes babysitting for the Bellaroses until seven. Back home, she's missing all the end-of-high-school rituals that feel far from her life: the prom and the parties and the ordering of caps and gowns, the group of parents taking photos in her friend Sarah's backyard. But she's not missing other things. She's not missing hauling those open house signs out of the back of her mother's Subaru, setting them up on street corners. Or, even worse: *I can't believe you're going to leave me home alone all weekend. What am I going to do by myself? Fine. Just go.* Or *You better not have some fabulous time in Seattle and not come back like your father.* The flip side of too much guilt is murderous rage, who knew?

She's having fun out here. Houseboats line the perimeter of this lake, and she sees them upside down. They're cheerful and shingled and they rock and sway. There's also a huge upside-down bridge, with tiny upside-down cars. She flips to her stomach. A woman drinks from a cup while standing at the end of a dock as a dog swims laps in front of her. For a second, Madison wishes she were that woman, or maybe even that dog. He looks like he's having the time of his life.

Okay, that's it. She's had enough. She decides to head back. Pancakes sound good. Swimming makes her so hungry.

Now. Think of this—what if she'd stayed out there just a few minutes more? Or what if she'd gone in just a bit sooner? It can make you believe in the Big Guy Upstairs, even if he seems coldhearted a good lot of the time.

She kicks hard, strokes with a power that would've made Coach King cross his arms and smile. She slows when she nears the bank. It's still deep there, but she begins to feel the slip of reeds by her legs. Mads is used to that feeling, the surprising slide of a slick cordy something past her calves, the quick what-was-that of plant or fish. It isn't anything that makes her uneasy. But after this day, even a long time later, *years*, whenever she thinks of this moment, she will shiver.

She ducks her head again. Her eyes are closed. It's best that way near the shore. Sometimes it's safer not to see.

She feels—well, it isn't a thud exactly, more of a bump, a wrong bump. She knows that—the wrongness—straight off. Her head has knocked against something, something that gives and then knocks again, and what comes to mind, oddly enough, is a life raft. A tight, inflated life raft. Is she at the dock already? Is this a float, or a buoy? She has an irrational image—that dog from the dock. She and he are colliding. This is his thick, giving side.

But she knows it isn't a float or a buoy. Certainly, it isn't that dog. Nothing she says to herself is true, of course. You always know when you're lying to yourself. Already she can feel the hair twined around her fingers.

Madison rises to the surface, opens her eyes, and sees her. She is so white she almost glows, and her face is vacant and still as the moon in a night sky, and when Mads shouts and flails, she drags the woman's head under. It feels awful to do that, and so sorry, the details are terrible, but it's the truth of this story. Mads's fingers are caught in the woman's hair, and her face dunks and dunks again until Mads untangles them.

A different person, not Madison but Madison, is making sense of this. She is crying out and flailing, but her brave and functioning self (*who is* she? Mads wonders) is putting the pieces together: the lake, the bridge, despair. Mads's terrified self tries to get away from this horrible, sickening body, while her strong self, hidden before now, has seen a woman. An actual human being. This is the self that understands things about the water—the way it can swallow you, keep you concealed, maybe forever.

This rational one, she is the person who reaches under the woman's arms and grasps her shoulders, while the other

Madison grimaces and pretends not to feel the cold flesh. Mads is now the lifeguard she was from age fourteen on, at the Apple Valley Estates neighborhood pool. She strokes and tows, strokes and tows that body, the way she never had to in the sparkling cement crater filled with shrieking toddlers in water wings and teenagers showing off.

The woman needs help, the terrified Madison thinks, while the other Madison knows this: She is beyond help. Mads hears a strong, clear voice. She realizes it's coming from inside her: *Bring this woman to shore. Bring her and bring yourself to shore.*

She will. She has to, because the woman, the body, will disappear if they don't make this horrifying swim together.

Madison kicks past the waves with her strong legs. The woman's own legs float and bob against her. Soon the two of them are near the bank, where Mads can stand. There are rocks underfoot; slimy, slippery rocks, and Mads is out of breath. The reeds are waist high, and the body skirts along their surface like a sled on ice. The woman has gotten so, so much heavier now. Mads sees that her body is bruised, splotchy, banged-up purple. She faces the woman's eyes, which she's been avoiding. They stare up toward the clouds as if they can look past them. Whatever has brought the woman to this morning's fate—it disgusts Mads. The woman herself does. Mads is angry with her, for causing this. But Mads's heart is sick and heavy with grief, too.

She hauls the top half of the body onto the bank, as far as she can.

And then she screams.

She screams and screams, the way you do in bad dreams, the way she always feared she might have to someday for a different reason, a desperate-mother reason.

Things happen fast after that. Suddenly, there is a man wearing a tie, and a young woman in jogging shorts, and then the spinning lights of a police car, and then an ambulance. A heavy blanket gets tossed onto her shoulders, and in spite of the sun now showing through the clouds, she needs that blanket, because she is freezing. Her own body is doing tricks—shaking out of control, her knee a strange entity that's clacking up and down like drumsticks on a cymbal.

"Maddie! Mads!" It's Aunt Claire, running to where Mads sits on the ground. Somewhere in there Mads called Claire, but she barely remembers that. It feels like she has been there for a week and for a second. There's the *thwack thwack thwack* of a helicopter overhead, announcing tragedy.

Two men carry a stretcher. The body is on it, covered in a deep-green plastic. There's the *slam-slam* of doors.

That's it, Madison thinks. *This nightmare, my relationship with that woman, is over.*

Of course, she is wrong. She is so wrong. Because traumatic events like this, acts like *that*, spread far and go deep. The water soaks delicate layers; the waves crash and crash again. So many people will break and change and stay changed.

Awful, yes?

Yes.

But don't misunderstand. While, true, this is a story about the horrible things people do (the way hurt people hurt people, if you want to get self-helpy about it), it is more importantly about what happens next.

This is what happens next as she rises from that grass with Claire's arm around her: Madison sees that dog. He is back up on the dock now. He shakes himself off on the woman with the coffee cup, who is watching all the commotion. He sits right down, as if hoping for a treat.

See? Life goes forward. More, much more, will happen after this. Things involving maps and books and true love and tragedy, tragedy like you wouldn't believe. But fine things, too. The best ones.

Even if it might not seem so at the time, even if there is something as horrible as a body and police and cold, life has some beautiful surprises up its sleeve, and don't you forget it.

Chapter Two

Sometimes, Billy Youngwolf Floyd plays real life like it's the video game Night Worlds. For example, right then as he's leaving to go to work, Gran gives him a Gaze Attack, which can curse, charm, or even kill. His options? He can avert his eyes from the creature's face, watch her shadow, or track her in a reflective surface. The glass of the coffee table works. It's better than meeting Gran's breaking-and-entering eyes, which are searching around, rifling through his head, hunting for the sign that he'll be the next one to jump off a bridge.

"You okay?" Gran asks.

"Sure."

In the reflection, he sees the old woman staring at him, but he also sees his own face. It surprises him, because it looks young. It *is* young—nineteen. After everything that's happened, though, he feels thirty at least, and some days, fifty-sixty.

"I don't have to send you to a bunch of doctors, too, now do I?" Gran says.

Billy shakes his head. That's one kind of magic he's lost belief in over the years. Doctors or no doctors, medicine or no medicine, his mom was sad and then okay, sad, okay, always coming back to sad. *Sad* sounds almost soft, but it wasn't soft. It was aggressive and mean. It was a gas leak that felt suffocating, when usually they were fine, great, making their way together. He feels bad thinking that: *suffocating.* He shoves the word away, imagines them watching the Hobbit movies together instead. He was still little, so she'd hide his eyes at the gory parts, but he'd peek through her fingers.

"Just as well, because look at all the good those shrinks did." Gran gestures toward the urn on the fireplace.

"Jesus, Gran!"

"What? Do you know how much money I paid those people? She had to have the last word. She always did."

"Gran, come on." She's lucky she's old, or she'd be on her ass! He used to think his mom was too sensitive about things Gran said, and he didn't get why Mom just couldn't move past the stuff from her childhood, stuff she told him about, like how Gran would yank her head backward by her ponytail when she didn't listen, or practically rip her arm from her socket when she asked for something in a store, or how when she was six, she waited for Gran for hours after school, crying and scared, because Gran wanted to teach her a lesson about being late. But shit, his mom was right. Gran won't even give her a break now that she's dead.

"'Come on'? Come on, what?"

"*You're* the crazy one. You should go." He makes it sound like a joke, because Gran can't stand being criticized. No one fucks with her. Depression doesn't even fuck with her. *Stop sitting around feeling sorry for yourself,* was what she used to say, like Mom's sadness was some kind of moral failure. Can you imagine being depressed and then being judged for being depressed? Who's crazier, anyway: people who struggle honestly, or the people who act like they never do?

"I worry about you, is all, Buzz."

His nickname plus Gran's small, tired eyes give him a weird stabbing in his heart. You know, a love stab. He instantly regrets his mean thoughts. She's about the only one he has left in the world. Gaze Attacks—they doubly affect ethereal creatures, even if that's a shitty, unfair rule. If Billy is anything lately, he's an ethereal creature. They can exist on the material plane, but everything there is gray and dim and ghostly. Only a magic missile can break through their walls. The most important thing about them, though, is that they do not fall.

"Don't worry. I'm okay."

Of course he's not okay. He's coping better, but the storm system still sits off the coast, waiting for the right temperature or unstable airflow. He watched that in a show about cyclones. It was more interesting than you'd think.

He gives Gran a hug good-bye. He can't stand to be an asshole. When he grabs his keys, Gran's old dog, Ginger, gets excited and hops around. "I gotta go. Sorry, Ging, you've got to stay and babysit the old woman."

"Never mind, smart aleck. See you later."

"See you."

He's taking off a little early, because there's someone he's got to pick up before work. He leaves Gran's houseboat and walks up the ramp that connects the dock to the parking lot, and he gets in his mother's black truck. The SUV has seen better days, but it's still fast. It has *get-up-and-go*, as his mom used to say. She used to love that truck. *A car is your own little capsule of freedom*, she said. He wanted a car of his own, but he didn't want it this way. He'd been saving up, and now he just has a bunch of money. It isn't have-to money anymore. It could be dream-money. If he tells anybody his dream, they'll think he's nuts. They probably think he's nuts anyway, after what his mother did a couple of months ago, but dreams seem extra important when life as you know it can be gone in a second.

Her radio station comes on. That station hurts his stomach. He isn't going to change it, though. He longs for more of anything she loved. He already knows all the lines of the Eagles songs, and the Doobie Brothers and Simon and Garfunkel ones, all the la's and oh's of crazy old nights and bridges and black water. He pictures her singing to the radio with the windows rolled down. He used to pretend it was bad singing, and plug his ears and make a face, but it secretly made him happy, seeing her just being herself like that. She'd say, *I know, it's too beautiful to stand*, and sing louder.

It's a good memory. Still, he gets so mad, driving that car.

Once, he pounded the steering wheel and screamed that one word, the only word, over and over. *Why.* But he feels close to her here. The her that was her real self. He slept in the car one night, but it worried Gran when she woke up and he wasn't in his bed.

Billy pulls out of the lot. He drives past the Fremont troll and goes up the hill, heads to his and his mom's old neighborhood. There's a FOR RENT sign on the house, he sees. Jesus! He barely just got their stuff out of it! His stomach clenches up again. He feels sick. It's a cross between a throw-up feeling and a crushed-soul feeling. God, he hates that! *Focus,* he tells himself. He has a job to do. That asshole Mr. Woods always lets Lulu out right around then. It's going to be easy, as long as Lulu doesn't flinch and hide at his outstretched hand. That's what happens to them after a while.

He parks in his old driveway. If Mr. Woods spies the car, he'll think Billy is just bawling his eyes out inside or something. He spots Lulu cowering in the corner of the garden. No problem.

Billy gets out. And that's when he sees her. Sees her again. That girl, parked on his street in that truck. The truck needs paint, bad. It has big bald spots of primer. Come on, get it fixed up! A truck like that deserves some respect. He knows shit about cars, but he knows that much.

The girl—her hair is shiny. He noticed this before. She has very white teeth; he can see them even from that distance. She's the kind of girl who smells good. She's all scrunched down, pretending she's doing something innocent, like checking her phone. What *is* she doing there? He's seen her before, the day he moved his and his mom's junk out of the house.

Oh, yeah.

Oh, yeah, of course. You know why she's probably there? That guy, a few houses down. It's got to be. Billy forgot all about him. Some senior; goes to one of the private schools. Blanchet? One of those Catholic ones. A real douchebag. Girls like that always have a thing for boys like him. He probably hurt her, just as she always suspected he might, and now, after proving her right about herself, she can't let him go. This is how it plays. He knows that particular story too well.

J.T., he suddenly recalls. J.T. Jones. What is it about assholes with initials instead of names?

The girl is going to be a problem, though. Usually, the idea is, make it natural, do this in the broad daylight, but not when you have a witness. He's going to have to act natural, is all. He'll use an Ability Modifier from Night Worlds, probably Charisma. He'll make her think this is the most regular thing ever. He'll be calm, smooth, decisive.

His heart is beating a hundred miles an hour, but ignore that. He could be in a movie, he thinks, 'cause he's precise as a laser, cool as a blade. Lulu is one of those cute little white dogs, so she's an easy one. He scoops her up in one clean arc. He sprints like a sharp breeze. He doesn't even look at the girl. What girl? Here's hoping she moves on to a better guy and forgets that douchebag once and for all.

Lulu is excellent in the car. She turns a circle on the passenger seat and falls asleep, as if she can finally rest. Here's hoping she moves on to a better guy and forgets that douchebag once and for all.

Billy pulls into work. Heartland Rescue is noisy as hell and stinks a lot less than you'd think. He loves this fucking place with all his heart. He carries Lulu under his arm and then sets her on the counter.

"Billy," Jane Grace says, and runs her hand through her short hair. "Not again."

"I don't know what you're talking about," Billy says.

"Where did you get this dog?"

"Found it. Lost. Walking around lost." Lulu's tags are in the pocket of his jeans.

"Lost."

"Uh-huh."

"Just walking around lost."

"That's right."

"Okay." She sighs. "Fine. What should we call her, do you think?"

Heartland Rescue always names their animals, and never ever puts them to sleep.

"She looks like a Lulu to me," Billy Youngwolf Floyd says, and then Lulu winks at him, the way dogs do sometimes. He swears it wasn't an accident. He knows a real wink when he sees one.

Chapter Three

Mads wants to strangle the kid. "Harrison, for God's sake. Stop following me. Find something to do. Don't you have school?"

"Half-day conference schedule till we're done."

"Well, go build a fort or something. Make a rocket with, I don't know, sticks."

"Mom said to keep an eye on you."

Harrison's mouth is still purple from a Popsicle he ate yesterday. He's a weird boy. Sweet, but weird. His eyes are too big for his face behind those glasses. His best friend, Avery, has the same ones. When Avery comes over and they sit on the couch watching TV, they look like a pair of owls on a tree branch. Harrison is the kind of kid you have to try to like until you do. Now Madison sometimes feels a surprising gust of love for him that makes her heart nearly burst.

"She just meant it casually. It's something people say. She didn't mean it was your *job*."

"Can I come?"

"Harrison, since when do they let ten-year-olds go to community college?"

She gets in and slams the door of Uncle Thomas's truck, and then feels bad. Mads can't stand to be unkind. She rolls down the window. "Hey, Smurf. Rematch later? Yahtzee champions don't stay Yahtzee champions for long. Not with this lethal weapon." She blows a puff of luck onto her clenched fist, shakes a pair of imaginary dice. "Yeah, man! Five sixes."

He grins, and Mads heads out. Thomas's truck sounds like a jet plane. No one is even supposed to be driving the thing yet. It's Thomas's project, and only the unexpected appearance of his niece changed that plan. The truck still has big splotches of silver-gray primer, from where he sanded off the paint, prepping it for a new coat. You wouldn't exactly call that truck incognito. Which'll be a problem when she steals the Bellarose baby. The law will spot her and Ivy in a flat second in that thing.

She drives across the 520 Bridge and takes the turnoff for Bellevue Community College. Otto Hermann will be there already, his white hair sticking out from his head in curled springs of who-cares. Good for it! Wouldn't it be fantastic, not to care? Otto Hermann probably even slurps his coffee with that accent, too. *Ve vill now dizcuss zuh vine art of zuh contrakt.* If you don't understand him, that's your problem. Otto Hermann is who he is. How about a few lectures on *that*?

She knows what she'll see when she arrives on campus.

18

People her age, finishing up spring quarter in all those enticing classrooms. Many people do not put the words *enticing* and *classroom* together, but she does. Dream of her dreams (don't judge; you don't judge a person's dream) is to be taking English classes, studying books, stories, poems, the stuff of life, maybe one day teaching that same stuff to others, like passing on the secrets of the universe.

But this will not happen. She is destined (*doomed*) to be in Otto Hermann's tired room, where the fluorescent lights twitch, and where the students are mostly older women who aren't wearing wedding rings anymore. There are a few men. One's name is Arthur. He still wears a watch. There's a young guy who reads books with titles like *Selling Your Way to Your First Million.* This is not college-college, but Continuing Education. Continuing Education is a good name for life in general, Mads thinks.

Here are the necessary details: After she finishes both Washington Real Estate Fundamentals and Real Estate Practices, Mads will take her licensing exam. She is in Seattle for this one purpose, to take this particular course, which is packed into two quarters and completed by summer's end. This is where they promise a "convenient and expedient" experience, and where 97.5 percent of graduates pass the licensing exam on the first try.

They are, after all, in a hurry. Speed is of the essence. Her mother forgets to return client calls, and important inspection deadlines are getting overlooked, and there was even that near miss with the Huntingtons' lawsuit, when the couple almost lost their fat wad of earnest money, thanks to Catherine Murray's lack of attention. Her mother needs her. Needs her *now*. Or, as she's told Mads more than once, *It'll probably all go under without your help, not that it matters.*

It matters. The business is her mother's livelihood. What would happen if she lost it? Disaster, that's what. Here is the ticking clock: The partnership papers were drawn up sometime in Madison's junior year, ready to be signed the minute she passed the licensing exam. The cap is off the pen. Feet are impatiently tapping; fingertips are drumming on tabletops. Mads graduated early for this. She ditched her friends in what felt like the middle of the party. Last year at the attorney's office, the lawyer, Mr. Knightley, didn't listen to Mads's (admittedly muted) protests. He said things to Mads like *You can make a real difference here* and *What would your mom do without you*, and thus sealed Mads's fate.

The problem is—and Mads would never confess this to anyone, even now consider this a whisper, consider it something you can barely hear—the classes, the papers, the signature . . . They fill her with a despair she senses she is no match for. Ever since she and her mother sat across from Mr. Knightley at his desk, a long shadow of sorrow has slipped over her like an eclipse. When people notice the half-moons under her eyes (sorrow keeps you awake), or the slow weightiness in her step (sorrow grabs your ankles), they say things like *Cheer up!* And *Look on the bright side!* These words are only sweet flowers that the dark ogre of depression eats in one bite.

She tries the "pep talk" (awful, awful, utterly useless phrase) on herself, too. Who, after all, is handed a business right out of high school? A mostly-paying-the-bills business! She could be set up for life! And she and her mom get along great, they do! Maybe later, she could try something different. Even her father, who is pissed she's not going to college, has occasionally said *It's not the worst thing, I guess* and *It will give you work experience, anyway.* Mads is not ungrateful. (She hates that word. Even saying *ungrateful* makes her feel ungrateful.) It's just that the idea of it all is like being in one of those horrible stories where people are buried alive. There's the crush of earth and the last squeak of oxygen. Still. She can't say no. You might not understand this, but *she can't say no.* Her mother would be furious. And she can't let her down. The guilt would kill Mads. She's the kind of person guilt could kill. It'd barely have to try.

Either way, her own self will be swallowed up, gone. Already, she is slowly disappearing.

As she drives to school, her required textbook, *Mastering Real Estate Principles*, 7th Edition, sits on the seat beside her in Thomas's truck. She has her completed homework assignment on valuation, too, which is tucked inside.

But something strange happens as they crest the hill where the school sits. It's as if Thomas's truck has a mind of its own. It speeds right on past the campus. The campus shoots by like

Harrison on his bike, when he pedals so fast the wheels blur. Thomas's truck screeches a loop. It goes straight back over 520, into Seattle. Mads attempts to talk some sense into it, but that truck is having none of it. She may be confused and despairing, but that truck isn't. It knows exactly where it wants to go.

The night of that horrible swim a few months ago, the woman was oh-so-briefly on the news. There was a small article in the *Seattle Times* the next day, as well, with a picture of the park. Half of Mads was in it—her arm, her leg, the right side of her face—in the distance. And then, after that, there was nothing. Nothing! The story was over. How could that be? Shouldn't there have been *more*? Shouldn't there have been *why*? Shouldn't everyone know the woman's past and what happened to the people in her life *after*? How could people just go on as if nothing monumental had occurred? Mads realized then how often she herself had gone on, after hearing news like that. How she'd just got up and made some popcorn, or changed the channel, or went back to her biology assignment.

But something important was revealed, even in the brevity. From KING 5 news at five, Madison learned this: Her name was (is?) Anna Youngwolf Floyd. And she jumped off the Aurora Bridge.

Since then—the body, the name, the jump—Mads sees Anna Youngwolf Floyd every time she shuts her eyes. No, wrong. She doesn't even need to shut them to see her. Anna is just with Mads all the time now. She is not a ghost who bangs doors and flutters curtains. She is just a thought that won't leave. She is a gnawing question. This is the most insistent kind of ghost of all.

"What is that, Mads?" Claire asked late one night, not long after the swim. Well, sure, she'd want to know, especially after Mads slammed the lid of her laptop down so she wouldn't see.

"I'm sorry. Am I keeping you awake?"

"It's late, honey," Claire said. She leaned against the doorjamb of Mads's room. "Really late. It's, what, past one?"

"I'm done now. Homework," she lied. She's a terrible liar.

"Homework, huh? You're on that thing all hours lately. Mads, was that her picture? That woman?"

Mads said nothing. Aunt Claire didn't deserve to be deceived, anyway. She's a nice person, same as Mads. She does yoga. She's the nice sort of yoga person, not the superior kind of yoga person. She wears yoga person skirts, and yoga person woven things, and she has longish, rust-colored hair. She tries to feed Harrison organic stuff, which is thankfully, what a relief, balanced out when Thomas sneaks him Doritos. Mads feels bad that Claire has gotten stuck with her all spring and summer. Thomas probably felt obliged, given that his brother, Mads's father, ditched them to work in Amsterdam, fleeing Mads's mother like she was the wreckage of a burning plane.

Aunt Claire sighed. She shook her head. "This isn't healthy," she said finally. "I know what you've been doing all these hours on the computer, Mads. Trying to look her up . . .

And you're not sleeping. Not eating . . . This whole thing . . . The other day, when you heard the water running—that's a *flashback*, Mads."

"I'm going to go brush my teeth," Mads said.

"She was just a woman. Probably mentally ill, you know that, right? There aren't always real explanations when people do stuff like that. Except that one."

"I know."

"If mental illness made sense . . ."

Mads waited. She hoped and hoped Claire would finish, because it might give her some sort of an answer. *Oh, please,* she thought. *Come on, Claire!* But Claire just waved her arms a little, luckless branches riding a sudden wind.

"Are you sure you wouldn't like to go see someone? A therapist? I don't want to keep bugging you about it, but I really think it might be helpful. I mean, you were already struggling, you know, um . . . depressed? And now this. Not to put a label on you, or anything! I mean, after something like that, it might all just be . . . too much, right? An expert seems important."

Mads snorted. She'd lost belief in that kind of thing a long time ago. Still, Claire and Thomas had been asking her this daily, watching her endlessly, looking for signs that she might be the one to jump off a bridge next. Even her mom was suggesting that Mads come home for *support*.

"Do you know how many psychologists and psychiatrists and other ists Mom has been to?"

"You're not her."

God. She hoped not. It sounded unkind, and she didn't even want to *think* unkind, but wow. That idea could make a person nervous. She loves her mother. Her mom is sometimes her best friend, the way they talk and hang out and joke; the way she's there for Mads like no one else. But Mads also has certain permanent images that knock-knock-knock. The constant, cruel jabs at her father when he still lived with them. The rages that cause Mads to flee to her room. The inability to manage, which Mads must manage. "I know."

"And you don't have to *become* her." Aunt Claire seemed angry. She shoved her hands down into her robe pockets. She's seen years of stuff she thinks is wrong, and she's had it with her sister-in-law. Mads should live her own life, Claire has told her. Mads shouldn't be the nurse or the mother or the best friend.

"Okay."

"All this time on the computer . . ."

"I'm just curious," Mads said.

Aunt Claire tipped her head and scrunched her nose, an all-purpose face that covered a lot of territory. *If you're just curious*, the face said, *you shouldn't be. But you're not just curious.*

And it's true. Mads is beyond curiosity. She is in need. Dire, downright *need*. She needs to understand just how sad a person has to be to do something like that. Not able to even eat scrambled eggs sad? Ex-husband in Amsterdam sad? Running off in the middle of an open house sad?

Or worse. Returning to Apple Valley forever sad? A signature that decides your whole life sad? Murray & Murray Realtors, the business cards already printed up and waiting sad? Hearing Suzanne and Carl Bellarose fight in the driveway as baby Ivy looks on with worried eyes sad? Because she is clearly this sad, this sad and more, and she has been for what already feels like a long, long time.

Every night since the body in the water (no, that, too, is a lie—more than that, every day and every night, many times a day), Mads has looked at the satellite image of the bridge. She zooms in, click, click, click. Anna Youngwolf Floyd would have had to walk up those stairs, right there. She would have stepped onto that narrow grating. There is the cement wall she would have put one leg over. What was she thinking, just before she lifted her second leg? On the satellite image, Mads sees the view she had. Worse, she sees the view she herself might have.

The thing is, there were two bodies in the water that day, hers and Anna Youngwolf Floyd's. What keeps Mads up at night, what keeps her on the computer trying to find out more, more, more, is the question, the big question, the only question much of the time: *why*. The *why* feels like something about to happen. The *why* is a mystery that might lead to a way out. Or else, to the last locked door.

Thomas's truck leaves the community college in the dust and heads away like it has an automotive mission. Mads rolls down the windows, and the breeze ruffles the bits of her homework that stick out from *Mastering Real Estate Principles*, 7th Edition. The truck heads to a place Mads has been before. Once she had Anna's name, the address was easy to find. Now she parks across the street from the house, in the spot where she usually studies it. She visualizes the layout, as always. Standard Seattle Craftsman bungalow: living room in front, kitchen in back, bedrooms upstairs. She'll say . . . two bedrooms. Three. Bathrooms need updating, probably. One fireplace; creepy unfinished basement where the laundry room is, she'll bet. She pictures Anna Youngwolf Floyd down there, tossing a load into the washing machine. At least, Mads pictures Anna as she was in the 1976 La Conner High School yearbook photo Mads found online. Anna had long, straight dark hair parted on the side, and she was wearing the usual dreamy-but-looking-toward-the-future 1 x 1 inch yearbook expression (as well as a white shirt with a collar big enough for liftoff). She was next to Steve Yepa, who had a grown-man moustache and was sporting a suit and tie, and Gene Yu, whose bouffy hair could have its own moons and orbit the sun.

Anna is about to pour the liquid soap into the washer of Mads's imagination when a black SUV drives up. Her heart lurches, and she scooches down in her seat, fast. She starts to sweat. She's seen that truck here twice before. The first time, a mattress was tied to the top, and the back was stuffed with boxes. The second time was very late at night. She likes this place best at late hours, when she can park in the dark space between streetlamps and gaze at the still, secretive house under the light of the moon. But that time, this same SUV had been in the driveway. And she swore someone was in it, sleeping in there, maybe. At least she thought she saw the truck rock slightly, and then she'd gotten out of there, fast.

Well, now she's been caught. Definitely caught. The truck drives right past Thomas's. She acts like she's there with good reason, punches nonsense into her phone, pretends to talk while sneaking glances. She may look small and cringing right then, but inside—here's the funny thing—there's an odd boldness rising. It fills her like some magical, powerful, pink-smoke summons. It's some kind of wish and wanting and it feels amazing. She wants to see who that truck belongs to. She wants to see a living connection, a face, a moving body. Someone who is proof that Anna Youngwolf Floyd was a real human being. Mads is scared to see what she might find, though. If it makes her feel worse than she does already, this will likely be a mistake.

Okay. It's a boy. He's getting out. Is this the son? Is this the *William* mentioned in the obituary? She pictured him older for some reason, but he's about her age. He has Anna's dark hair; it's thick, but not straight like Anna's. It goes a little wild around his face. He's thin as a new tree, and his jeans ride his hips in a way that says he doesn't give a flying fuck.

He runs his hand through his hair. If Mads had hair like that, she'd do the same thing all day long, it'd feel so good. He looks at her then, right straight-on at her, and she says, into her phone she says, "Yes, I'm so sorry I can't meet you because something's come up and a train is coming at me right now on a track," so her lips will move.

He seems nervous. His eyes are darting around like a bank robber's. Mads narrows her own eyes to see better, tries to locate the signs of devastation in him. What is his life like now? He has his mother's nose, too, she notices. It's a slightly hooked nose. But why is he shooting weird glances over to the neighbor's yard and pacing around by his truck? The house, his house, his mother's house—it's an afterthought. No, it's just an after. Not even a thought.

His face looks determined. So determined that a different curiosity stirs in Mads. He saunters across their old yard. Truly, this is the word, *saunter*—his thumbs are all casual in his pockets. He's trying really hard to look like he's cool as anything. But then he trips over an old garden hose left on their lawn. When he stumbles back up, he presses his palms to the legs of his jeans as if they sting. Now he runs like hell. The run is all guilty bumbling. He unlatches his neighbor's gate and scoops up a little white dog and bolts back to his truck with one shoelace untied. He screeches and swerves down the street like an awkward firefighter off to save a family in a burning building.

Mads is stunned. Her mouth may even be open a little. She has no idea what she just witnessed. She tosses her phone over to the passenger seat, where it sits with *Mastering Real*

Estate Principles, 7th Edition. She puts her hand to her heart to see if it's working, because it feels changed enough to wonder. The neighbor's gate is flung wide, and she can see how Anna's old garden hose, so recently moved, has branded a large snaking *S* onto the lawn. The house looks different to her now. It doesn't seem sad and finished. It is still breathing.

Chapter Four

It's stupid, and it looks stupid, too, he knows, but Billy puts his arm over the map when Amy skips down the steps of Heartland Rescue where he sits. It's what he used to do in the third grade when that bully, Devon Wilson, would cheat off his spelling test.

Amy isn't a bully but she's something close. Billy's known her since junior high, when he and his mom moved from La Conner to Seattle to be closer to Gran after that asshole Powell left them. Mom needed someone besides him, even if Gran greeted her with a *What did I tell you?* and a *Why do you keep trying to get things from people you will never get?* On his first day at Eckstein, Amy and the blond girls (they weren't all blond, but that's how he thinks of them) teased him about his name and about that old shirt of his father's he'd decided to wear. Grateful Dead. It's a pretty sicko name when you think about it. His mother might be grateful now, but who knows for sure. He sure as hell isn't. He'd always thought of it as his lucky shirt, though, and fuck 'em, even after that, he still would.

"Whatcha got, Wolfie?" Amy nudges his leg with her toe. She started being friendly to him sometime in their sopho-more year. Now they both work at Heartland Rescue. Amy wants to become a veterinarian, so she takes classes at the U and hangs around Dr. Mukherjee when he comes in, but she still has to pick up shit like everyone else. She'll go to veteri-nary school next, but she'll never be the type of veterinarian Billy would ever take his dog to. He likes to think he has the true Seeing Spell, where you can cut through illusions to tell what a creature actually is.

"Nothing much," he says.

"Looks like a map."

"Yeah."

"Wow," she says. "That's it? 'Yeah'? You know, if you don't let people in, they can't be there for you."

"I let people in."

"Whatever." You know what? The less attention he gives her, the more she wants him. He doesn't get this. It's a mys-tery. She stomps off to her car. Now she'll probably go to some restaurant and spend twenty bucks on a lunch she'll barely eat. Even Jane Grace doesn't let Amy *in*. If anyone has the true Seeing Spell, it's Jane. Billy's noticed that Jane only lets Amy deal with the flighty, small dogs, not any of the more sensitive ones like Jasper or Zeke. Not any that have soulful eyes.

People can be mean same as dogs can be mean—there are

the ones that have always been that way and will always stay that way because that's how they came. And then there are the ones that get mean after they're treated mean. He feels bad for those dogs, but truth is, they can rip your face off, same as the others.

You need theories about people and dogs and most other things when you have a mother who was a bridge jumper. He is trying out the phrase: *a bridge jumper*. It sounds weirdly casual and purposefully cruel, but then it makes the knife twist. His stomach gets that feeling again. In comes the horrible rush of love and longing and hatred and *why* and *you left me*. Fuck!

Go back to the map! He does. He's so full of self-hatred and hatred for his mother that he could gouge his own eyes out. He feels so bad right then.

But as he spreads the map flat once more, the Big Guy Upstairs (or fate, or the universe, or whatever you believe in—it's helpful to believe in something) is moving the pieces around. Billy doesn't know it, but some stuff is about to happen. Like, right about. Stuff always happens, whether a day from now or years, stuff that will make a person glad to be alive, if you can somehow just ride through the self-hatred and the gouging and the bad. Here he is, feeling like shit, sitting on a cement step with a stupid map on his knee, and big plans are in the works. Tick, tick, fate looks at its watch and smiles. Billy's clueless. Pretty much most of the time, this is how it works.

The map has a lot of creases, even if he's tried to be careful to fold it along its original lines. If he concentrates hard enough, it's like he's inside the actual museum just by looking at it. The asshole doctor in his head reminds him that the video games and the map and the book are just places to escape, but so what? Who cares? He already knows that! He's not stupid. Give a guy a break! They're lucky he isn't drinking his head off or shooting up drugs. He's not sure who "they" are, but they are!

He moves his finger from the entry of the American Wing to Arms and Armor. In the book where the map comes from, Jamie picks Renaissance art to study instead of Arms and Armor like his sister, Claudia, guesses he will. But Billy would definitely pick Arms and Armor. He looked it up online to see the actual pictures. Those long, mighty swords, those chest plates of steel—he can't imagine walking around with so much stuff on, he doesn't even like wearing a coat, but no one could get to you behind all that iron.

Amy's not out of the parking lot yet. She pulls up next to the steps in her daddy's old BMW, rolls down her window, and gives it one more try. His friend Alex keeps saying, *She wants to blow you*, but Billy just tells him to shut up.

"I could bring you a sandwich," Amy says, leaning her head out. She makes her voice all breathy. She does that a lot, and she totters around on heels and shows off her boobs and bare stretches of stomach. It reminds him of those baboons he saw on that nature show, who always flash their red asses. (He was just flipping past. He only watched maybe a half hour.)

"Nah," he says. His cardboard cup from Java Jive sits next to him. He isn't all that hungry lately anyway.

"Never mind," Amy says. "Just forget it." She rolls up her window, mad. Her tires actually scream out of there.

Jane props the door open with one foot. "Wow. What was that about?" Billy doesn't answer. Jasper and Bodhi and Olive and Runt race outside, yanking Jane out, too. The leashes aren't twisted up yet, but they will be soon. She holds them in one fist, and that's just asking for trouble.

Within two seconds, Bodhi lifts his leg on a tall weed, and Olive is sniffing Jasper's butt, and Runt starts barking his head off at a passing car. Runt is no runt—he's a Bernese mountain dog. He was turned in after someone found him sitting at a bus stop near Highway 99, as if he'd had enough of a bad situation and was moving on.

"I was hoping you'd take these guys for a walk," Jane shouts over Runt.

"Sure."

Billy stands, folds the map up, and puts it in his back pocket. He reaches for the leashes, sorts them out. Runt and Olive go on one side, Jasper and Bodhi on the other. He gives Runt's leash a firm but gentle tug, which is dog language for *knock it off*. Runt listens. Still, he eyes the back end of that car like it better not forget who's boss.

"Get out of here for a while," Jane says.

"Sounds good."

"Did I ever tell you I went there?"

"Where?"

"The museum. The Metropolitan Museum of Art."

"You did?"

"Yeah. Dave and me. We took a trip to New York for our twenty-fifth." Jane and Dave have been married forever, since they were his age. They don't act like it, though. Dave will pinch her butt, and she always greets him with *Hey, handsome* whenever he comes by the shelter. Sometimes, it's old people kissing, which is disgusting, but also kind of nice. After his father and Powell and a few losers in between, he thinks Jane and Dave are like the golden tiger or albino crocodile in Night Worlds—singular and rare animals. If you had a life like that, it might be better than having a million dollars.

"Cool."

"We were there a whole day and it wasn't enough. We skipped the Empire State Building so we could go back. You could spend weeks in that place."

"Yeah."

"You've got to go."

"I'm going to."

"I mean, really. One day you ought to decide to just do it. Get in the car and go. Ditch this place."

He grins. "Someday." It's his dream, but then there's the reality. He can't just take off and leave Gran. And the dogs need him. Zeke, and even crazy Bodhi, and now Lulu, too. But Jasper, especially. And then there's Casper. No way he can leave him right now. He can't do anything until he finds a way to save Casper from that bastard H. Bergman.

"Someday *soon*."

"Yeah."

"A change of scene would do you good. I think that's the line of some song."

If he doesn't start walking, Runt's going to pull his arm off. Jasper has already had enough of the other dogs, Billy can tell. Jas is like a professor stuck with a bunch of inmates. The dog decides to sit and ignore them. He lifts his nose and sniffs all the scents of summer coming. That's the kind of guy he is. That tells you everything you need to know about him, right there. Runt, on the other hand—Runt's the muscly dude leading the barbarian army.

Billy crushes his cup in his hand, tosses it into the trash can by the steps. He heads out of the lot, then looks over his shoulder and calls to Jane. "You trying to get rid of me?"

"I'd only keep you forever if I could," she calls back.

Certain people are your people, that's all. That's one thing he's sure of.

Walking the dogs is Billy's favorite thing. He especially likes how their heads bob as they trot along. They look so happy and serious at the same time. There are a lot of stops to pee. A tall grass clump, bushes, piles of bricks, whatever, they all have to be marked, like posting comments online. Every single dog, they all need their pee-voice heard. No one wants to be forgotten, even the most polite of dogs like Jasper. *We are here*, they each have to say.

Bodhi's black lips are pulled back in a smile, and Runt's big tongue hangs out. Olive has the shortest legs, so the poor girl pretty much runs the whole way.

Billy admires Jasper's coat, which is thick and healthy now. The dog's nose is still working hard, taking in every fabulous second from the garbage cans at the Mykonos restaurant to the deep-water-and-goose-shit-and-who-knows-what-else of the ship canal. Billy feels like a proud dad when it comes to Jasper. When Billy snatched him from the yard with the junk pile, Jasper had been chained up so long that his fur was gone in big patches. For a while, he walked all hunched, too, a slave crouch from chains, but now his neck is tall and straight. It pisses Billy off so bad. It makes him fucking furious. He doesn't get it, he just doesn't get it, and he never will. Why would you keep someone from leaving you, and then treat them brutally? Power, control? Was the cruelty some bloodletting leech (nature channel, but, Jesus, never mind that now), sucking out some dark wound? God.

He walks all the way down Canal Street. Bikers zip past; a jogger or two or three huff by. He arrives at the famous Seattle landmark, the one on all the postcards, the group of statue people who look like they're waiting for a bus. They're always decorated—wearing hats or grass skirts and leis, draped with streamers or balloons. Right then, they're in swimsuits (the woman with the iron shopping bag is wearing a bikini), and they all hold a sign that reads BON VOYAGE, JACKIE!

It's a hub; all nearby streets converge here. A decision has to be made. Cross the Fremont Bridge, or not? This is not a small decision for Billy. Not since his mother did what she did. If you walk or drive over the Fremont Bridge, you have a perfect view of the sister bridge beside it. It's five times the size and five times the height of Fremont. Hundreds of people have jumped off the Aurora Bridge, and his mother was one of them. It looks evil.

Where he lives—it's hard to avoid that thing. Gran lives in the houseboats along Westlake, which is in the bridge's shadow, and their old house and Heartland Rescue are right nearby. If you want to go anywhere, there it is. What does it matter, which way he goes? Because, really. Even if he doesn't actually see it, it's everywhere, all the time. It's in his dreams, and in a flash of dark hair in a passing car, and it's in certain smells (Ivory soap, barbecue sauce, the singe of a candle going out). Now he feels the rise of courage and *Fuck it!* He will stare right into the mean, steely face of it.

He takes his crew onto the wide, generous sidewalk next to the Fremont Bridge's blue towers and helpful bike lane. It's a friendly bridge compared to that other one, which is high, fast, and ugly. A guy strolls past him with a backpack slung over one shoulder. Cars and trucks ba-bamp over metal plates. It's loud as hell here, too. It smells like city—onions frying and piss and car exhaust. Even on this smaller bridge, the water is so far down. He can see the same shoreline she must have seen, just before, with the houseboats below. The view is horrible and it's sacred. He never wants to see it again, and he wishes he could see it every second.

He stares that other bridge down. He needs to know he can look right at it and take it. Some days, he can take it. A girl on a bike calls, "On your right," and the walkway gets too crowded for him plus all the dogs, so he turns back.

He and the dogs are a well-oiled machine. If Amy or Lee or any of the interns tries to walk more than two dogs at once, it's a shit show, let alone in a place like this. But the five of them, hell, they're like ballroom dancers. They're a flock of birds flying in a V, with him as their leader. They're a . . . Wait. What? His heart almost stops.

At the small park at the foot of the bridge he sees that truck again. He'd know it anywhere. He recognizes those silvery bald patches, and the big, sturdy hood that looks like a friendly face with surprised eyes. It's that girl. The one who was dumped by J.T. Jones.

What happens next—he doesn't have words for it. He's taken up, as if struck by a spell. A Fear Spell, likely, where an invisible cone of terror causes a living creature to panic, unless it succeeds in making a save. He's terrified, all right. Panic has its hairy hands out. He has no reason to suspect what he does, none at all, no one even jumps from this bridge, but she is looking up at it, right at where he's been standing, and he is sure, *sure*, he knows what she is thinking. The asshole dumped her, all right, and now look.

He starts to run. He flies around the corner of the stair

rail and down the steps. She is heading toward him, heading *up*. The dogs feel his fear and energy and start to bark as they run beside him. They are a team of speeding superheroes. They need to stop her. His insides *insist*.

"No!" he yells. "Please, no!"

He'll be so glad later, *so* glad, that with the roar of engines and clatter of steel, you can't hear a damn thing down there.

Chapter Five

Suzanne Bellarose cries. Actually, literally *cries*, with one percussion hit of a sob. "How can I stay with him when he's always taking off?" She blows her nose into a paper towel that has seen better days and tosses it (ick) onto the kitchen table. There's a bunch of bills on there, too, and another unopened box from Amazon. She gets at least one a day. Mads is always at their house when the mailman comes. The packages pile up; the smiles on the sides of the boxes stack up against each other.

"It's good you're meeting Denise for lunch," Mads says. She's playing counselor. She's gotten good at that. If you've gotten good at playing counselor, you probably need one yourself.

"Denise doesn't understand. Denise has perfect Ben. And perfect Sophia. Do you know Sophia is walking already? She's not even ten months. *God.*"

Mads wants to cup her hands over Ivy's ears. She wishes for the millionth time that she could take Ivy away from here. The baby sits in her high chair, a handful of Cheerios spread out on the tray. One plump hand hovers over them, but she's lost interest. Her blue eyes are wide, fixed on her mother's face. There's a single crease of worry between her brows, and her little rosebud mouth is half open, suspended between squall-or-not.

"Oh, look, Suzanne. It's almost twelve thirty."

"Great. Just great. Now I'm going to be late. Denise is always on time, of course." Suzanne shoves her chair back, stomps up the stairs to the master bathroom. "Do you know how long I waited to find the right man?" she shouts. Mads hears a bathroom drawer slide open and slam shut again. "I could have married Zach Shelton. I could have had Terrance King. Carl doesn't even realize." Her voice tilts. It's the sound of a chin lifted for a quick application of mascara.

Mads can't wait for her to leave. Honestly, she can't stand that woman. Mads is there every day for Ivy and Ivy only. She feels a duty. Duty is complicated.

Ivy tosses a few Cheerios from her tray and then looks down as if she can't imagine how they got there. Another handful flies to the floor. She checks Mads for her reaction.

"Good trick, buttercup," Mads says. She smiles at Ivy. She smiles tons to make up for all the upset Ivy's seen. Mads is pretty sure every human being has a tally sheet on their spirit, so she does what she can.

"Gah," Ivy says.

"Couldn't agree more. Want to get out of that thing?"

Mads unsnaps the tray of Ivy's high chair, and then unfastens the belt. She lifts the baby up. This makes Mads's arms truly happy. Ivy smells of smushed, ripe fruit, and Mads has to stop herself from biting Ivy's fat cheeks. She walks into the living room with Ivy riding her hip. Claire and Thomas helped set her up with this job, and out the front window, she sees their house. Olivia Watson is next door to them, and next-next door is Ned Chaplin, who lives alone with cats. Mads stands by the wall of photos, wishing Suzanne would hurry up and leave. Until she does, Mads has to be Perfect Babysitter, which feels like wearing tight pants. Ivy reaches out a hand and a framed wedding shot tips crooked on its nail.

"Aarl," she says.

"A metaphor, huh?" Mads says.

"Dah."

"I can see that. Look, there's your dad. And there's your mom. And Kitty. See Kitty?" Mads points now.

"Kee."

"Exactly."

Suzanne rushes down the stairs, heels clicking, handbag bouncing. "Come here, sweetheart! Come to Mommy."

She swoops Ivy out of Mads's arms. "Mommy will only be gone a little while. I will miss you so, so much! You be a good girl for Madison? Your mommy loves you so, so much!" Suzanne buries her face in Ivy's neck as if she's a soldier going off to war. Then she hands the baby back to Mads. Ivy starts to wail.

"It's okay, sweetheart! Mommy will be right back! You'll be fine! Oh, God, I hate it when she does that. I can't stand to leave!"

"Bye, Suzanne," Mads says. Ivy's face is red from scream-ing and Mads is losing a few years of her good hearing.

"You call me if you need anything. If she doesn't stop, I want to know."

"We're fine."

"Bye, sweet girl. Mommy loves you, you know that, right?" Suzanne turns her back and shakes her head as if it's all more than she can bear. She rushes out. Mads hears the car door slam.

The exhausting part of babysitting isn't the baby. Any babysitter knows this. Probably every teacher, too. Ivy sobs as if her days have ended.

"Come on, chickadee."

Mads opens the sliding glass door to the backyard, takes the deck steps down to the lawn. "These are roses," she says. "Beautiful, right? Yellow. Yel-low. Prickly, though. You have to be careful. All thorny things in general." Mads uses her calm voice, but she is sick of people, and she's crushingly sad, and full of love for Ivy. Mads's flip-flops are off now, and there she is, stepping across the grass barefoot with a baby on her hip, totally unaware that the Big Guy Upstairs (or fate, or beautiful circumstance, or who-what-ever) is moving the pieces around for her, too.

"Another rose. Pink." She says *pink* as if it were the most cheerful word there is, and, yeah, it's probably in the top ten. "This one? Don't know what it's called, to be honest. Look at those big, fat flowers, though." They're cheerleader pom-poms, or the ball of fireworks that drips down like tears. Mads pats one, just a few hours before her life is about to change again.

"Your mom ought to water these." The squall has turned to a hiccuping sob. "Okay, fine," Mads says. "I'll water them."

With Ivy balanced on her hip, Mads squeak-squeaks the faucet on, and they stand together, watching the hose trickle. Ivy leans down to grab the water, and Mads sprinkles some on her hands and toes. "Funny girl, funny toes. All right, miss. You want to get down, huh? Now that the crisis is over, you're ready to roll?"

Mads turns off the water, sets Ivy down on a blanket in the shade of the willow. Ivy takes off, crawling fast as a little bullet. Mads grabs her before she can eat a rock or something, sets her down so she can speed away again. This is a great game for only a little while, because Ivy's ready for her nap. Abandonment is exhausting. So is being an object and not a person.

There's a night-light in Ivy's room in the shape of a moon, and there is wallpaper with bunnies, and a mobile of fleecy lambs. Ivy's real life is crashing dishes and a silent dad who stomps off, and a mom who clutches her like a security blanket. It makes a person furious.

Ivy falls asleep fast. The house is quiet.

Back home, when Mads babysat, she'd snoop around the houses, trying to locate the secret everyone seems to have. She found a sex book in the Rowells' dresser drawer, and bottles of Valium in the Chens' medicine cabinet. With Suzanne and

Carl, though, she has no desire to snoop. She wishes she could take away some of the things she knows, not add more.

Now, here's what Mads intends to do: read the chapter "Contracts, the Fine Print," study for Otto Hermann's quiz. Here's what she does do: opens her laptop. Looks at stuff. It's all preamble. The things you do to cover the things you're going to do. Even your own self needs a little fake-out before sliding into personal destruction.

She checks her e-mail. Sarah sent a bunch of pictures from a camping trip her friends took. They make Mads feel the same way every phone call or message from her friends does—as if that life is in the past. Even though she's returning home eventually, that version of Mads is a sweet, gone thing, painful enough that it requires steady ignoring.

There's a message from ColeSlaw1, too. This post-breakup reconnection is her fault. She called her old high school boyfriend, Cole, after the body in the water. She wanted to hear his familiar voice, wanted to feel like her former self for a minute and not a person who swam with a corpse. But since then, he keeps calling and texting. *Why are you ignoring me? I just want to know you're okay. I have to send a flipping e-mail? You sounded so awful. You scared me. . . . Come on, please!* This is why clean breaks are best. The guilt-anger fills her. Sometimes, right or wrong, she can want just what she wants from a person and no more. She wants people close until they're too close.

Next is an e-mail from Mads's mom, who also calls every

day, sometimes multiple times a day. This time she sends a link. It leads to a listing for an apartment near the Murray Realtors office. This is actually progress. Or maybe just a small negotiation for a larger gain, because before this, she hadn't wanted Mads to move to a place of her own at all. *Look at all the room I have! Free rent! It makes no sense to move out for the sake of moving out!* Now she writes: *Been on the market for eight weeks. I'll go by and have a look. Maybe he'll pay for this instead of college.*

Of course, Mads knows who "he" is. "He" is her father, a fun, great-to-be-around guy, a hardworking, kindhearted, can't-hurt-a-fly type person, who nonetheless swatted Mads right down to save himself. Her mother would prefer she not love him, but Mads does anyway. In secret. Even if he ditched her, she does. Even if he's in Amsterdam, permanently ducking whatever flare his ex-wife shoots him, writing checks he's able to write because of his whirlwind, busy-busy journalist job. He is fatherly by phone. Fatherly by long distance, something he may even have been when he lived with them. "He" gives practical advice, is disappointed that she isn't going away to school, and will never understand that she can't go away to school because he is in Amsterdam. A husband might ditch the joint, but a daughter never can.

None of these e-mails hold Mads's attention, of course. It's all picking at appetizers before the anticipated meal. Finally, she digs in. It's like succumbing. It's almost relief, the way it is with all obsessions. Anna Youngwolf Floyd. The eyes staring up, her cold skin—typing her name into the empty search rectangle makes Anna come alive. And now there is William Floyd, too, if that's who that boy was. He ran like hell with that dog under his arm, drove off with him in the passenger seat, and now he is another lead, another inroad to an answer. Of course, Mads doesn't even know what the question is, but that seems to be beside the point. Plenty of times there's *need* with no clear reason at first.

She types in *William Youngwolf Floyd*. Types it in again, for the millionth time. She hopes some miraculous new bit of information will appear, but there's only the same *Seattle Times* article. There's a photo with it, two guys at the top of a snowy hill, a pair of flattened cardboard boxes under their arms. *Roosevelt students William Youngwolf Floyd and Alex Banning take advantage of the record snowfall.* She makes the picture as large as she can. It's hard to tell if it's even him, through the Lite-Brite speckle of pixels. His hair is shorter than on the boy she saw. He doesn't even have a coat on! Still, his dark eyes stare right at Mads from the black-and-white snow day from two winters ago.

Where to look next? It doesn't seem possible that with all the bits and volumes of information on the Internet there is only this. She hunts for other ideas. She clicks and pecks like a hen searching for an overlooked corn kernel. *Seattle woman jumps from bridge. Son of. Seattle woman suicide.* This leads her to a quiz. *Are you depressed? Welcome to the Goldberg Depression Screening.* Fine. She'll take the stupid quiz. Why not? Maybe she isn't even depressed! Maybe she's just very, very tired. *Number one. I do things slowly.*

She pauses. It is a very slow pause. *Not at all. Just a little. Somewhat. Moderately. Quite a lot. Very much.* She answers after much time has passed.

My future seems hopeless.

Mads's mind shoots her an image of those Murray & Murray business cards, all printed up and waiting. Do you know how many come in a single box? Hundreds. Hundreds! All in a row, smelling new and begging to be let free so they might circulate in the world. *Here's who I am and will always be*, they shout. It'll take her years to get through the ones her mom already ordered. Finished basements, empty rooms, the losses and leavings of other people—all of that will be hers as her mom leaves work early because her head hurts.

The big ogre of despair starts stomping around, now that his name has been called. He's a familiar beast, and so is the way he pulls Mads in and shoves her down and makes her feel out of options. Damn you, Goldberg Depression Screening! *It is hard for me to concentrate on reading*, Mads reads, and then reads again because she can't concentrate.

Enough! She moves on. Next, there's a confessional article by a famous person about their *struggles with depression*. It is always worded like this, like Harrison and Avery wrestling after they make each other mad. It seems about right. Mads's own arms feel locked behind her back, and the ogre has his chin in the soft place between her shoulder blades. Now another confessional article by a famous person, and another. No one can get out of bed, and there are lots of people curled up on bathroom floors. This also seems about right. Every day, Mads experiences a forced unfurling, the fight to rise; the ogre has his big, rib-eye hand on her chest.

These confessions—Mads knows they're supposed to make her feel better. They're meant to send helpful messages like *You're not alone* and *Me too* and *It can happen to anyone*. But they don't make her feel better. Maybe she shouldn't even admit it, but the articles only feel like despair stacked on despair (Suzanne's smiling Amazon boxes, upside down), and she needs to hear the *okay* part. She needs her famous people to conquer. She needs people older than her to cope. That's unfair, but she does.

A scratching and rustling blares from the baby monitor. It sounds like a space traveler making contact with Earth. When Mads goes into Ivy's room, Ivy is sitting up, her cheeks rosy from sleep, her hair sweaty.

"Well, hello, sunshine," Mads says.

Ivy lets out a string of babble that might be a highly intelligent foreign language.

"Let's get you changed."

And then Mads finally does it. The thing she's thought about since the first day she started working for the Bellaroses. The thing that will maybe-just-maybe keep her from being some bathroom floor person from the Goldberg Depression Screening. She packs Ivy's bag. It gives her a weird release, relief from what feels stuck and immovable. She puts in Ivy's favorite toys—the stuffed frog, and the ball that makes music. She fixes a bottle for the road and gets the formula powder to make more. In go the container of Cheerios, and diapers. She packs a change of clothes for every season. And then she grabs her keys.

Mads's father always says that if you have your phone and a credit card, you've got what you need for a trip. He said this whenever they went on vacation and her mom got all anxious about forgetting stuff back home. It's also nearly all he took with him as he left when Mads was nine. (And, yeah, one other thing, too, but she doesn't like to think about that.) This demonstrates the hurry he was in. Mads has her phone and the Visa her dad insisted she get to *build credit*. Pretty sure he didn't have *kidnap baby* in mind.

"Cap-a-bility," Mads sings, a song that just comes to her. She tries to rhyme it, but oh, well. She buckles the car seat into Thomas's truck and lifts the strap over Ivy's head. "What do you think about that, missy?"

"Burble gah."

"Burble gah! I'd have said the same thing myself."

Ivy rides along next to Mads. Mads has her window rolled down a bit, and Ivy's wispy hair waves farewell. The baby slaps the glass with her hand, two smart smacks.

"Bah," she says.

"Good riddance." It's an old-fashioned expression Mads

remembers from scary, hunched Grandma Mary, Mom's mom. It's no wonder Mom is the way she is. Still. Mom had a bad childhood, which means, so did Mads. "Good riddance to bad rubbish."

She has no plan, but Thomas's truck does. It zips through Wallingford, where Claire and Thomas and the Bellaroses live, and then it heads toward the adjacent neighborhood of Fremont.

"Look, Ivy. See the water? See the boats?"

"Pree."

Mads smiles. Ivy's new words have lately been falling like snowflakes. "So pretty."

God, it feels great. It feels fantastic, to get out of there, to flee. She's as thrilled as Harrison was on the last day of school, his papers and school supplies already part of the past by the time Claire poured the celebratory Gatorade. Joy rises up, and Mads could fly on that joy forever, but Thomas's truck has other ideas. It pulls off into the little park just before the Fremont Bridge. The lot is right underneath it, and the cars roar overhead. Mads feels the rumble and shake of metal.

She needs to stop and think. Stop a minute and *think*. Sure, running off is an understandable plan, but it's not a good plan. They'll arrest her, and she'll be a terrible prisoner. She'll be terrified and she'll cry every day. Jumpsuits are a bad look for anyone. This whole thing made her feel good for all of five minutes.

Mads gets out of the truck. She unbuckles Ivy from her seat. She carries her to the grass by the water. From where she stands, she can see two bridges, the friendly, blue-towered Fremont right beside her, and the high, intense Aurora Bridge beyond.

"Boat," she says as one chugs past. She jiggles Ivy on her hip. Her mind is not on boats, though. She knows where she is, of course. She knows exactly what she's looking at. Anna Youngwolf Floyd jumped from that huge bridge, and her body floated across the lake to where Mads swam that day. It was all too horrible, and it's too terrible for Ivy to see. She isn't sure why Thomas's truck led her here. There's a park with a few geese walking around and gawking, and there's a guy eating his lunch, and a mom with a pair of twins tossing rocks into the water, but there's that bridge, too.

"Tell me," she says. Who knows who she's even asking. Or what she's even asking. There are just questions and more questions here. That's the way it is a lot of the time. No one tells you how often you just have to sit in the not knowing.

"Ives, I'm sorry," Mads says. "We're going to have to go back. I forgot your sunscreen at home. And Kitty is there. And I didn't bring Blankie." Mads feels a crush of failure. She isn't sure how anyone ever saves anyone.

And then . . . she sees something. When coincidence is that beautiful, you might as well go ahead and call it fate. Because, just before she crosses back over that goose-pooped lawn, she glances up at the Fremont Bridge, and she swears it's him. William Youngwolf Floyd. She's not sure. Her eyes are bad. She should wear her glasses all the time, but she doesn't.

54

It seems crazy. Is it even possible? It's a fast-pass of rebel hair that gets her attention, and a bunch of dogs. Tons of them! She shields her eyes with her free hand so she can see better, but then she stops all the hesitating and wavering and heads for the stairs. She hurries, walking with intent, because he'll be gone in a second, and if it's him, it's the most important coincidence of her life. Sure, we're talking about a ten-mile radius circling William's life and Mads's, but never mind. Cynicism is for cowards.

Mads wants to see if it's him, but also, she *has* to see. Ivy grabs a handful of her hair and tugs, but Mads barely notices. Wait. He seems to be looking her way. Is he? Is it even him? She still can't tell. With eyes like that, she should never drive without her glasses! If she doesn't get a move on, he'll disappear.

But look. He's changing direction. Suddenly, too. He's running! Rushing toward the stairs like there's some kind of emergency, and with all those dogs. One of them is as big as a sheep. What a disaster. It's *a bloody mess*, as her London-born father would say.

The guy is at the top of the stairs. The leashes are wound around his legs, and the dogs are barking their heads off, and he stops to untangle everyone. One of the dogs squats right there, and the guy has to dig a plastic bag out of the back pocket of his jeans. There's the briefest pause to take care of business, and then they descend. Why he's in such a hurry, she can't begin to say. It's calm at the park. One of the twins chases a goose who hops away, bored with that old game.

As the guy and those dogs barrel down the steps, though, everyone stops to look. The twins, the goose, the man eating his lunch, who watches the chaos with half of his sandwich stopped midair.

How they make it down without him breaking his neck, Mads has no idea. She is busy being frozen in place. There are three reasons for this: One, anyone would be shocked at this commotion. Two, it is most definitely William Young-wolf Floyd barreling in her direction with a cyclone of dogs. Three, it has suddenly occurred to her that she is the reason for his haste. He must know who she is. The girl who pulled his mother out of the water. The girl outside his house. The crazy, obsessed stalker, who he's about to confront.

Ivy's eyes are huge. A glossy stalactite of drool drops from the corner of her mouth. "Dah?" she says.

"It's okay," Mads says, though she doesn't know if this is true. Maybe she should run.

But she is too compelled to run. They are coming toward her, this unruly gang. William Youngwolf Floyd has one arm raised, and at the end of it is a fistful of leashes, as if he's hailing the most important taxi of his life. His T-shirt has come untucked, and there are rings of spooked sweat around his underarms. He's thinner up close. Those dogs could pull him right over, but Mads notices the muscles in his arms, too. His mouth is open. He's shouting something. She can't hear him, because it's loud near that bridge.

He stops in his tracks. It's the sort of sudden halt that the phrase is made for, a cartoon slide, which causes all the dogs to ricochet back in a humiliating way. The one in the lead makes a little heck-heck choking sound from the rapid yank of the leash. They bump into each other like a five-car pileup.

They're all winded. The big dog has an enormous tongue that lolls out his mouth. William Youngwolf Floyd is right in front of her now, breathing hard. Up close, his dark eyes are something from the universe, a star in reverse, deep and old, black-intense.

He leans down to catch his breath. One of the dogs sits. He's a sweet boy, with fur the color of a gingersnap.

Mads is speechless. She doesn't know what to do. She is saying silent prayers that he doesn't know her identity. Her guilt (guilt for the stalking, guilt for her role in such a private family matter) is making her face burn red hot.

"Can I help you?" It's the very first thing she says to William Youngwolf Floyd, which is funny when she thinks about it later.

Well, it's funny to him right then. His face twists up, and Mads wrongly thinks he's about to cry. Anna Youngwolf Floyd's son stands near the bridge where she jumped, and he is now going to burst into tears. It's what Mads expects, to see the way he's wrecked. But then he starts to laugh. He's laughing so hard. He shakes his head as if he can't believe himself and tears roll down his face, all right, the kind from the shock of the ridiculous. He wipes them away with the back of the hand still clutching the leashes. The biggest dog flops down and causes earth tremors in Central America as the boy gasps and tries to speak.

Mads doesn't know what's right in front of her. He is a laughing mess of tears, and she is a stunned mess of confusion. Two strangers gaze upon each other's real and fucked-up selves. Somewhere in the universe, a couple of stars collide. They aren't fancy stars, or even ones with names. Just regular old stars. Two of millions. Still, just like that, some of the best things begin.

Chapter Six

"I thought . . . ," he sputters. Jesus, he needs water, bad. His stomach hurts from laughing so hard, and from twisting something on that last step. Shit, maybe it's his back.

He doesn't know the last time he's laughed like that. Maybe the day Alex went with him to Gran's to pick up her old TV. Alex misjudged the corner of the houseboat dock and fell right in the water. It was hilarious, and Alex was *pissed*. He was dripping wet, but Billy just stood there pointing at him and cracking up. That was, what, last year?

But, wow, talk about a first impression. Way to go. Great job. He's even holding a plastic bag of dog shit, which he attempts to hide behind his leg.

"You thought . . ." She's trying to help him. Her eyes are kind, though when he ran toward her, they were squinched and her nose was squinched, too, like she was trying to see better. But, yeah, it's the same girl, all right. He'd recognize that shiny hair anywhere.

"Forget it," he says.

"Forget it?" She shifts the baby to her other hip. Wait. Baby? He takes in the baby for the first time. She—it's a she, he can tell from the pink shirt with the cat face on it, the ears in quilted yellow—hides her face in the girl's shoulder and then peeks at him. She holds a clump of the girl's hair and then brings it to her mouth and sucks on the ends.

"I thought you were someone I knew." The lie comes right up, nice and handy and fully formed. Probably thanks to that coffee he had back at the Rescue Center. Maybe that's all this was. A java-fueled hallucination.

"Oh."

"Is that your baby?" he asks, as if he has a right to know. He hopes J.T. Jones hasn't spawned a kid.

"We were just going for a ride! I was bringing her right back."

"Hey, I'm not the baby police. I was just wondering."

"Okay, sure. Of course," she says. "I babysit her. I thought we'd get out of the house for a while, you know? It's a beautiful day, we were cooped up. . . ." She has brown eyes, but not just brown. Oh, man. He loves soulful eyes like that. "It's complicated."

"I like complications."

It's a line from The Book. Jamie says it to Claudia before they run away to New York to stay in the museum. Billy pictures this going differently—tossing off the phrase like they do in the movies, quoting some line from a classic film, or

60

a famous poem. It'd be kind of smooth. But of course, she doesn't know The Book! Probably no one in the world knows it like he does! She turns her eyebrows down. Not in a scowl, exactly, but confused. Shit, it sounds like he's hitting on her, and he sort of is but isn't. It's not even true. He doesn't like complications! He wants way, way fewer complications from here on out.

They just stand there looking at each other. She's staring at him hard, like she recognizes him from somewhere. Shit! He doesn't know what to do, so he silently prays she doesn't recognize him from that day she was spying on J.T. Jones, the day he stole Lulu. Him plus the dogs, she could put two and two together.

Her mouth opens as if she's going to say something. Her lips part the way lips do when they're about to speak the truth.

"Well."

"Yeah."

"I better get back. The mom'll be home any minute."

"I better get these guys back, too." Bodhi's eyeing a goose, and Billy knows what that means.

"Are they *your* dogs?" She raises one eyebrow. Something passes between them, like a wrapped gift handed over. Maybe it has an explosive inside. He can't tell if she's saying some-thing more than she's actually saying.

"They're rescues." Jesus! Why'd he say that? Now she's really going to remember him in Mr. Woods's yard, if she hasn't already. He needs to get the hell out of there. "Well, hey."

"Hey."

Bodhi's pulling toward that goose, making his usual hecking sound as his collar strangles his stupid neck. Billy acts like this is just a regular part of the job. No problem. It's all easy and fine. He turns to leave. As he does, a voice inside starts yelling at him. It's not the usual doctor in his head but a different tough guy, one who seems to be on his side. *Go back! Say something to her! Do you think a coincidence like that, like seeing her here again, at this bridge, happens for no reason? Don't be a fool!*

He keeps walking. He can feel her eyes on his back. *Come on! Turn around! Say something!*

He hasn't seen eyes like that since Abby Millicent in the sixth grade. Abby and Billy were best friends. He was in love with her, actually. Even at twelve, he could tell that Abby Millicent was the kind of girl who could make him happy. She wore glasses and read mysteries and collected anything with whales. They kissed, and he gave her that necklace, and his heart was broken when he and Mom moved away from La Conner after his dad basically drank himself to death in that speedboat.

If you ever want to see that girl again, turn around! Right this minute!

Wow, fate has it rough, dealing with us clueless, stubborn humans. We refuse to listen and refuse to listen until we're practically knocked over the head! It's lucky that fate is even more stubborn than we are.

But Billy's mind is not on fate. It's on defeat. He doesn't even look back. Who wants to get their heart broken again? Billy's has been broken so many times, he isn't sure he has one left. He can hear it beating, but that's about all.

He gives the dogs big bowls of water. What a day. There's a note on his desk. Well, it's not a desk exactly, but it's the part of the table near the cubby where he puts his stuff. *Party, Andrew's. Tonight. Be there, would ya?* She doesn't even sign her name, but he knows Amy's handwriting. Billy balls up the note and tosses it in the trash on top of someone's lunch bag. There's an envelope with his paycheck in it on the desk, too. He takes out his wallet to put it inside, and that's when his heart falls.

It can't be.

Oh, no. Please, no.

He checks all his pockets and dumps everything out of his wallet. His chest is caving in. His heart is a rodent being squeezed by a snake. He saw that on a . . . Stop it! Who cares right now!

The map's gone.

He's such a fucking moron. Losing the one thing that's important to him! What kind of an idiot lets that happen? He wants to run right out and retrace his steps. After everything that went on at the park, no wonder he lost it! God, what a moron idiot dumb-shit fool. He could sob like a big damn baby, so instead, he shoves the lost map away in his head, to some place where it doesn't fucking even matter.

The way it matters (so much *matters*) still simmers, but whatever. Just, whatever. Okay? You can't keep someone with you by holding on to some stupid map in a stupid book anyway.

On the way home, Billy makes his usual stop: H. Bergman's house, to check on Casper. He looks around to see if anyone's watching before he says a few loving words. He makes Casper the same promise he makes every day, and then he tosses the beef sandwich from Paseo's over the chain-link fence. He's gotten good at that, for someone who sucks at most sports. He can lob anything pretty much right at Casper's feet. The first time he tried it, he flung a pork chop and it landed just beyond Casper's chain. It still kills him to think about this. He worried, too, what would happen when H. Bergman (that's the name on the mailbox) saw it. But when he went back the next day, it was gone. Casper was still there, though, of course. And this weighs on Billy. It weighs on him heavy. He's got to get that dog out of there, only he has no idea how.

That night, Alex and Drew come over to the houseboat. No way he's going to go to some party with Amy. Drew brings his own controller, which is good because Billy only has two. They play Night Worlds. Gran makes a big casserole dish of macaroni and cheese. She's trying to fatten him up, because he hasn't felt like eating much lately.

When Gran goes to bed, Alex runs to his car and gets the beer. Billy isn't much of a drinker (his father, Daniel Floyd, has pretty much killed any desire for alcohol) but he has a couple. Alex and Drew stay past midnight, quitting Night Worlds after Alex advances from Dragon Disciple to Duelist. You'd think he just won the presidential election. Billy has to tell him to shut the hell up before he wakes Gran. "Do you want me to kick your sorry ass?" he says, which makes Drew and Alex snort and hit each other because Billy's never kicked anyone's ass in his life.

Still, they shut up, because basically they're good guys. Drew has those tattoos across his knuckles that say *Your Next* but they don't mean anything. He tries to hide them now, since Alex's old girlfriend, Leigh, told him it was spelled wrong.

They leave, and after he goes to bed, Billy stays awake for a long time, feeling the houseboat rock. He stares at a beam of moonlight. It shoots through the window and lands right on the Chucks his mother gave him for his last birthday. All his stuff is there now, in Gran's spare room where she keeps her old computer, which is from the days when computers were big enough to anchor ships. There are his Chucks from Mom, and the action figure from a cake Mom made him when he was a kid (it still has the frosting on the bottom, dried to cement), and his clothes, and the lamp he's had forever, made from a big rope. The lost map tugs at his spirit, twisting it like a shirt left on a clothesline in a storm. Still, it's strange. All his shit looks weirdly new. Maybe it's the beer, or the full plate of food, or maybe something else. Yeah, he knows it's the something else.

It's those eyes. Hers, the girl with the shiny hair. He feels changed. He's been carrying this change around since he turned and left the park. It's a quiet feeling, but in this quiet of night, he's more sure it's real. Because of those eyes, his heart has lifted a little, like the corner of a page in a book, right before it turns. His Chucks are magic in that light. The moon sends him luck. He drifts off, and dreams of knights and maps and girls with bad eyesight.

Chapter Seven

Mrs. Erickson slides her phone over to Mads and sneaks a look at Otto Hermann as if she's going to get into trouble. This is probably what happens after you leave an abusive husband, which is what Mrs. Erickson—*Linda!*—has done. Mads will have to get over the discomfort of calling adults by their first names if she's going to be in business for herself. When she tells clients that their house won't sell for the price they want, she'll have to sound like an authority. Otherwise, she'll get bulldozed, and the property will sit on the market for months, money for flyers and open houses and advertising bleeding Murray & Murray dry. At the word *clients*, she hears the sound of bones clicking and rattling in a grave, but never mind.

Mads looks at Mrs. Erick—*Linda's!*—phone. There's a picture of her little girl sitting in a blow-up pool.

Mads makes an *Aww!* face and slides it back. Listening to Mr. Hermann is like sitting through those movies in AP history about World War II. Same accent, same droning, same low-level dread of the inevitable. Her stomach starts to hurt. She glances down at her flip-flops and her woven bracelet, makes sure they haven't been transformed to sandals with insoles and a Swatch. She's not middle-aged, okay? Even if all those shiny, sunbeams-of-the-future graduation shots her friend Jess posted look like something from long ago. Even if everyone she used to hang out with is starting a summer (the summer before college!) that seems frivolous and mysteriously carefree. Even if her life story is already written, she's only eighteen.

This realization always surprises her, because she feels thirty at least, and some days, fifty-sixty. While her friends drift further away into rah-rah fun-fun, Mads is swooped time-machine style into her mother's office, a few years from now. On the wall above the two desks, there are two paintings of Roman ruins. The clock tick-ticks. Here, in this room, the clock tick-ticks, too. The ogres turn up the heat and spin the room. She might throw up. Or pass out. There's a suffocating feeling, sweaty palms. She hears the rumble of that bridge in her head.

Otto Hermann hands out a work sheet, and Billy Young-wolf Floyd's eyes are on it. Stars turned inside out. A black that's old and that comes from somewhere far away. It's not some sort of a crush. It isn't! That's the last thing she needs or wants. Even people who like complications wouldn't like that one. She'll be back home by the end of September. Those papers the lawyer drew up are thrumming, silently shrieking, same as those special whistles for dogs.

Billy Youngwolf Floyd isn't even her type! Not with those thin arms, with the muscles that look hard and round as baseballs. Not with the shaggy hair and sallow ashtray cheeks and white skin from too much time indoors. Not with all that tragedy, hanging around like an apparition. Not the least bit her type. Cole Fletcher is healthy and bright as a stack of just-washed clothes. He's always ready to go out there and conquer something with energy and good attitude, whether it's a running track or a car repair or Mads herself.

What is love anyway? (Everything.) What's the point of it, even? (All.) Something is burning. The dark eyes are turning that paper to flames, and, too, the map in the pocket of her shorts is all glowing, red heat. She found it after he left. It was folded up flat and waiting on the pavement, like an invitation. She knew where it came from the moment she saw it. *From the Mixed-up Files of Mrs. Basil E. Frankweiler,* one of her favorite books of all time. She used to stare and stare at that map when she first read that book in sixth grade. She imagined herself in those rooms, sleeping in the museum bed, solving the mystery of the angel statue, same as Claudia. She knew *what* his map was, but she didn't know *why* it was. Ever since the body, it's been that way—the what but not the why. Every morning, though, the *why* is the thing that draws her up from the magnet bed.

Throbbing head, tumbling center, fire. On that work sheet, Mads sees star eyes, but she also sees Ivy in her car seat as they drove home from the failed kidnapping, her hair sweaty and head dropped in sleep. And she sees something else from that day, too, something that's a nagging worry, a potential problem: two familiar bikes pedaling so fast they're a furious haze, a passing comet of metallic blue, helmets white and curved as eggshells, rows of knuckles gripping handlebars. Ten-year-old spies, too far from home—had they seen her and William Youngwolf Floyd? When she got home that early evening, Harrison was nowhere in sight. He stayed the night at Avery's house. The next morning, he smelled like maple syrup, and his hair was wild and exhausted and jazzed, like it'd been at the clubs until all hours.

Now, though, there is only the sound of a waiting classroom—a cough, a rustle. *Linda, Linda, Linda!* kicks Mads with her wide-buckled sandal. Otto Hermann has asked her a question, and he stares down at her as if she's a misbehaving soldier in the German youth army. His mouth is moving, but all she hears is *You're cruisin' for a bruisin'*, which is what Harrison sang as he passed Mads on the stairs this morning, bumping her on purpose. Thomas says this when he's about to scoop up Harrison for a tickle attack. But he also says it in warning when Harrison's mouth gets smart with some daring comeback, like *Big whoop* or *Make me*.

That kid could get her into a whole, whole lot of trouble.

"I'm sorry." Mads pushes her chair back. "I'm not, my stomach . . ."

"That flu can last a long time," Linda says.

Mads bolts.

Goldberg Depression Screening, number eight. I am agitated. I keep moving around. Not at all. Moderately. Very much. Outside, spring is officially turning to summer, and the air smells sun-soaked, and students sit on benches in a redbrick square, talking and looking at books with little white headphone buds in their ears. The scene is so different than her gray, tumbling insides that she suddenly wants it for herself, and oh, so badly.

Mads's phone rings in her purse. She doesn't answer. It's got to be her mother. Across the miles, Catherine Jaynes Murray feels Mads's betrayal, Mads is sure. She can sense it, like some people can sense an attacker in an empty parking garage. Sometimes— she's said it before, but it's true—her mother is the best friend Mads has. Her mother may need Mads, but Mads has always needed her, too. She can tell her mom almost anything, but not how happy she'd be if she never saw Otto Hermann's classroom again.

Scratch the smooth, cinematic running off. Mads forgets where she parked. Hopefully, they cut this scene in the movie of her life. She wanders around for a long time, and then she has to go up and down every row in the area. When she finally finds Thomas's truck, she's mad, like it's the truck's fault. She dumps her stuff inside, listens to her mother's message. She has to. Her mom might be checking up on her, but she also might be *struggling with*, or curled up on the bathroom floor like the famous people. There was that time when her mother stayed in her dark room on Christmas Eve, under the covers, unwilling/ unable to come out, and it was all so scary, Mads had no idea what to do. She plugged in the tree lights and tried to cook a chicken, but she was only ten and didn't know you had to defrost it first. It was pink and cold when she put it on the two plates.

False alarm. Her mother's voice is the highest car on the roller coaster. *I got asked on a date! You know that guy from Windermere? We saw him at the broker's open with the pool? Remember, last April? He does all the east valley. James Beam. Don't say anything about his name, he gets that all the time. Call me. I need your advice. I think he's too short for me. I can't decide if that'd be a thing or not. It could be a thing.*

Mads throws the phone onto the passenger seat and then sticks her purse on top, and then her backpack on top of that. She thinks: *I hate her.* The words are so clear. Crisp, even. And then comes the sucking mud of wrongdoing. *Number eleven. I feel that I am a guilty person who deserves to be punished. Just a little. Somewhat. Quite a lot.*

"Go," she says to Thomas's truck.

Puget Sound Rescue and Heartland are the only two animal shelters within walking distance of the bridge. Mads learns this one night when she can't sleep. Can't sleep *again*. Ogres love to keep you awake with their chanting. Insomnia bonus fact: She can tell you exactly when the streetlamps click off—4:45, just before the sun lifts.

She checks her pocket—yep, the map's still there. Two days ago, she parked in the PC Fix lot across from Puget Sound

Rescue and sat there for a good few hours before she decided it was the wrong place. She tells herself she's not a creepy stalker lurking in her car. She's more a private eye, solving a case. A head case, maybe, but still.

On the other hand, the body of Anna Youngwolf Floyd floated to the very spot in a 571-square-mile lake (Mads looked it up) where Mads had been swimming. This is too large a happening for mere coincidence. Coincidence is seeing your friend at Target when you both like Target. Coincidence is your boyfriend calling right when you're thinking about him because you think about him every couple of minutes. What happened in that lake was *meant*.

A why without an answer is the worst kind of lost thing— a lost thing you never had to begin with. You will endlessly, futilely try to find it between the couch cushions and in the pockets of the coat you last wore. You will retrace your steps and retrace your steps, and still nothing. You will toss and turn at night. You will run stop signs and put your keys in the refrigerator and wear mismatched shoes from distraction. You will shout *why* into a canyon and only get a *why why why* back again.

You will go to Heartland Rescue and park across the street at a Wing Dome. You will sit way longer in a Wing Dome parking lot than anyone ever has in the brief history of fast-food chicken. Long enough to worry that someone might call the police. Long enough that your hair will smell like smoke and hot sauce after.

But there—his truck. What a relief to see it! He hasn't disappeared forever after all. Mads feels the surge of victory. Great detective work! Well done, stalker!

She expects to park there for a good while, until she heads to the Bellaroses' to babysit. Step one is finding the right shelter, maybe communing with William Youngwolf Floyd's truck, and trying to learn about his life and his mother's life from the outside of the Heartland Rescue building. Giving him the map is another step altogether.

Mads still has lots of time. She rolls down her window, because it's warm out. A crowd of smells marches in, garbage and barbecue and city. She can hear the dogs barking from across the street. Stupid Wing Dome is actually making her hungry. Toe food (Harrison's name for tofu) can starve a person. Sadness can steal hunger. Mads takes her flip-flops off. Settles in for the non-show.

But then there's a rustle of activity. Mads shoots upright and then slouches down again with a confused jolt of energy. It's supposed to be a boring stakeout, and now here's some real action.

The front door opens, and there he is. It's the actual *him*, and it's crazy to say, but Mads never expected this. He's with a girl. A really beautiful girl, the kind that can pull off an exposed midriff, her hair the shade of blond that makes you think of money and beach volleyball and confidence. Exposed midriffs make Mads feel like she's shrunk stuff in the wash. She's not sure her own body is meant to be seen. It should stay hidden, she thinks. A girl's story about her body always involves her mother.

The blonde tugs on William's sleeve and then ruffles his hair. He moves his head away, but he grins. It's not a grimace, but a grin, right? She doesn't have her glasses, so she can't tell. But, you know, *of course*. Guys love that kind of thing. Mads wonders why the girl doesn't just throw him to the ground and climb on.

With all the fabulous amazing fun he's having, Mads is safe behind the Wing Dome Dumpster, she's sure. She never pictured him with a girlfriend for some reason, or at least, not with one like that. The girl gives him a little push before he gets into his SUV.

He's leaving! The girl heads back inside. He watches her go, checking out her ass likely, that's what usually happens. He looks in his rearview mirror, sticks his chin up, and examines it. He starts the car.

Mads stays a discreet distance behind. She follows him to the Lazy Boar, a brewhouse with a big copper tank in the window. He disappears inside, comes back out again a short while later with a square Styrofoam container. He's probably taking his lunch back to Heartland Rescue.

No. Instead, he winds through the center of Fremont, away from Heartland. He drives up Troll Avenue, past the huge cement troll statue with its long cement fingers. Mads stays a couple of blocks back. They're in a neighborhood now, and he'll surely see or hear her if she gets too close.

He pulls over. Mads stops. Veers behind a row of parked cars. They aren't too far from his old house.

He jogs down the block a bit, nicely in Mads's view. He reaches a tall cyclone fence. The small yard beyond it is all has-been grass, dried, heartless grass, grass that has given up green dreams long ago. It's brown and pebbly. Mads sees a gate with a padlock. And she can see a dog. A big white dog on the end of a chain. A dog that's also seen better days. At least, he's scrawny for his size, and he's dirty, and he has the rangy look of the forgotten. The house makes her think of cans of soup and faucets that spill rusty water before the clean comes out.

William Youngwolf Floyd pops the top of the Styrofoam. He lifts a thin steak and steps back as if he's the pitcher and the meat is the ball. It's a little awkward to watch. He attempts to fling it over the fence, but on the first try, the beef hits the chain link with enough force to make it clatter. He catches it on the bounce back as the white dog gives a halfhearted wag, as if he isn't sure what might happen next.

William tries again. The meat clears the top of the fence but lands for a split second on the dog's head. The poor creature wears it like a silly wig. Mads feels embarrassed for him, but luckily that fashion statement lasts only a moment. The dog shakes it off and then has the meal of his life from the looks of it. He gulps it down in three bites, and then over the fence come a baked potato and a roll.

Now William's talking to the dog. Mads rolls, rolls, rolls

her window down and tries to stick only her ear out, but she can't hear what he's saying. There's a crooning rhythm, though. And something is happening in Mads's chest. Her heart splits in half, like an atom. The story—Anna's story, William's, their family's—is larger than she ever imagined. The details tell her this. There are his black Converse shoes, and the careful closing of the Styrofoam container. There's the half-wave to the dog, the saggy-assed jeans, the trot back to the SUV. There are thousands upon thousands of these details, she realizes. He's a real person, and so was his mother. She's not two seconds of news, or a cold wrist, or the lumpy object under the thick green plastic with the zipper on top. She's not just a body in the water, or a suicide.

It takes great effort for me to do simple things. Get up to go to class, yes. Answer texts from friends at home, yes. Have a conversation with Claire about her day, yes. Turn the key, put Thomas's truck in gear, follow William Youngwolf Floyd to his next destination, no.

This is how the world saves you. This is how it shows its love. One small thing. One reason.

Where is he going now? Are there more deliveries to make? A list of dogs? Is this part of his work for Heartland Rescue? Bringing aid, like the Red Cross for canines? Or does William Youngwolf Floyd have an obsession of his own?

He backtracks. Goes down through the neighborhood, back past the troll on Troll Avenue. Mads loses him for a second when she gets caught behind a biker by the Fremont

Branch Library. She has to stop at a red light. She glimpses that SUV, turning by Sustainable Sandwich.

Now only the disappearing back end of the SUV is visible on the other side of the Fremont Bridge. It drives off, just as the maddening red warning lights begin to blink and the arm of the bridge gate folds down. Great. Terrific. Just Mads's luck—she's lost him for sure. She is stuck there, right in the shadow of the bridge his mother jumped from. How can he even bear to pass it? Mads waits, dum, dum, dum, tra-la-la, as the bridge slowly, slowly rises. A sailboat passes beneath, and then the bridge lowers again. A few eons pass.

The cars are set free again, but there's no way she's going to find him now. Stupid to even try. He could be anywhere. Thomas's truck is pointed over the bridge, though, and so over the bridge she must go.

She ends up on a fast and confusing road that hugs the lake, so she pulls into one of the parking lots by the water to turn around. There's a marina, and a place that sells yachts; there's a bookstore with boaty-looking books in the window, and there's a set of wooden stairs heading to the shore.

Turning around is tight. And, then, shit! Oh, man, really? Thomas's truck dies when Mads puts it in reverse. A car waits to pass, and Mads gets all panicky. She gives it too much gas, which makes the situation worse. Flooded—she knows that much from Cole, who's worked after school at Rainier Auto Repair since he was like twelve. The other car backs up, shoots away in anger. Mads swallows another dose of guilt-fury. It swirls around, blends with the memory of the blond girl in the crop top, and with Mads's entire past, and probably with hunger of all kinds, and now she's in a bad, bad mood.

"Thanks, truck," she says. "Thanks a whole lot."

She tries to start the damn thing again. She is refraining from smacking her fist against the steering wheel. And then she sees it. The SUV. William Youngwolf Floyd's SUV! The SUV should have God rays coming down on it, it's such a miracle. She didn't see it at first, because it's parked by this monster of a restaurant called China Harbor. It's one of those places that probably had packed tables back in 1977. She's sure there's a big, sad aquarium in there.

The truck's in a slot marked RESERVED FOR RESIDENTS OF DENNY COVE.

"You crafty little devil," Mads says to Thomas's truck. "I owe you an apology." What a big hunk of metal goodness. What a true friend.

Mads gets out. She's nervous, but that weird boldness is with her again, too. She listens like a good detective. A seaplane lands with a roar, so that's all she can really hear. She sees that set of stairs, but not what's beyond them. It's an excellent way to get caught.

The stairs lead down to a swinging wood gate. There's a sign: PRIVATE. RESIDENTS OF DENNY COVE ONLY. No one is around. She's a person who always turns her homework in on time, who mostly drives the speed limit, and comes home by curfew. The kind of kiss-ass, honestly, who always cares if the teacher likes her.

Fuck *Private*.

Everything is different after you find a body in the water. Everything is different with a pounding, pulsing *why*.

She pushes open the gate. On the other side, there's a dock of houseboats—small shingled shacks and larger two-story homes all angles and skylights. Pots of flowers and hanging baskets decorate nearly every porch. At the end of the dock is the lake, with its choppy waves and boats. Straight across, nearly exactly, is the dock where Mads took her swim.

She hears voices. She stops; closes her keys in her fist so they won't jingle. Yes, two people are talking somewhere down the dock. She recognizes one of the voices, all right. It's him. She ducks into the entryway of a blue houseboat with white trim. A cat stares out from a window, bored and unmoving, as if he sees creeping intruders on a regular basis.

Mads peers around the big basket of drooping fuchsias that are right in front of her. The flowers, shaped like little pink and purple ballerinas, dance on her cheeks. They *smell* pink and purple. She parts the leaves so she can see.

She squinches her eyes because it's all a little blurry. She sees William and an old lady, whose silver hair is in a ponytail. The lady has a green watering can in one hand. She grabs William's chin with the other. "What's this?"

"What," he says.

"You growing a beard?"

"Nah. Maybe."

"Get rid of it."

He shakes free of her. "Stop."

"Shave it off. You got two whole hairs. A gerbil's got more."

Ha! Mads gives a little laugh-sputter behind the hanging plant, even though her heart is galloping like mad.

"Give it a week. I'll be like . . . Who's that old cowboy singer you're so crazy for?"

"Which one? Kenny Rogers? Willie Nelson? I'll call you Gerbil Man. Get the razor."

"You can't stand how handsome it is already, that's all. Your eyes are practically falling out, it's so handsome."

The woman chuckles. Mads smiles.

"Give me that can. You're going to hurt yourself lifting that heavy thing."

"I'm stronger than you," she says, but lets him take it.

Mads is in trouble now. He moves toward a row of pots where he'll surely see her. She slides flat against the house. The cat's water dish is by her foot. A boat drives by too fast and causes the houses to rock and slosh.

And then a little white dog starts to sound the alarm. He's closed inside the old lady's house, but Mads can see him through the window. He's up on the back of the couch, barking his head off. He's staring right at her.

That's it. It's over. Either they'll see her face, or she can run like mad, giving them only the view of her fleeing back. The choice is clear. She steps over the dish, races down the dock.

The gate squeaks as she pushes through. Her keys are in her hand. Her heart goes from a gallop to a crash. Just as she reaches the huge sheltering side of China Harbor, she hears the slap, slap of shoes running on the steps behind her.

Oh, God. Her hand shakes. All of her is shaking so hard. Why did she lock the door of the truck? Someone's really going to steal her backpack or her phone in the five minutes she's away? Only Goody Two-shoes lock their door for five minutes. Only girls who can't stand five minutes of risk.

"Hey! Hey!" he calls.

Wrong key!

She feels the tug as he grabs a pinch of her shirt. He spins her around. Thank God she's got an explanation ready, there in the pocket of her skirt. She expects the star eyes to be furious, but instead they're just sloped down into a question. His face is close to hers.

"Who are you?"

Right then, Mads has no idea. Honestly, right then it is an excellent question.

Chapter Eight

"Are you some kind of reporter?" he asks. It's the first thing that comes to him, even if no one gives a shit about his mother and never has. But he's struggling to understand why this girl is everywhere he is lately. Is she even J.T. Jones's girlfriend after all? With the way she keeps showing up, he has no idea.

"Do I look like a reporter?" Okay, weird—she sounds mad. Her cheeks are flushed, and her hands are little earthquakes. What the hell—she's creeping around his house, and *she's* mad at *him*?

"A junior reporter, maybe?"

"Why would I be a reporter? And if I *was* a reporter, why would I be a *junior* reporter?" She's jabbering, she's so pissed. Taking big, deep breaths, like she might pass out from anger, or something.

"I saw you at the bridge that day. We talked—"

"*You* saw *me* at the bridge and now *I'm* a reporter?"

This isn't going well. She's right. He's not making sense.

He saw her on his street, sure, but then *he* was the one who spotted *her* at the bridge. "Well, who are you? What are you doing here?"

"Madison? Murray?" She says it as if she's not sure. "I have this." She shoves her hand down into her skirt pocket. Pulls out the square of folded paper. "Of yours. You dropped it."

Can it be? *Please, please, please, God*, he thinks, *even if you never listened before, let it be. This one small thing, come on!*

He sees the yellowed pages, folded and folded again so that only the words on the back side show. Yes! YES! He tries not to do a spin plus a fist pump. He thought it was gone for good. He searched and searched between the couch cushions and in the pockets of his jeans, and the next day, he decided to retrace and retrace his steps after all, and still nothing. Now his heart rockets with relief. All this time, he's imagined it lost on the bridge somewhere, run over by cars, carried off on the tire of some truck. Or, God, worse—fluttering *down*, and here, the shiny-haired girl has had it the whole time.

"You," he says. It all seems like a miracle. A small one, but who cares about the size of a miracle? The map has probably been resting comfortably on a white dresser in a pink room with a canopy bed. He doesn't know shit about girls' rooms, not really. Abby Millicent had a Power Rangers bedspread handed down from her brother.

"It's yours, right? You said the dogs were rescues, so I went by . . ." She waves her arms a little, as if she just walked into a spiderweb. "So I went by . . . A girl . . ."

"She told you where I lived?"

Madison Murray rubs her neck. It's turning red. "I didn't want to . . . just toss it or something. It looked important."

It is. It's really important. He can get another map anytime he wants, but he can't get this exact one.

"Yeah. Thanks. It belonged to someone . . ." He's such an idiot. He even chokes up a little. He clears his throat. He can't say anything more. First off, he just met this girl. You're not going to say your mother jumped off a bridge, you're not going to tell her about the arrows that rip through your heart nearly every second you're awake. Still, tears gather up like an army of mummies on an Energy Attack. He's just so glad to see that map, he can't even say.

"It looked old. I think it fell out of your pocket when you bent down. . . ."

He gets it now. He gets all the beautiful, fantastic coincidence of it. She's here to give him back his map after they talked at the bridge, and he was likely right all along about that first time he saw her. He should tell her. Like, this second. About spotting her outside J.T. Jones's house. Not saying anything is kind of a lie, but saying something will be pretty awkward. It means having information he shouldn't have yet. *I saw you before that day at the bridge, you know, stalking some douchebag who broke your heart.* She probably has no idea how many girls he's seen going over there. Plenty, all the time. He's heard about those Blanchet guys and drugs, too. What is it about Catholic school guys? Yeah, he gets that rules can make you want to break them, but going out of your way to piss off a nun? Why not just piss off a rainbow or a basket of flower petals? Come on, assholes.

Madison Murray looks down at her feet, scrapes the asphalt with the toe of her flip-flop. Then she meets his eyes. "I know what it is," she says.

"You do?"

"Yeah."

"Oh, heh heh." That's actually what his laugh sounds like. Heh heh! Jesus, how embarrassing! How's he going to explain this? It's a stupid book, meant for ten-year-olds. But it was his mom's favorite, and it's the only book he's ever read all the way through for fun. More than that, he gets it, why his mom loved it. He'll never admit that, but he does. The museum, sneaking into it like they do . . . Spending the night with those objects all around you, stuff that has lasted through Roman times and wars and every fucked-up thing the human race did . . . That stuff tells anyone who looks at it that you can keep on going, no matter what.

And The Book itself—it's lasted. It's so awesome, because here it is, talking about a happy family, man, how retro, hot fudge sundaes, a mom and a dad, the time when kids could just get on a train and no one freaked out, a time when you could break into a museum and not get fucking Tasered or something, and here he is, Billy Youngwolf Floyd, with a dad who drowned drunk, and a half brother he met only once, and a mother who jumped off a bridge after being depressed for years, and he chuckles like hell reading how Claudia and Jamie hid in the toilet stalls from the guards. He loves (shut up if you don't get it) the running away and the need for a larger life, and the mysterious angel statue and the chauffeur and the lifetime of mess and secrets in the files. How every piece is a part of a bigger experience, and how you should never forget that. You know when that book came out? 1967! The Vietnam War, people! That long ago! Kids and kids and kids have read it, when there've been protests going on and presidents resigning and communist walls crashing down. When the book first came out, there were barely computers! It could blow your mind. They didn't even have Pac-Man yet, let alone Night Worlds. They didn't even have the Internet, which you can barely imagine. Today, though, little children are still reading the damn thing and wishing they could sleep in that fancy museum bed. You gotta love something that *stays* like that.

Mom didn't take a lot of things from their place in La Conner. Furniture, yeah; his stuff, but barely any of the crap that had been hers and his dad's. But The Book was one thing she did keep. It had her name written in it, Anna Youngwolf, in a kid's fat, loopy handwriting, and underneath that, the year she'd read it, 1985. When he saw the book again the day they packed up her things—her sweaters and her balled-up socks, the bottle of pills that didn't do squat, her shampoo, her magazines, her last check from the stupid car rental place that fired her, the pans and those plates made of some plastic you could back a truck over and they wouldn't break—he plucked it from the

Goodwill pile. It was yellowed and it smelled like an old closet and some of the pages were scrunched, but she had kept it, and so he would keep it. She didn't have jewelry and shit like that. He didn't have some ring to wear on a chain. So he carried The Book with him for a few days, until the cover started to come off, and until it started getting awkward, carting it around. Then he took the map from the middle, taped the two halves together, and kept that with him instead.

"*From the Mixed-up Files of Mrs. Basil E. Frankweiler,*" the girl says.

He can feel the heat rise in his face. His cheeks burn. He's struck with some deep shame, as if she's just seen him naked, or found out he sucked his thumb until he was seven.

"Well, it's . . ." There's no good explanation. He wishes he could be the fuck-you-who-cares kind of guy, but he's never been that. His dad used to say he was too sensitive. Once, Billy cried when he got hit with the kickball during recess. Second grade. Kelsey Rodgers would squawk *waaa-waaa* whenever she saw him after that. He could never be with a girl, he has so many secrets.

"I love that book," she says.

He takes her in for the first time, truly looks at her outside of his own dead-mother panic and his own shiny-hair, knowing-eyes need. He sees *her*. Yeah, there's the straight brown hair, and those eyes, but there's also a trickle of freckles over her nose that make her look honest. She's in an orange T-shirt and a tan patterned skirt, and she wears a woven leather bracelet around one small wrist. Her neck is blotchy from heat or nerves or something, and her nails are bitten down. He's never seen anyone quite so beautiful.

"Oh, yeah?" he says.

"The way they run away. How they become a team . . ."

"It's the only book I ever read for fun," he says. He hopes this will clarify things. At least, it'll make him seem less like a moron.

"Really?" she says. "You're kidding."

"I mean . . ." Shit!

"Oh, no, it's totally fine. There are just so many amazing books, is all. Don't even get me started."

He doesn't know what to say to that. They stand there silent, and, God, it's awkward. A Disappearing Spell would be awesome. Finally, Madison Murray brushes her hands together. "Well!" she says, all brisk. It makes him think of Mary Poppins, the way she got in there and got everyone going. Same with the nanny that sings in the mountains in that movie, he can't think of the name right then, because he's sinking fast and the girl is so beautiful.

"Mission accomplished! You have your map, and my job is done!" She's so superconfident that she's done with him, he's sure. "Wow, what time is it? I'm probably already late! I've got to babysit."

"The baby in pink."

"The baby in pink. Nice to . . . you know. I was going to say meet, but we already did sort of meet, though . . ."

"Billy." He holds out his hand. "Officially Billy." It sounds like a brand of jeans or something.

"Billy? Right! I guess that's short for William." Her hand is small and, truthfully, a little sweaty.

"Hey, thanks so much for bringing this." He waves the little folded square. "It belonged to someone I knew," he says again.

"No problem."

She inches away from him. She's trying to get the hell out of there. He hopes his breath isn't bad.

"See ya!"

"See ya."

She tries to wiggle the key in the lock of her car. It looks upside down to him. In a second, she'll be back inside, driving off, and all he'll have is her name.

Idiot! Stop her!

The voice is back—it's turned deep and Mafia, so he knows it means business. He shoves his hands in his pockets, heads back down the stairs and through the gate to the dock. Whatever. His mom hasn't been dead long enough. You don't go hit on some girl. *This is not just some coincidence!* The Mafia voice has a point. You have your regular old coincidence-coincidence, like when one of his friends, Evan, actually does his Algebra II homework on the one day Billy doesn't, saving his butt, or when some guy starts a fight right as they're checking IDs at Corazon, so they get in. But this—seeing her after seeing her after seeing her, it does seem like a sign. Maybe his mom . . .

Stop! He doesn't like to think all woo-woo and stuff. If she wanted to give him some guidance, she should have stayed around. You're not supposed to be critical of people who do what she did, but try being their kid.

You're gonna lose your chance!

Who even believes in love? Fine, fuck. He does. A person *should*.

He turns. He's a blur; he's a heroic streak of long-shot passion as he runs up the stairs. "Wait!" he calls. But no need to worry. She hasn't gotten far. Her truck is having trouble starting or something. She's sitting in the seat with the windows rolled down, her head in her hands.

"Hey," he says. She looks up. "Is it the battery?" It's his only guess. He doesn't know shit about cars.

She seems surprised to see him. "Kind of starts when it wants to start."

He chuckles. The truck has a big, smiley hood that makes you smile back. Or maybe he's just suddenly feeling really good. Singing bluebirds kind of good. Dancing penguins good. Ladies running around Alpine mountains good.

"I was thinking," he says.

One of her hands rests on the wheel with that bracelet around her little wrist. It's delicate and determined, like the wing of a bird.

"Maybe we can . . ."

She waits. Her eyes are brown and deep as Jasper's.

"Meet for coffee or something."

"Sure."

"What's today?" Stupid! Like he has a full calendar or something. Like he's a CEO whose days are full of meetings!

"Wednesday?"

"How about Friday?"

"I babysit until seven. Maybe we can . . . I don't know. I'm never very good at this part."

"Um, pick up food? Take it somewhere?"

"Sure."

"Do you want me to pick you up? In case your truck . . ." What's he saying? He has a flash of meeting some father at the door. He's never met a father at the door. Mariah, she picked him up for that dance and the few times after, and he and Zoe always met somewhere. Zoe, well, you know it's not right when her mouth feels wrong.

"No. No, no, no! We can meet! How about somewhere like . . ."

He's supposed to fill in. "Okay, let me think. Agua Verde? Mexican? By the Montlake Cut?"

"I can find it. Seven thirty?"

"Yeah. That'll work. They make great burritos." He never realized it before, but *burritos* is the least romantic word there is.

The truck starts up. Blasts his eardrums. She drives away, gives a shy wave. Her arm is tan as caramel, and oh, no, she's going the wrong way, unless she wants to get on the express lane of the freeway heading south.

Outside the houseboat, Gran's still watering those plants. Probably trying to listen in with her eagle ears. "Who's that girl?"

"No one."

"You didn't go running after her like it was no one."

"Mind your own business."

He's giddy. He's suddenly starving. Gran's down-turned mouth is just a mean pebble in a nice shoe.

"Fine sight, I'll tell you that."

"What?"

"A smile. You smiling." She makes it sound bad. No, she makes it sound *mixed*. It's confusing. The words say one thing, the tone another. Choose which to believe, and the other will slither under your skin.

Gran sets her watering can down. She pinches dead stuff off flowers. Her silence jabs him with shame. Her silence tells him what a bad, disappointing person he is. He just doesn't get what she wants from him. The dock rocks as a boat passes, and he hears the clang of Glenn and his husband Craig's sailboat. They have the biggest house on the dock, and it's pitching and rocking. He doesn't feel too well, all of a sudden. It's anti-magic. He can feel an Ability Drain, levels turning to red.

"Buzz?" Gran says.

Shit! A Breath Weapon, Devil Chills, a Red Ache, Mind Fire. His stomach clutches up and his chest squeezes. Gran is right about him. What was he thinking? His mom is dead, and he's going on some date?

God, just like that, he's sobbing like a baby. It comes out of nowhere, an invisible creature. He is felled, and he clutches his bony little gran and cries into her shirt, and it's pathetic. You never know when these things will happen. One time, he was just brushing his teeth, looking at his frothy mouth in the mirror, when all of a sudden, bam. Grief clutched him in its fist, and he banged his head over and over and over into the bathroom wall. There's a crater in the plaster still, like a meteor struck.

"Buzz." She sighs. "It's okay. It is. You can be happy." Now that she has what she wants from him, now that she's dragged him down into feeling like shit, she changes her tune. Her voice is all soft and loving, yanking him back up again. He can see how Gran operates, but it doesn't matter. You can understand a volcano, but it'll still burn and bury you. You'll still give it thanks if you're not entirely destroyed.

"I can't."

"You need to."

"A few months is all it's been."

"So much longer. Years. It's been *years*."

Poor Ginger is losing it inside. She hates when people get upset. She's scratching at the door and whining, and Gran lets her out. Ginger jumps around his legs. He feels her little toenails, trying to say *It's okay! I'm here!* Dogs just give and give. No matter what's happening in their own life, they look after you.

He picks up Ginger. He gazes at her white shag rug face. "Stupid dog," he says, but he means it with so much affection, his heart hurts. One thing he knows, he can love like you wouldn't believe.

Chapter Nine

Mads is lost. She realized that already, but now she is actually, literally lost. She got on the wrong freeway entrance and has ended up here, in some industrial graveyard. There are big warehouses and chain-link fences. There are huge, mysterious metal parts, the knuckles and knees of iron giants. An airplane swoops low and there's a shuddering roar. She should never have turned off on that exit. Everyone gets confused down here. Night will fall by the time she finds the freeway again.

She's late. So late. See what trouble that boy has caused already? He distracted her like crazy, and now look. She pulls over into the parking lot of a huge, blank building labeled CTC. Anything could be going on in there. Mads's phone won't connect to the Internet. She hunts in Thomas's glove box for a regular old map, but only finds a pair of winter gloves and a stack of Burger King napkins. Mads calls Suzanne. She tells her she's having car trouble (true), that the truck has stopped (true) and that she'll be right there (mostly true). Suzanne is pissed. People who are always late are the least understanding about you being late.

Mads ventures back into the vast dystopian land of cranes and bridges and manufacturing. She chooses a street. To her new eyes, the sign says EUROPEAN PAINTINGS and not 1ST AVENUE SOUTH. She drives through DUTCH AND FLEMISH 17TH CENTURY and decides to turn down AMERICAN PAINTINGS AND SCULPTURE (S. SPOKANE STREET), which leads her neatly to the freeway. A person needs a map, is all.

Thomas's truck shudders over sixty-five. Mads arrives at the Bellaroses', sweaty and out of breath. Suzanne basically shoves poor Ivy into her arms and then takes off, tires screaming. Suzanne always speaks through objects. Tires and doors and Ivy.

"It's good to see you. It is so, so good to see you." Mads says this to Ivy, but in her mind's eye, she is also saying it to Billy Youngwolf Floyd, the moment he runs up to Thomas's truck, the moment he speaks four words she never knew were magic: *Is it the battery?*

"You can just go out with him and see what happens. Having a date doesn't mean you're marrying him. You can take it slow." Mads sits on the edge of the bed in her room at Claire and Thomas's house. It's their former office/spare room, where they put in a twin bed for her. There's a big oak desk, too, and on it, a picture of Claire, Thomas, and Harrison standing near a fountain. Also—Harrison's first-grade school photo in a frame. In it, he looks serious and responsible, like he's about to come fix the air-conditioning unit in the apartment complex.

"He's so short, he's up to my eyebrows! His wife cheated on him. That's why he's divorced. He *wanted* to stay married. He's not the type to just up and leave, like some people we know."

Mads likes that room, but right then, listening to her mother on the phone, she feels as if she's somewhere else. In a lake, where water-words are drowning her. In a desert, where her mother's voice rolls over her like waves of heat as she slowly melts.

"Good, then," Mads says.

"Well, I'm in no hurry to be with a man. I like things the way they are, with you and me. Us girls. Boys just bring complications."

I like complications, Mads thinks.

There's a rap on the door, and Claire pokes her head in. "Dinner," she mouths.

"Gotta go, Mom."

"We barely got to talk."

"Dinner's ready."

"You hardly have five minutes for me anymore."

Mads's chest squeezes with the bad/ungrateful/guilty feeling. She can be so selfish, she thinks. Selfish = bad person. She should be more generous. Even this guy, Jim Beam, will be gone soon enough. She knows this. Her mom will pick at him; she will jab and belittle. One day, he'll strike back, because he doesn't understand the rules, how you're supposed to keep the waters calm, and then it will be over. Everyone leaves Catherine Jaynes Murray, which means Mads never can.

On the other end of the phone, their home sounds empty and abandoned. Of course, Mads worries about *abandoned*. She's seen what it's done before. It turns her mom into all of the fairy-tale characters at once—the small, scared Gretel lost in the woods, and the angry, consuming witch with the oven and the house of candy. *She's a grown woman*, Mads's father would say, Claire would say, Thomas would say. But she isn't really. Mads understands that even the witch is just having a very large tantrum, even if it's hard to say what's worse, the small and scared or the angry and consuming.

"We'll talk tomorrow."

"I wanted to tell you about a new listing I got."

"Claire's calling."

"I think it can go for over four hundred. It's got a view. The seller's a bitch, though. You know what she said?"

"Mom, I've got to go."

Mads's mom sighs. The wind whistles through the desert. "Well, I'm off. I have work to do."

"Love you."

"I love you. I miss you so much. We'll talk tomorrow."

"Mads, you barely ate anything," Claire says. She slides the casserole dish of vegetarian lasagna toward her. "Thomas, give her another scoop."

"I'm fine, Claire. It was delicious, thanks."

"She's fine, Claire," Thomas says. "A person gets to say whether they're hungry or not." Thomas and Claire catch eyes, like television parents. Mads likes that.

"I'm just worried about you, sweetie. Not worry-worry—I know you can handle yourself. Just, you've gotten a little thin."

"Lean and mean," Thomas says.

"Bean and green," Harrison says. "Weenie and peenie. Weenus and penis."

"Harrison."

"I just want to get to the library so I have enough time before it closes." Mads pushes her chair back. She stacks Thomas's empty plate onto hers, gathers the utensils.

"I'm going, too," Harrison says.

Claire shakes her head. "No, buddy. You and me, spelling words."

"*C-O-N-C-E-R-N*. Extra-credit word. I don't need to practice. Mads said I'm the copilot."

"Not *every*where," Claire says.

"I take a really long time in the library," Mads warns from the kitchen as she lines up the dishes in the dishwasher.

"I'll stay in the kids' section," Harrison says. "You won't even have to watch me. I'll make sure no one kidnaps me. Someone tries to snatch me—"

"Put that down," Claire says.

Mads hears the *Ha-hoo* that is Harrison getting the bad guy with his samurai sword/butter knife.

"You can't follow me around," Mads calls.

99

"I wooon't!"

It's still light out. As they drive, Harrison announces every license plate from another state until Mads tells him to shut up. He rides with his wallet on his lap. He loves that wallet, but there's not much in it, Mads knows. A couple of dollars, and his library card, and an old movie ticket to *Space Fighters*.

Mads strolls around the kids' section with Harrison for a while. "You don't have to stay," he says. "Who's following who?"

"All right." She's already found what she came for anyway. "Be free, big man."

Mads collects a few other books. This time, they're camouflage, the way guys in teen movies buy Red Vines and car magazines along with their condoms.

"God, Hare," Mads says. "How can you even carry all those? Do you need help?"

"I'm done. Let's get outta here." He sounds like a gangster after the holdup. The library always makes Mads feel like she's just pulled off a big score, too.

At home, Harrison lays his stash out around him, same as Mads used to when trick-or-treating was through. Thomas pats a spot on the couch and Mads sits with him and Claire as they watch some show. She's being polite. She laughs when they laugh and grimaces when they groan, but she's not paying a bit of attention to that TV. The book is calling to her, as books do. As stories do. As Billy Youngwolf Floyd's story does, especially.

She makes her escape as soon as she can. Now that she's finally alone with the book in her room, she takes her time. Anticipation is a warm bath to soak in. She tucks her knees in just so. She reads the back of the book, then the front pages where the reviews are. Finally, the first lines. *To my lawyer, Saxonberg: I can't say that I enjoyed your last visit. It was obvious that you had too much on your mind to pay any attention to what I was trying to say. . . .*

Then: *Claudia knew that she could never pull off the old-fashioned kind of running away. That is, running away in the heat of anger with a knapsack on her back.* Mads loves how it's written with a God voice, a voice with all-knowing wisdom. In this case, God is Mrs. Basil E. Frankweiler, but still. These are E. L. Konigsburg's words (and what is *she* like? The book says she lives in Port Chester, which sounds like a perfect town with perfect green lawns and definitely, most definitely, television parents), but they're not just her words anymore. They belong to Mads now, and to Billy, and to a million other people. It's strange, because the story seems to have stayed exactly the same since Mads read it last, but it has changed, too. It's new again, read with older eyes. It's strange how a book is both steady and mutable.

Mads stops reading, looks at the black, chicken-scratch pictures. And, then, finally, she opens the book to the middle. She squinches—her glasses are here somewhere, but whatever—and makes out the tiny words. *French Impressionists.* Where is Billy's own map right now? she wonders. Back in his pocket?

Set on a nightstand? In his own hands? Could they be gazing at *Far Eastern Art* at the same time, like distant lovers with the moon? He said the map had belonged to someone, and Mads can guess who. She is certain it was his mother's. She studies it for what it might have meant to them. *Greek and Roman Art. Great Hall. Arms and Armor.*

Mads can almost hear the tap of her own heels on the floor. *American Wing. Art of India.* She feels the cool hush of history, the secret tales of jeweled swords and necklaces in the shape of tigers and oil paint so real that you're sure a king's eyes follow you. She's filled with a longing to *be* there. A map can make you want things, and a book can open a door—a door to the main staircase of the Metropolitan Museum of Art, which leads to a long hallway with a velvet rope, heading to an angel statue that might transform you. Like Anna Youngwolf Floyd, like Billy himself, Mads wants to stay there for a while. In that place, there are no parents and no guilt. No ogres are allowed in. There is only a boy and a girl who become a team, whose ordinary lives fall away because one day they decide that it will be so.

Oh, Billy Youngwolf Floyd and his mother have gotten inside her, settled right in to disturb her soul and rustle her heart. They are there to cause some trouble, big trouble. Map or no map, fate or no fate, trouble has a job to do.

Wreck stuff. And wreck it good.

Chapter Ten

He should have picked her up. Just because he didn't want to meet some father in a tie, it was chickenshit not to do it. Billy's not a tie-type person, and he doesn't know tie-type people, so the whole neckwear idea makes him nervous. His dad wore one only once, in that box, which is a pretty bad place to finally try to straighten up, in Billy's opinion. Billy's glad he didn't have to see his mom all waxy and *gone* like that. Better to remember her the way she was, at least, the way she was when she was doing okay. Like that day she got the job at the rental car place and she brought home burgers and shakes from Dick's and said, *Life is funny*, in a way that meant it was good. Like when she'd hug him hard and he'd say, *Mom, stop*, even though he didn't really want her to. Or when she'd do something silly like sock him with a pillow or pat his head or tell him, *You're the best, that's what you are*, and he knew, no doubt, how much she loved him.

The only guy he knows who wears a tie is Uncle Nate, his

dad's half brother. At least, he wore one in that newspaper article about him and the software company he started. Billy doesn't really know him. Couple times he's called to see if Billy needs anything, like a job. He seemed like a really nice guy. But Billy never called "Uncle Nate" back because it feels disloyal. His mom could get almost jealous about his dad's side of the family, and Gran doesn't trust his uncle, says he's up to something. She says, *Blood may be thicker than water, but what do you want when you're thirsty?*

These particular thoughts make Billy more nervous than he is already. He pretends to study the menu in the plastic box outside Agua Verde. He tries to look casual. He used some of that cologne in the bottle with the horse-head cap that Gran got him one Christmas, but now it's all he can smell. He tastes it, even. It's going to give Madison Murray a headache. He tried to splash it on his cheeks, but it got all over the front of his shirt. The cap always makes him think of the *Godfather* movie, with the horse head in the bed. First time he watched that, he cried his eyes out, like some big-ass baby. He was eight, okay? The babysitter let him watch it, and his mom was *pissed.*

Tonight, no matter what, he's going to tell Madison about seeing her stalking J.T. Jones. It feels like a lie otherwise. It's funny, but he's got this weird thought: He wants to do everything right with her. He doesn't even know her. Maybe she's lazy or thinks she's hot shit or maybe she's a cat person. He doesn't think so, though. It's dangerous to *hope* like this.

Already, there's a little flame of it, and he wants to cup his hands around it so it doesn't blow out.

She's coming. He hears that truck two blocks away. He acts like he doesn't notice. He's calm and casual, just looking at that menu. He puts his hands in his pockets and rocks back on his heels, like some young Hollywood mogul. He feels Hollywood; things are going his way. His hair turned out good. He's all Charm Spell.

Billy's been looking at that menu so long, he can tell you that you can add chicken, steak, or pork to the taco ensalada for four bucks, and shrimp for five. She's walking across the parking lot now. Even if he didn't see her coming, he bets he could feel it. *She's* the one with a Spell-Like Ability. She probably doesn't even know it. She *should* know it. If you can use a Spell-Like Ability at will, it's limitless.

She's hurrying, breathing funny, in and out, in and out, like Mom did after she signed up for that mindfulness course they gave at the hospital. He hated that class, because his mom would chew her food real slow, and gaze out at some cloud like she'd never seen one before. Jesus, it was annoying. Thankfully that lasted about two weeks. It would have been great if it was some amazing cure, but staring too long and chewing too slow didn't look all that different from her bad days, only with the fake-ass smile of fake woo-woo bliss.

Stop! No more of these thoughts. This is his night. A person who jumps from a bridge goes out making sure you know how unhappy they are, and you'll never forget it. They have the final say, and you'll always remember how you let them down and weren't enough to stay for. But what they did shouldn't wreck everything even if it wrecked everything.

"Hey," Madison Murray says. "I'm sorry I'm late. I hate being late. It's so rude."

"Hey, no worries."

She wears a blue skirt and a flowered top and sandals and that bracelet. He really likes that bracelet. Maybe it's his favorite piece of jewelry a girl ever wore, if you can even call it jewelry. It's just leather strands woven in a braid. It makes him think of tree branches and nests.

Madison takes a pinch of her shirt and waves it in and out. "Whew. That was crazy. The people I babysit . . . Man, sometimes . . ."

"Yeah?" Wow, she smells good. Even over all his own cologne, he can smell it. Tangerines, or something else that's summer.

"Big fight. I didn't think I'd get out of there."

"Other people fighting is the worst."

"Really."

"I'd rather be fighting myself than not fighting and hearing other people fight." Ugh! Mouthful of moron.

She laughs. "Exactly."

The restaurant is packed. It's a casual place, stuck out over the water. You order at a counter, then bring your own drinks to your table. He starts to worry. Plastic cups, someone's napkin on the floor . . . He hopes she can see past how regular it is. He's

106

a plastic cup guy, not some thin-stemmed wineglass guy. Is it possible she doesn't want a thin-stemmed wineglass guy? Maybe he'll be that when he's forty, but probably not. The food is great, that's the point.

"This is great," she says. They've carried their food to one of the outside tables by the water, and now napkins are piling up, because the burritos are good and messy. She's talking with her mouth full, and this makes him so happy he can barely stand it.

"Isn't it?"

"Fantastic." At least, he thinks that's what she says. He can't really tell. She's downing that thing like she hasn't eaten in days, but so is he.

"I could eat five of these right now."

"Mmphh," she says.

They sit near the path off Boat Street, which curves along the narrow channel of water in front of the University of Washington. A couple passes, pushing a stroller, and two girls ride by on bikes, their wheels going *zzzz*. It's the perfect time to tell her that he knows all about her and J.T., so he'd better snag it. Perfect times are always numbered.

"You go to school?"

"Community college. Bellevue."

"You trek over to the Eastside, huh? That's a bitch." He's trying to work it into the conversation, but it's not easy. *So, I saw you stalking some guy, and hey, it's fine. I get it.*

"It's not too bad."

Just be natural! Acting natural is hardly ever natural, that's for sure. *Come on!* "Did you go to Blanchet?"

"Blanchet?"

"I mean, I'm guessing. I never saw you around Roosevelt."

"Oh! A school! I thought maybe, I don't know. A store or something. I'm not from around here."

"You're not?"

"Eastern Washington. I've only been here a couple months. I'm staying with my aunt and uncle while I do this real estate licensing course. I'm going home in September."

He doesn't even hear this at first, the true and most important point, the declaration of The End. He can only think what a fast mover that asshole J.T. Jones is. Make a girl fall in love with you practically right when she sets foot in the city and then ditch her so her heart breaks before she barely gets a chance to fucking unpack . . .

"I think you might know someone I know," Billy says.

Madison knocks over her drink. He always gets too many napkins, so no problem. He pats and soaks, and she's half-standing and red-faced. "I'm sorry," she says. "I'm so sorry."

"Hey, it's okay."

"I should have said something before."

"You couldn't have known I knew the guy."

"The guy?"

"J.T.! What a douche."

Her eyebrows bow down like two caterpillars being introduced. "Such a douche," she says. She looks shocked. Shit! He doesn't want to make her feel bad. Everyone falls in love with an asshole at least once in their life. Look at his mom. More than once. People who think they're above that—they're idiots, if you ask him. He hears people, girls, say it all the time. I *would never* . . . Oh, yeah? Congratulate yourself all you want, but you don't know what you might do when you look at someone and they look at you and they're everything bad you've ever secretly wanted. Humans are human, even the ones who think they're so smart.

"I saw you a couple times. Outside his house. I used to live near there."

"Oh my God! I feel awful. . . . I have to explain."

"Don't feel bad, feel glad!" He sounds like an advertising jingle. "He's gone! You deserve better. I can tell that already."

"I don't know about that."

"You do. J.T.'s an asshole."

"I'm not the greatest myself."

She looks right at him with those eyes. They're a deep pool, they're a long drink of water, they're—

"Billy . . ."

She has that look, like she's going to spill a bunch of stuff, confessions about J.T. and her, maybe say stuff he doesn't want to hear, how she's not ready yet for anything new. Whatever. He doesn't give a shit about J.T. Jones. Right then, sitting with her there as a seagull hops around by their feet and a squirrel runs up a tree like a Disney squirrel in a Disney movie, he's full and floating as a balloon, and there will be *no popping*. "Hey!"

he says fast, to change the topic. "You don't even know my last name. Or my phone number. Give me your phone."

She fishes around in her purse, hands it over. He types. "Give me yours," she says. He does. They hand them back. It's like a ritual has been completed. Like they've exchanged rings or something.

"Billy Youngwolf Floyd," she reads. His own name sounds like music when she says it. "That's beautiful."

"Really?" His mom always said Gran wanted to change it, but she wouldn't let her. Mom said you shouldn't be ashamed of who you are and where you came from, but talk was one thing. You could do your best to teach your kid the right stuff without being able to do the right stuff.

"Really."

"Mads," he reads. "Not Madison?"

"That's what my parents call me when they're upset."

"Got it."

"So. Billy Youngwolf Floyd." She leans forward. You should see how cute she is when she does that. "Tell me about the map."

"The map?" Of course he knows what she means. She lifts her eyebrows to say she's onto him. Heh heh—he loves it. "It was my mom's."

"Yeah?"

"She's . . . gone. Not here. You know, she passed." It sounds almost like *she's past*, but those two words don't go together at all. Passed is never past.

"Oh." Mads's voice is soft, and she doesn't ask a bunch of questions or go on and on like she feels sorry for him. It's nice. Really nice. If he wants to talk, he'll talk, and she seems to get that. People, they think they have to pull stuff out of you. He likes his stuff where it is.

"I want to go there, though."

"The museum? Doesn't it sound amazing?"

"I guess, yeah. Arms and Armor sounds cool."

"Sleeping in that awesome bed!"

They crumple up their garbage. They just sit there. Awkward busts in, makes itself comfortable. He doesn't want the date to be over, and maybe she doesn't, either, because she finally says, "Do you want to walk?" He runs their trays and cups back inside, and then they take the trail along the wharf at Boat Street. He should maybe grab her hand or something, but he doesn't. First off, they just met. Second, it's probably good to be a little more distant, harder to get, like J.T. Girls love that.

And he doesn't want to be one of those assholes who only talk about themselves, either, so he asks her about school, and where she's living now. She tells him about her real estate course, and community college. She sounds pretty excited about it. He tells her about Heartland, and staying with Gran at the houseboat.

They walk, and the evening light is all golden. It's that brokenhearted yellow of a summer day ending, and it's so tender or something that he has to be careful not to cry. It makes him think about everything his mom will never see. The water has little white diamonds dancing on it. Right there, the way the water sparkles—she's missing out on that.

His heart is full. Madison Murray walks beside him, and right then he practically has everything. By the time they get back to the parking lot at Agua Verde, the sun is almost down. Darkness edges in fast. It uses its weight and its elbows, the sneaky bastard. He wants the night to go on and on and on. He wishes he had his own place. In spite of how loaded those words are (he can barely think of those words without wanting to throw up), he wants that.

"I better go."

Ah, she fells him. It's a bow, a spear, a found object like a rock or a log—whatever it is, he's struck. It can't be over— it's such a great night. He wants to pick her up and carry her around the parking lot.

"Billy, um . . . ," she says. "I'm not going to be here very long. Only until Septem—"

Fuck that! And fuck distant and hard to get! He kisses her. He leans right in and kisses her hard, and, holy shit, her mouth is all sweet yellow light and fate and nearly missed chances. Her breath is warm, and they are shoved up against the car, and their hands are on each other, like that kiss has been wait-ing somewhere for years. She tries to say his name again, but his own mouth is over hers, and the soft whisper of *Billy* dis-appears. Maybe he does like complications, same as Jamie. Bring 'em on. Bring on every last beautiful one.

Chapter Eleven

What a mess, what a mess, what a mess! *Please save me from myself*, Mads thinks as she drives away. She sets her fingers on her mouth, and sure enough, it's different. Those lips are not her lips. They're lips that want things, bad. They're the lips of a girl who might stand at a gas station in a faraway place, with only her phone and a credit card.

She has never in her life, not once, wanted anyone like that.

This is awful. What is she doing, and what might she do next? She's heading for certain doom, that's what she's doing. She can't tell the boy who just kissed her like that (oh my God, that kiss—stars imploding, planets aligning) that she's the person who pulled his dead mother out of the water. Not *now* she can't. She can't tell Thomas or Claire about this, either— they'll have her hauled away to some place with locked rooms and rolling lawns. There is so much they don't know already— how deep her sadness is, the extent of it, how she thinks about oncoming cars and sudden swerves and bridges, how her anger is rising like a seaweedy creature. What's just happened, though—that was not another private thought tossing and turning like an insomniac. That kiss was a choice. An *act*. It feels powerful and amazing (and horrible and shameful) to act, but never mind that now. We're in the middle of a crisis, here.

This situation will only have one end, and she's well aware of that. Mads can never be with Billy Youngwolf Floyd. She reminds herself (as if she needs reminding) of all the reasons why. One: the dead body, his mother—this urgent fact she now can't reveal. Two: Murray & Murray Realtors, waiting for her in September. This is not some romantic comedy where he'll chase her down a traffic-filled street so she'll change her mind. *She is going home.* She has to. Her life has a fixed course, and there's no way she can envision him following her to Spokane to sell *real estate*.

Three: Billy Youngwolf Floyd himself. Ignore that kiss for a minute. Even if they met the way normal people do, what do they have in common? Nothing, that's what. All they have is that weird bond to Anna Youngwolf Floyd, and to a *book*, of all things, which brings Mads full circle to number one again.

The window of Thomas's truck is down, and Mads's hair is blowing all around, and she's distracted. So distracted that it takes her a moment to realize she's going south again on the freeway instead of north. Really, she should wear her glasses when she drives. In a panic, she takes the next exit. She told Thomas and Claire she was going to the library to study, and now, *now* she's going to be so late that the lie will crumple. The library closed hours ago. She's giving herself a lecture as the turn signal click-clicks: *If you're going to become a liar, you're going to have to get better at it.* This will never happen. Some people are just terrible with lies (like some people are terrible with plants, or TV remote controls, or love), and Mads is one of them.

The self-lecture, her hair, the turn signal, that kiss—it's several more pieces than her burdened mind can handle. Sometimes, we just keep doing the same thing again and again until we stop. Yep, she's once more down in the land of airplanes and machine parts and big, empty lots. Out there, there's nothing a person can do but change direction.

Otto Hermann is bent over his PowerPoint. He's having technical difficulties. He mutters something in German as a fat lock of white hair drops over his forehead. It's been a whole week since Mads got home, flopped on her bed, and pleaded for one pass, *please, just one,* after her date with Billy. If no one found out about this, she vowed, she'd get back on the right path, go to class, refocus her energy. No more Anna Youngwolf Floyd and her sad and complicated life. No more Billy and tragedy and museums and kisses that blindfold you and spin you around. No more lurid (but great, really great) peeks behind the scenes.

And, yeah, everything's been quiet; Claire practically whistles with her usual good cheer. It appears that Mads has gotten away with her crime. So it's her turn to fulfill her side of the bargain.

But there's a problem. She hasn't heard from Billy Youngwolf Floyd. And now all those vows about class and the right path, et cetera, et cetera, are totally gone, because she's caught up in the cruel, tormenting mystery of *why hasn't he called*. Not seeing him again was a great idea, until it was no longer her choice. Goddamn him! It's driving her crazy. The blank stretch of *What happened?* fills with the usual nonsense. Maybe he's sick, or has been in an accident. Maybe she said something stupid and unforgivable that night without realizing it. Maybe that kiss meant nothing to him. He probably does stuff like that all the time, and she's just another girl in a line of girls, serving her purpose by feeding his ego. Yeah, those guys just spend enough energy to prove a girl likes them, and then they vanish, because they got what they needed. Of course he'd treat her like an object! Who *really* saw her? Who *didn't* just use her for their own purposes? Not to get all waaa-waaa about it—the opposite! *Get it together*, she tells herself. *Stop letting shit like that happen. Stop letting users affect you. You don't even* want *him! It's a* relief *he's gone!*

She's not going to call him, either. She won't be that girl.

Mads hates distant and hard-to-get types. Game players. She's known a few, and her friend Sarah liked that jerk, Jake, for a while. She rubs her thumb over her lips. They still feel changed, but they'll go back to the way they were soon enough. Guys like that never have true and long-lasting importance anyway.

Mrs. Erickson (*Linda!*) slides a note across the desk. Poor Linda, trying to go back to the point in her life before everything went wrong, back to her high school days, when passing notes was risky behavior and pot was shocking. *His computer's probably not plugged in*, the note says, and Mads nods, rolls her eyes in the direction of the struggling Otto Hermann, who has begun to sweat.

The room has no real smell—maybe bodies and the slight tang from a Snapple bottle in the trash. But any lull in smell or sound or sight seems to fill up with images of that night, and *damn it!* now the room is overtaken with the musky-something of the cologne Billy had on. God, he smelled good. This kicks off the film, because the cologne was the first thing she noticed when she hurried toward him, sweaty and rushed after Suzanne and Carl had made her late. Mads kept Billy waiting so long that when she arrived, he had his hands in his pockets and he was rocking back and forth on his heels like he desperately had to pee. It was a little awkward-looking, actually.

Then came the great food, and the talking, and then (here it was, probably; the reason he didn't call) the horrible realization that he'd seen her that day on his street. He'd come to some crazy, awful conclusion about a guy she didn't even know, and as soon as she got back home, she looked him up— J.T. Jones. Sure enough, he lived two houses down from Anna and Billy. There was his picture in a *Blanchet Bugle* newsletter; he'd made some winning play in a football game. Mads with a football player? Hilarious. No way. Football players never paid any attention to her! She doesn't even really understand big guys crashing into each other. Mads is a quiet, book-reading girl who believes being nice will get you places, which it usually doesn't. J.T. Jones had self-important cheekbones and don't-give-a-shit eyes. She prefers star eyes and cheekbones like ledges you could fall from.

Stop! she yells to herself. The thing she doesn't get about the not calling is that Billy was great. He was. Looking at him, you picture a guy who smells of cigarettes and bad ideas, but he was *sweet*. And the whole thing with the museum was . . . Yeah. Just *yeah*. How was it that he seemed to understand her as no one else had before? The night was so twilighty and weirdly special that Mads forgot how tragic he was and how sad his life was, and how sad she herself was, because he was just being himself (she thought) and she was just being herself (for once). For those few hours, she felt some twilighty, sparkly-waterish sort of lightness. She felt (ugh, don't think it) hopeful. And then the kiss blazed through her forest and burned it all down. In a good way. In a *holy shit what just happened* way.

Well, he didn't call—no text, no nothing, and she should count herself lucky. She played with fire, and though her inner landscape feels altered, she is still intact. No one found out what she did or who she really is. Call it a near miss. It's great, actually.

She hates everyone.

Ryan Somebody, a twentysomething guy with religious

newscaster hair, bends to help Otto Hermann. "The plug?" he says. "Your laptop battery is dead, Mr. Hermann. You need to plug it in."

Linda slides her foot over and crashes it into Mads's. Her eyes gleam. Mads tries to give Linda a smile from 1985, even if Mads's mood says it's the end of the world.

Carl's home for lunch. He throws the loaf of bread on the counter, bangs the mayonnaise jar down. Suzanne is folding laundry in the family room, pretending that's what she actually does all day.

The silence is so loud Mads can barely stand it. In the strained hush of the Bellarose house, the *What happened?* of Billy grows louder. Mads feels pissed and restless. Over the week, her old, overwhelming despair has crept back in, too. The big ogre sits in a corner, casting his shadow, examining his fingernails and humming a tune. Mads has been waking in the night again, and not eating, and she's so anxious, she can't even read. When books can't comfort you, you know it's bad. Carl and Suzanne aren't helping anything. Fury plus despair is a bad combo. It makes you do crazy things just so you do *some*thing.

Outside, Ivy uses the chaise to pull herself up. She's so proud of standing. She lets go, and wobbles like a building in an earthquake before plopping down. Mads applauds. Suzanne joins them outside, like they're a team against Carl.

They are not a team. "See, Ivy? See the bird?" Suzanne says. Her voice is righteous as church bells.

Carl appears. He lets the screen door slam shut behind him. "Daddy has to go to work," he says. "Daddy's got to go pay the bills." Suzanne and Carl must have been crazy about each other once. They must have stared in each other's eyes and had passionate sex, and dreamed of forever, and now they can't stand to be in the same room. It's hard to understand.

Carl lifts Ivy, kisses her, sets her back down again. Ivy starts to wail. Mads hears the front door slam as he leaves.

"Ivy, come on! Jesus, stop it! Please!" Suzanne rises. The damp grass has soaked her shorts, proving once again that the world's against her. "Great. Terrific. Now I have to change."

"I got her," Mads says.

Mads wonders how one arranges a hit man so she can do in Suzanne and Carl. She needs to watch more *48 Hours*. Is Ivy ruined already? She's so perfect and so sweet, with her eyes the color of violets and her skin soft as tulip petals and a chortling laugh that makes you happy as a bluebell. But this is what Ivy sees and hears and takes in every day. This is the news she gets about love. No one is hitting her or sticking her in a closet, but no one is protecting her, either. She deserves better.

Ivy stops crying and studies Mads's face. That's what babies do. They look. And if they see anger or peril, or if no one really looks back, they've learned something about the world they live in, Mads knows. And so she smiles, sends messages of safety and love.

"You are one great baby, Ivy."

"Bee you," Ivy says. "Ibble be you."

"Be you? Ives, you're right. You're so right. Let's make that rule number one. Be you, no matter what. Fight for yourself like a samurai. Be your own noble warrior. Take it from me."

"I'm gone!" Suzanne calls.

Gone. It sounds like an answer.

Carl left the mayonnaise jar out, and the TV is still blaring in the family room. Mads shuts off the screaming (un)reality housewives. According to her father, she has what she needs—her phone and a credit card. She adds *book* to that list, since, like a true reader, she never goes anywhere without one. Lucky she's still got *From the Mixed-up Files* in her backpack. She needs a map, too, even if she never hears from Billy again.

A phone and a credit card are not enough for Ivy, though. You should see all the stuff they bring to go to the park. And they aren't just going to the park.

The diaper bag already has the basics, but Mads stuffs a couple of grocery sacks full of extra diapers, changes of clothes, the chime ball, the frog, the toy telephone, the book with the talking bookworm in the center. Also: a box of cereal, and a few bananas, and graham crackers. Bottles of juice and milk.

She sets Ivy in her crib and runs outside to strap the car seat into Thomas's truck. Across the street, Claire and Thomas's garage door rises, and Harrison speeds out on his bike. Great. Terrific. This is all Mads needs. Harrison shoots right up to the Bellarose driveway and skids. The bike tires make a satisfying long black mark along the pavement, an expert, superhero arc.

"So, where're you going?" he asks.

"Where's your helmet?"

"I'm just coming here!"

"You still need your helmet."

"You didn't say where you're going."

"None of your business."

"What's in that bag?" He drops his bike. Now he tries to snoop through the open door of the truck.

"Don't you have anything better to do?"

"That's a lot of stuff."

"Yeah? So? Hey, Harrison, I think Claire is calling."

"I'm too old for that trick."

"Ugh!" This is not meant for Harrison, but for the stupid car seat. It's like wrestling a stubborn toddler.

"You're buckling it in the wrong one," Harrison says. "That's for the middle person."

He's right. She finds the right buckle shoved down in the seat. There. The satisfying *click*.

"Hey, Hare, I gotta go. You be good."

"You better not be meeting some boy in secret."

This stops Mads. It stops her cold. She feels a thud of dread. She's right to worry. This is all it takes to send a person's whole life into a hurtling catastrophe—one weird kid, one wrong move, the butterfly effect, where the flap of far-off wings causes a hurricane across the globe. Harrison's owl eyes stare at Mads from behind his glasses. They are large enough to make you believe he knows things.

"What are you talking about?"

"Hmm, I wonder." Now he has one knee up, picking at a scab. He hops around to keep his balance. His shins are bruised and bumped as an old peach.

"Harrison."

He stops hopping, examines the scab as if it's a new specimen for the books.

"God, you're gross."

"You wouldn't be nervous if you didn't have anything to feel guilty about."

"Who says I'm nervous?"

"You're practically pooping your pants."

"What are you even saying? Maybe I have friends you don't know about."

"You don't have friends."

"I have friends, all right?"

"What do you think I am, stupid?"

"You just better mind your own business, mister."

"This *is* my business." He reaches into a pocket of his cargo shorts. Pulls out one of those small spiral notepads. He waves it at Mads.

"What is that?"

"Wouldn't you like to know." She tries to snatch it. She lunges, but he's too fast. He takes off, sprints a loop around the Bellaroses' front lawn. "Can't get me."

God, he's infuriating! And, whatever! It's not like she's ever going to see Billy again anyway. "Hey, this has been fun, but I'm at work. And I have somewhere I need to be."

Inside the Bellarose house, her phone is buzzing. She does not want to even *think* it might be him. Yeah, well, no worries, because it isn't. It's her mother. Three texts, one phone message, which is what she does when Mads doesn't answer right away. *Made appt. with attny. Knightley the week you return to sign papers! So exciting! Tell me you got my text about signing papers when you get back!*

Fury is some weird, out-of-control engine. She squeezes the phone, jams it down into her purse. Now she's back outside with Ivy on her hip. Harrison is still on the front lawn. The Bellaroses' cat lies across his shoes. Harrison's hunched over the spiral notebook like he's calculating the formula that proves the big bang.

He spots her, checks his watch. It's nearly as big as a hubcap, with lots of circles and dials that do various things he's tried a million times to tell her about. You could scuba dive with it on, he's said. Which is very handy, since Thomas and Claire barely let him take a bath without supervision.

"Two thirty-eight," he reports aloud. "Eleven thirty-eight p.m. in Cairo. Nine thirty-eight p.m. in the Reykjavik, Iceland."

"Watch your head, Ives." Mads pulls the car seat harness over the baby's head and buckles her in.

"Two forty-one," Harrison says.

Mads starts the truck. She sticks her head out the window. Harrison's glasses are skewed, as if he's had another unfortunate run-in with the Nerf darts. She better be nice to him. Someday he'll discover how to live on Mars in the event of a nuclear catastrophe. "Two forty-three, suspect leaves the premises," she calls. "You're wasting your time, anyway."

She takes off. Her general rage and despair do not fade, but her nerves about Harrison do. She stops worrying about him.

She shouldn't.

She's not nearly worried enough. The weird kid has a mission and a camera phone. He's trying to protect her, and the urge to protect can cause plenty of trouble. Plenty. Some clueless butterfly flaps in Panama. The hurricane begins to swirl right there on the Bellaroses' front lawn.

Mads *will not* get on the southbound freeway again. She'll head north. It'll be an entirely new beginning!

Ha. New beginnings are nearly impossible with the exact old you. Mads thinks: *a ferry, islands, Canada.* She feels the city fall behind her. Now she passes the towns of the north suburbs. Just as she sees the first sign for the ferry terminals, she notices the thin, small arm of the gas gauge. It's flicking back and forth, shaking as bad as Derek Carson's hands whenever he had to give a speech in their ninth-grade public speaking class.

Honestly, Thomas's truck? Mads thinks. *You would be this cruel?*

She takes the first turnoff, winds down a narrow, treed

road. There's a Bartells pharmacy and a Starbucks (of course), some yoga place and a chiropractic clinic, but no gas station. The road leads to the water and the ferry terminal. The signs say so, but she also can just tell. It's beginning to smell salt-watery, and the sky is getting larger. She's silently praying that she makes it to the town below, where there's sure to be a gas station. Where is Cole when she needs him? He knows everything about cars. He'd know why the half tank of gas she's sure was there has basically disappeared.

It smells like the sea out there, all right. You could bite right into that smell. Ivy's fallen asleep. Mads sees the ferry terminal a few blocks away, sitting at the quaint end of a quaint town.

What are you doing? Mads thinks. *What, what, what? You are stupid. This is pointless. You are a loser, and forgettable besides.*

Of course, despair isn't just one big ogre sitting in a corner; it's an army of ogres. They've been gathering, hiding behind every tree, and now they swarm, smack into her and take her down. All at once, she's too defeated to move. She's so sad, she can't even cry. The ogres drop a blanket of sad over her. She's at a stop sign with the engine idling. She wants to lie right down on the seat, and the only thing that stops her is Ivy. Of course Mads won't be getting on that ferry. Of course every single toy and jar of food will be returned to its usual place. Kidnapping Ivy is only a dream that keeps her feeling like something can be done and someone can be saved, she tells her loser self. But it can't and no one can be; at least, this is what the mind-sick ogres chant. Their job is to keep you in place with their force and the tethers around your wrists and ankles. Your job is to do the impossible and fight the bastards.

She can't fight right then, because you need weapons and tools and spells to be a warrior—potions are good, and so is an outstretched hand, a narrow window of escape, and, most of all, the shout of your own voice, yelling for help. The voice, saying *me, I, mine.* But that's so hard, because the voice is rusty from lack of use, and now the ogres have their big ham-slice hands around the vocal cords.

She's stopped at a railroad crossing. Crossroads, really? Please! Still, obvious is good, in her condition. Subtlety would surely fly right past. A Shell station is just on the other side of the tracks. Solutions, okay, maybe not *solutions*, but first steps toward solutions, are just *beyond*, if she would *just* . . . These are the words other people say and the ones she tells herself: *just*, and *knock it off*, and *you think you have it so bad?* One person against all those ogres is impossible. As far as weapons go, she's got a smile shield and a guilt umbrella, and even her anger is still just a burp she covers behind her hand.

She wonders if trains even come through here anymore. She feels bad thinking about this with Ivy in the car. But later, alone, a train might work. It might do the trick. It's not that she imagines exactly what would happen if she stepped out in front of one—the horrible details, the trauma to the driver of the train, to everyone she knows and doesn't. She just imagines the burden that she has and the burden that she *is* being lifted. The mind-sick stuff that the ogres gleefully toss in the air makes her believe that there is only one story possible for her life. What a lie that is. You must never forget how ogres love a lie.

Only a single element needs to shift: carbon, nitrogen, a violin case, a museum ticket, the loud and frantic *beep-beep!* of a car horn. The loud and frantic beeping of a car horn? What? What is that? Jesus! Mads jolts out of her own head. There is some kind of screaming emergency. She looks around in panic—is a train coming? Is she on the tracks after all, putting Ivy in worse danger than she's ever been in at home? But no, she's just sitting at that stop sign, and there's no train, and the tracks only disappear off into the quiet distance.

Still, the honking seems to require some action, so she swerves over into the first place she can, an adjacent restaurant lot, same as you might for an ambulance. The gas gauge, she notices, has returned to half full. Her heart is pounding. Who's honking like that?

She checks her mirrors, cranes her neck.

No.

It can't be.

She thinks she's seeing things. Is she imagining this? She could swear that's Billy Youngwolf Floyd's truck barreling down the hill, honking like something's on fire.

It's him, all right. This is crazy. He pulls up right beside her, his tires spinning in the gravel. They're in the parking lot of the Fog Horn Grill. Out her open window, Mads smells fish frying and the sunken, mysterious odor of kelp and deep water.

This—this is a coincidence definitely too strange to ignore. Billy leaps out of his SUV. He runs around it, leans right down into Mads's window. She is speechless. His face is right close to hers. His eyes are a little wild. They look just like his mother's in that yearbook photo from 1976.

"What are you doing!"

"What do you mean, what am I doing? What are *you* doing? What are you doing here?"

"I was just . . ."

"Just?"

Wait. He looks awfully guilty. Like he's been caught. What was she thinking? This is no coincidence. It's about as much of a coincidence as her seeing him at his own house. See? There's fate, and there's agency, dancing together beautifully, like a couple in sequined costumes.

"The baby is with you," he says.

"Of course the baby is with me. I'm babysitting. Are you *following* me?"

"No! Jesus, come on. I mean . . ."

"Who is that?" A tall dog with shaggy bangs sits in Billy's passenger seat. The dog gives her a quick glance, as if he's too polite to stare.

"Rocko."

"Rocko?"

"Look at him. It's a fucking shame."

"What?"

"He's starting to get bald patches, see? By his—"

"Wait."

"What?"

"He looks familiar."

Ivy stirs. One thing about Ives, she wakes up like a champion. She opens her eyes and beams like the sun, and then she looks right at Billy Youngwolf Floyd and—clear as day—she says, "Dog."

"Dog! Did you hear that?" Billy says. "She called me dog! She remembers me! You're right," he says to Ivy. "Wow, you're amazing."

Ivy chuckles. Mads does not know what's going on here. She hunts around in one of the bags, finds Ivy's bottle of juice, and hands it to her. Ivy sucks a little and then smiles and says *dog* again, through the squeak-suck of the bottle.

Mads narrows her eyes. "That dog lives in my neighborhood. I've seen him. I recognize his bangs."

"Every day for a week, that owner—"

"Every day for a week?"

Billy rubs his forehead with his palm, runs his hand through his hair. Then he reaches into the open window by Rocko. "I wanted to leave you this. Like, a surprise."

It's a Whitman's Sampler box. It's yellow, and there are flowers in the corners of it and there's a bird and a basket that look embroidered on. Chocolates.

"They're my gran's favorites, and I thought . . . Shit."

"Chocolates?"

"I tried to leave them a few times, but once your uncle was mowing the lawn, and then there was this kid . . ."

"Harrison, my cousin."

"He took my picture."

"He did? I'm sorry. He's a little protective."

"And when I was on your street, I saw Rocko, you know? Pretty obvious what's going on with him, the state he's in . . . And so today—"

"You stole him."

"I wouldn't say stole exactly."

"Kidnapped."

"Fine, kidnapped. I don't like to call it that, but whatever. And just as I'm getting him in the truck I see *your* truck pulling out of your street, and I thought—"

"You thought you'd follow me."

"You make me sound like a creeper." He's right. Who is she to talk?

"I mean, you could have just called."

"I tried!"

"You did?"

"I thought maybe you gave me the wrong number on purpose."

"Let me see your phone."

He digs it out of his pocket and hands it over. Ivy sucks her juice bottle and watches like Billy and Mads are Bert and Ernie in a riveting episode.

"Four five four *eight*, not seven. I'm an idiot. I'm so sorry."

She's still astonished that he's standing here in front of her now, but all at once, she's relieved, too. Relief washes over her, pours and pours like a waterfall. She wants to tip her chin up to it in gratitude.

"Sometimes girls do that, the number thing. . . ." He blushes.

Ivy slurps the last of her bottle, flings it to the seat. "Duh," she says.

"Do you want to get out of this car? Go down there?" He crooks his head toward the beach. "Walk, or something? Rocko probably has to pee."

She shouldn't. She remembers in a rush why even spending time with this boy is wrong. All that remembering pushes in and shoves at her conscience. But the relief is so great, and she's just really so happy to see him. "Sure. Let me change Ivy first."

"I'll get Rocko on a leash."

Mads changes Ivy and then slathers her with sun lotion. Ivy's hair is stuck up all sticky and sweet-smelling. Mads pops a hat on over it, ties it underneath Ivy's chin. Ivy grins like she's having the best day ever.

Billy and Mads and Ivy and Rocko cross over the tracks, to a soft sand beach. Kids dig and build castles and fetch water from the shore in pails while moms unwrap snacks and keep a watch out. Mads puts Ivy in her pack.

"Want me to carry her?" Billy asks.

"Okay. Thanks."

He lifts her to his shoulders.

"Want me to take him?" Mads asks.

"Sure. Appreciate it."

He hands Mads the leash.

They walk. Ivy's floral hat bobs as she checks it all out. Rocko sniffs coils of seaweed on the sand.

Mads doesn't even really know where she is. She's far from home, and everything around her is unfamiliar. At home there are farms and vineyards and pastures rolling out like seas, and here there's the real ocean. At home, there's her mother and her friends and a boy who still loves her, and here there are strangers, and an unusual boy with a stolen, long-limbed dog. But in this strangeness and in this *away*, some part of her sighs. The sigh is very nearly *rest*, such a needed rest that it's almost a potion, and the ogres sit their big bodies down and get a little sloppy. The sun and salt air make them sleepy. They loosen the ropes around her wrists.

A ferry pulls away from the dock. There it goes, leaving for Canada. Billy Youngwolf Floyd slips his hand into hers. It feels both shy and bold. Mads will have to break it off with him. She knows this. Right then, though, she accepts the hand that reaches.

Now a train is coming after all. The arm of the gate turns stern and folds down. Red lights flash, and the train rumbles through. Ivy points out the astonishing sight with one chubby finger. Even from the beach, the train seems to shake the earth. Mads and Billy grip hands and watch it pass. As it does, Mads does not imagine that train smashing into anything or anyone. Instead, she imagines the places it could go.

Chapter Twelve

Billy's palm is getting a little sweaty, but so what. So the hell what. He wishes he were on that train with her right now, and he wouldn't even care where they were going. It could end up in Tacoma even, right at the smelter, and he'd feel fabulous.

"I love you!" Mads shouts. Okay, she doesn't actually shout this. He can't even tell what she's saying, because the train is freaking loud. He can only see her mouth move, and she's smiling, so he nods and smiles back.

He's just so relieved, he can barely stand it. Relief's like a spell of Fast Healing. His Ability Points practically pour back in. All week, he's been in agony, thinking she gave him the wrong number on purpose. It didn't make sense, not after that kiss. And now—he was right! It was a misunderstanding! He never knew misunderstandings could be this awesome. And he was wrong, too, about the truck and the train tracks. The minute he saw the baby, he knew he'd been wrong. She loves that kid. That day at the bridge, he saw how she put their cheeks together and how she pulled up the baby's little socks.

Relief throws a party in his whole body.

He was wrong about the train, but still, he's glad she's walking right next to him as it passes. He anchors her down by holding her hand. When he saw the truck stopped at those tracks, he thought the same thing he did that day at the bridge. The doctor in his head, the one with the idiot box of Kleenex, tells him he'll see his mom in every girl, but he's not that stupid. This is more than a head game. Mads has those tan arms and those adorable freckles, but he sees the spell she's burdened with, the secret coat she's wearing. Once you know about the secret coat, you can spot another person wearing it. Mads is sweet and cheerful, but she buttoned her sweater wrong during their date when the night got cool, and her eyes have those thumbprints of dark circles under them. It's something out of Night Worlds. He'd call it a Despair Spell. The weight of the coat would slowly drain your energy before killing you off.

But this is *not* why his heart cracks right open every time he sees her, he tells the doctor in his head. It's the possible joy, not the sorrow, that draws him, asshole. This is no freaky mother-thing, you loser. He is not attracted to the coat, but to the real person under the coat.

The train disappears into the distance. "Where's it going?" she asks.

He has no idea. "New York. Metropolitan Museum of Art." She laughs. "Yeah. That's exactly where it's going." The baby pats the top of Billy's head as they walk again. Rocko pees on a boulder and then on a washed-up tennis shoe.

"Rocko's walking funny," Mads says. She's already getting a little sunburned. She put lotion on the baby but not on herself.

"It's a sign? That he's been abused. Hair loss, too. That sore by his ear . . . He's got another one under his front leg. Our vet will take care of that. Right, Rocko? You're gonna have a new life, friend."

Rocko's ear twitches at the sound of his name. "That's so sad."

"Sometimes they won't even walk around like he's doing. They don't play. Or else, right away they bond to you. They don't want to leave your side. You should have seen Jasper." Billy's talking a lot. Something about that girl just makes his voice pour out.

"Was Jasper with you the other day?"

"Yeah. He's my buddy. You saw him, the big golden? He wouldn't get off my lap for like three weeks when we first got him. Jasp, I'm going to take him when I get my own place." The words *my own place* come out like nothing, but they're not nothing. He uses those words on purpose, because saying them to her, saying them in all this *light*, might make them okay again. In spite of what those words now mean to him, he feels a graze of desire for them, too. God, it'd be so great. A place with a yard for Jasper and Casper. Freedom. It's the first time he's let himself imagine it again.

She has no idea about any of this. She just sits down so

cute, doesn't even see him fighting off the slam throw-up feeling, doesn't even see that he *wins*. He wins, because he lets *the future* in. They sit on a big piece of driftwood, and then the baby, Ivy, gets squirmy in her pack, and they take her out, and Mads walks her around holding her little seashell hands. She keeps heading for Rocko, which makes Billy slightly nervous.

"I don't think he's aggressive. But she probably shouldn't pet him or anything."

"Okay."

"He needs some time to just, you know, be himself."

"What's going to happen to him?"

"My boss, Jane—she'll make sure he gets a good home. We're a no-kill shelter, so however long that takes . . . Sometimes she'll bring charges against the asshole. And generally I'm not supposed to just—"

"Steal them?"

"Not steal them exactly. Remove them from the situation. Without permission from the owner."

"Steal."

He doesn't know how to explain it. "I can't help myself."

"I get that."

"Yeah?"

"Definitely."

"It feels so great out here," Mads says. "It makes me just want to—" In one sudden move, she picks up baby Ivy and runs like hell down the beach and then runs like hell back. Ivy bumps along on Mads's hip, and the baby's laughing so hard, you can't see her eyes. Mads's face is so happy and open that Billy's heart just busts. It cracks, because whatever is in it has made it crazy-full. It hasn't felt that full in so long.

"Come here," he says when she's back again, panting. "You come right here." He wants to lift her right up off the ground, but he can't. Not with Rocko on the leash and Ivy on her hip. He yanks her hand instead, pulls her toward him.

They grin at each other like idiots and then she says, "I'd live there." She points to a small white house on the bluff.

"Not there?" He indicates a big damn mansion.

"Too much vacuuming."

"You can come here and sell a bunch of real estate and buy it."

"No way. It might look small, but I'm guessing three bed-rooms, with an attic and a basement. Twenty-seven hundred square feet, at least, and with that view? Practically waterfront. Okay, there's the train, but still."

"You sure love real estate, huh?"

"Me?"

"Yeah, you. Rocko's a dog and Ivy's a baby, so they don't even know what real estate is."

"I don't love it."

"You don't?"

"No."

"It seems like it. You seem so happy talking about your class. And the whole Murray and Murray thing."

"I didn't want to seem all negative."

"Do you even like it?"

"I sort of like it. I maybe like it. I don't know. I don't think I like it. Let's just call it a family obligation. It's complicated."

He grins.

"Oh, great. I know what you're thinking." She can't help but smile now. "I know exactly what you're thinking."

"You're a mind reader, huh?"

"Don't even say it," she warns.

He raises his eyebrows, wiggles them. Man, he likes her.

"If you say it, I'm going to punch you."

"Say what, something about complications? Something with the word *like*?"

"I'm going to punch you a good one."

"I'm a lover, not a fighter." It sounds stupid, but kind of just right, too. She laughs. She play punches his arm anyway, and he wishes he could grab her so hard and kiss her and pull her down on the sand.

Ivy's squirming again, getting cranky. She's making little monkey screeches.

"This is going to get ugly," Mads says. "Jeez, what time is it? I've got to go."

"Yeah, me too. I better get Rocko over to his new digs."

They head back to their cars. When they reach the tracks, he takes her hand and runs everyone to the other side. No train is coming, but still. You don't want to take chances. Every one of them, Madison and Ivy and Rocko, and even him, yeah, even his fucked-up self, is worth protecting.

She buckles in Ivy. The baby twists and reaches for Billy like he might save her from the torture of the car seat. Shit. Now he kind of loves her, too.

"That's very dramatic, Ives." Mads hands the baby a round Tupperware container of Cheerios, and Ivy decides she likes the car seat after all. "It was really nice to meet you, Rocko." He likes how Mads looks at the dog. Like she's trying to give him all the love she can with her eyes.

He wants to kiss her so bad. He's trying to find a moment, but she's rushing all around, settling the baby, and before he knows it, she's in the truck. She rolls the window down, fast. After this great day, now she's all hurry-hurry, like she's trying to get away. "Well, thanks so much for the chocolates, and for, you know, stalking me."

"Hey, no problem. Anytime." He's not feeling the kiss coming. In fact, if he doesn't do something fast, she'll be gone. He doesn't get this. A second ago, it was like they were practically a couple, a possible couple, walking down that beach.

"Um, Mads. Wait. You want to get together later?"

No answer. Shit. Shit! She just runs her hand along the seam of the window ledge, as if checking the quality of workmanship.

"Or tomorrow?"

She stares out toward the water where the ferry disappeared.

"Or another time?"

"Billy—"

"Don't even say anything."

"No. No! It's not you."

He groans.

"No, I mean, this has been a great day. I was so happy you found me! But I can't come here and sell real estate, you know? I've got to go back home in September."

"You don't know what might happen between now and then."

"I've got to go home in September. I know *that*."

"Okay."

"And I'm not . . . I don't know. I don't want anyone to get hurt here. I don't know how to explain it."

"We're just hanging out." He's such a liar.

She rubs her forehead. "Ugh."

"Hey," he says. "No problem."

"I'm so sorry. I'm such an idiot."

"No worries. I'll just have to find someone else to go to New York with." He tries to make it seem like a joke, but his voice is cheery as a crime show.

"Just remember to keep your feet up in the bathroom stall so the guards don't see you." She looks like she might cry.

It takes three, four times for the engine to start. He stands around looking lame. He's not one of those guys who can lift the hood and fix the problem. He knows the chassis is the body, and the engine is the heart, and that's it.

She waves. He waves. In two minutes, he's gone from soaring to crash. He wants to swear and kick tires, but Rocko is with him, and Rocko has seen enough explosive shit. He's got a responsibility to that dog, even if the world is mean. He swallows that meanness and hopes it doesn't burn an acid hole in his own rusty engine.

He's in a bad mood. Even Night Worlds sucks. Drew knows someone who knows someone who's having a party, so he decides to go with Alex and Leigh. Supposedly, Alex and Leigh aren't back together, but going out together looks back together to Billy. He doesn't like Leigh. She's one of those people who always make little corrective statements, laughing at how Alex pronounces something or telling him to close his mouth all the way when he eats and shit like that. Next time, he's going to say something. He's not going to fucking sit back and watch Alex be humiliated. His mom's old boyfriend Powell used to do that to her.

He's in a hurry, and he's not hungry anyway, so he takes a few swigs out of the milk carton. Gran gives him a Gaze Attack. It's not about the milk, though. His mother didn't like when he didn't use a glass, but Gran couldn't care less.

"Billy."

"What."

"You aren't going to eat? What's the matter?"

"Nothing."

"Slamming the fridge door as you say *nothing* is not nothing."

"I'm just in a hurry."

"Is this about her birthday coming?"

Swear to God, it's like someone punches him. An actual punch, right in the gut. He's socked with pain. It bends him over. He deserves it, too. He forgot! He fucking forgot his mother's birthday was coming. How could he? How could he be such a dick? He wants to hurl that kitchen chair through a window, but he just jerks it away from the table and flings himself into it. He puts his head in his hands. He presses on his eyeballs until he sees stars.

Gran's hand is on his back. "You ever remember my birthday? No one ever remembers my birthday. It's okay."

It isn't. Nothing is okay right then. He starts to cry like a big baby again. His stomach heaves with grief. The wracking sobs give him the beating he deserves. First, he couldn't stop his mother, and second, he wasn't enough, and third, he almost forgot her. He knows he's not supposed to think like this. Depression is a disease, yeah, okay, but a person still makes choices! Even in that darkest of dark places, a choice was made, and he can't get past that fact. No matter how hard he tries, he keeps coming back to the wrong, black logic his guilty mind insists on: It's something she did to him, something he did to her, something people do to each other, which means it could have been different.

He forgot her birthday, and Madison Murray basically told him to take a hike after he already had started to fall for her, and now he's going to end this fucked-up day by going to a party when he hates parties, and a tornado of sadness is ripping through him.

"Billy. Look at me."

He doesn't want to look at her.

She forces his chin up with her hand. He hates when she does that. It makes him feel like he's six and not a man.

"Quit," he says.

He yanks his chin away. But she's already seen his eyes.

"It's not just that, is it?"

Sometimes she doesn't know when to leave a person alone.

"It's a girl, too. That girl."

"For God's sake," he says.

"Where did you say you met this girl, anyway?"

"We just ran into each other. It doesn't matter. I'm not going to see her again."

"You ran into her twice, you said. At home. At the bridge."

"She knew someone on our street. So what."

"Oh, really."

This is another thing he hates. Gran's paranoid. There's always some big plot, some way a person will do you wrong. Occasionally, she's right, but usually, she's just looking for a reason to hate people. Like her neighbors, the time they used her dock for like five minutes. She was pissed and held a grudge for years, because they didn't ask first. Like his old friend Jacob, who stopped coming over after Gran said he smelled like weed. He was a good guy, straitlaced, went to church even. He just lived with his dad and they didn't do a lot of laundry. Billy didn't like to think about it.

He loves Gran, but she has a mean streak. It's different

between Gran and him than it was between Gran and Mom, he keeps telling himself. Easier. But he wonders, you know, what it'd be like to grow up being told you should think the worst of people. If every person was bad, how did you ever feel safe?

"I don't know what you're thinking, old lady, and I don't care. I'm outta here."

"Don't be a fool. If something seems strange, it's usually strange."

"You're strange," he says.

At least he's done crying now. Also, he's just pretty much done in general.

The party's at this girl Becka's house. She and her friends were sophomores when Billy and his friends were seniors. It's weird, being at a party with people still in high school. He feels too old for this. He's only been out of school for a year, but hanging out with them seems like something you could get arrested for.

Becka's parents are gone. The house has a backyard with neighbors on all sides. The music's loud. The dining room table is filled with beer and open bags of chips and a bowl of dying guacamole. A few broken chips stick up from it like headstones.

Billy cracks the top of a bottle of beer he doesn't even want. Alex and Leigh are kissing. It pisses him off. "They have a hot tub," Drew shouts next to him.

"Did you bring your bathing suit?" Billy asks, and then

feels fifty. Drew pretends to choke on a swallow of Corona and gives him one of those looks that says *What the hell?*

"Whatever," Billy says.

He doesn't want to go home, but he doesn't want to be here, either. He should have taken his own car. A bunch more people arrive, and a guy sets another case of beer on the table. Bags of chips get thrown on top of other bags of chips, stacking up like bodies in a war movie.

The door is open and cool night air shoots in, and suddenly arms circle his waist from behind. They shove his T-shirt up, and icy hands press against his skin.

"Oh my God! Wolfie, you're here. Warm me up," Amy says.

He doesn't push her away, but he doesn't exactly encourage her, either. She rubs his bare skin for a minute and then gives up, tugs his T-shirt, gives him a little shove.

"Get me a beer," she says, even though they're right in front of her. She's the kind of girl who expects you to do stuff for her.

He hands her one. She hands it back. He unscrews the top. She grabs it, takes a drink. "I can't believe I haven't seen you at work in a week. I swear, Jane's putting us on different schedules on purpose."

"Nah." Yeah.

"Look around. It's a baby party. We should get out of here."

"You've been here two seconds."

"Long enough to know I have a better idea." She takes another long swallow, displays her neck like he's a vampire.

Now she meets his eyes, draws close. She sticks her hand in

his back pocket. "Show me that thing you don't want me to see."

Yeah, double meaning, whatever. He can feel her fingers wiggling against his ass. She has the wrong pocket, and he's glad. He pulls away.

"Don't you know what secrets do?"

He'd never tell her about the map. She'd never understand. No way. Not in a million years.

"You want to dance, or something? People are dancing." She's right. The music's gotten louder. He can see through the kitchen and out the open back door to the patio, where guys and girls and girls and girls dance. Leigh and Alex are out there. Drew stands on the deck of the hot tub, lifts off his shirt. Jesus. How much time does he spend at the gym?

Amy grabs Billy's hand and leads. They pass through the kitchen—there's a row of cookbooks, a fancy mixer, a microwave with its door swung open and something recently exploded inside. The parents are gonna love that. Just as they reach the back steps, Billy's phone vibrates in his pocket.

"Just a sec."

"You're going to get that *right now*?"

You don't just let a phone ring. After his dad and all the times with his mom, he always looks, at least.

His stomach flips, right as—*Jesus!*—Drew takes his pants off.

"I gotta get this," he says to Amy.

"Wolfieee. Ugh!"

She stomps away. Drew gets into the hot tub. His bare ass descends like the setting sun.

"Hello?" Billy ditches his beer on the kitchen counter, plugs his ear with his finger to hear better. The music's so loud, it's like being beat up around the head.

"Mixed-message phone call." Mads's voice doesn't belong here. It's like an angel in a head shop.

"Hey, it's you."

"Where are you? Sounds like a party. Of course you'd be at a party. I mean, it's Friday night."

"I can't hear you. Let me get outta here."

He passes the food table, spots packages of hot dogs and buns. Some naïve high schooler thought this was a barbecue. He grabs the dogs, elbows past a couple making out by the front door. More cars pull up; more kids pile out. "Hang on, I'm almost—"

"Wow, what was that?"

"Just this girl. Whistling." Amy's on the front lawn, hands on her hips. The whistle is *pissed*.

"It sounds like a car alarm. Like someone's stealing something."

Ha—Amy seems to think so. He jogs the hell out of there. The party retreats, and the street gets quiet. God, he's glad to be just walking under the streetlamps with Mads. It's just him and her, and a raccoon that skitters behind some garbage cans.

"So, you called." It comes out wrong, like he wants her to get to business.

"I'm sorry. I didn't mean to take you away from your party."

"No, I mean, I'm surprised. I'm glad."

"I was just thinking. There's no reason we cabefu."

"Cabefu?"

"Sowwy. It's the carmwa."

"Caramel? Are you eating—"

"Chocolates."

"Oh." He pictures her: She's wearing some cute soft paja-mas, and sits on her canopy bed with the yellow box on her knees. She's adorable.

"Friends. We can maybe be friends, even if I have to leave. Is there anything wrong with that? Not really."

"I don't see anything wrong with it." Friends. He's okay with whatever she wants to call it. His heart is already doing a little dance.

"Do you have to get back to your party?"

"I'm outta there." Who needs a car? He can walk home. He can *fly* home. "I don't even like parties."

"You don't?"

"You sound so surprised."

"I just thought you would."

He likes that, how when you meet new people, you can be anyone. You can be a regular guy who likes parties. Something about that makes him feel good. He swaggers down that late-night street holding the package of hot dogs like it's a briefcase full of money.

"Nope," he says. "Not a party person." The moon is out, reminding him that there are permanent things. The night smells like dark sky and dewy earth, and he wants to know everything about her. He wants to know her first memory and what she's scared of and what she looks like when she's sleeping. Where do you begin, when a whole new person awaits? "Do you have any brothers or sisters?"

"No," she says. "I guess that's another thing we have in common, right? I forgot about that. We're both only children."

He doesn't remember talking about this before, but maybe they did. He repeats himself all the time. Probably because he sticks to the few safe topics he's got. "I've got a half brother. But I only met him once."

"Oh, wow. Your mom had another kid?"

"Dad. Some high school thing. Made my mom all insecure."

"That must be weird."

"Nah, whatever. What about pets?" They have a lot of ground to cover. But, hey, he could walk all night. He could walk until daylight, he could walk to New York, because love is fuel, and his is burning.

"We used to have a dog, Mimi. But when my dad left . . ."

She doesn't want to say more. At least, she stops right there. "What?"

"This sounds bad. I've never even told anyone this before."

"It's okay." Are you kidding? If she only knew about his dad *and* his mom, she wouldn't feel embarrassed about much.

"When he left, he took the dog. He didn't think my mom could take care of her."

She waits to see if he understands without having to say more. He does. He wants to punch that asshole in the face.

"Sucks."

"Yeah. I still love him, though."

"I'm sure."

"We kind of look alike. I take after his side of the family. I used to spend time with him in the summers, before he moved so far."

They're silent for a while. He can hear her breathing. He can hear her trying to love, when love is hard. He tries to think up something fast to make her laugh. He says, "Okay, Mads, when do we bust out of here. And how?" If she doesn't get it, he'll just sound like an idiot.

"Just stuff some clothes in your violin case, and I'll stuff some in mine, and I'll meet you after school tomorrow."

He'll never tell a living soul this, but when she says that, he skips. He actually skips a little, he feels so good. Every day since . . . *Don't think about it!* Well, let's just say he never thought he'd feel happy again. But he could spin around a freaking lamppost right then, like the guy with the umbrella in that old movie. It's possible that he loves her already. People who say you can't fall in real love that fast, poor sad suckers, it's never happened to them.

The minute he grabbed those hot dogs, he knew where he was heading. He keeps walking as they talk. He learns that she's afraid of being buried alive and of leeches and home invasion robberies, and he tells her he's not afraid of anything, until she forces him to admit he's scared of crane flies.

"Crane flies?"

Crane flies, with their thin, threadlike legs. "No matter how carefully you pick one up, you know you're breaking its legs."

He thinks he hears her shudder. They move from fears to dreams. She tells him about filling out those college applications in secret, but how she never sent them. How she was going to use the money she earned as a lifeguard to apply. A lifeguard! This distracts him for a sec. He imagines her in one of those red suits, sitting up high and unreachable in one of those tall chairs. Holy shit, he wants to see that. He'd put his hand—

"I wanted to go so bad."

The longing in her voice stops the mouth-to-mouth he was just performing in his head. "You've *got* to go."

He'd be in her corner. He'd carry her books and help her study. He'd hold the flash cards. Probably there would be flash cards. He tells her about registering for community college, how he had his schedule and everything, but then his mom was doing bad and things were messed up and he never went. She tells him about wanting to be an English teacher. Man, she loves books. You'd never think it, him in love with a bookworm, but there you have it.

Billy arrives. Casper stirs. There's the slide-clink of his chain.

"I can't quite hear you," Mads says.

Well, he has to keep his voice down. Usually, he waits until that asshole, H. Bergman, makes his daily trip to the Quik Mart at the end of the block to buy cigarettes. Billy's got the timing down perfect. He rushes over from Heartland instead of taking a lunch hour. H. Bergman leaves only to go there, or to make his biweekly outing to Fred Meyer. Either way, he's never gone long, which is exactly the problem. Billy can't rescue Casper, because he'll never be able to break through that fence before H. Bergman gets back with his TP and frozen dinners. But now, tonight—love has made him brave. Here he is in front of the house, with H. Bergman's car right in the driveway.

Casper looks like hell. Food is one thing, but Billy can't be around all the time for whatever else H. Bergman does to him.

"It's wrong," he whispers. He means the whole real estate thing, but so much more, too. Mads and her mother, Casper and H. Bergman, all the shitty things people do. He opens the package with his teeth, flings those hot dogs to Casper, one by one. In his mind, they rain down like valentines.

"Billy, I should go," Mads says.

Never, he thinks but doesn't say. "Okay."

"Man, chocolate sure makes you thirsty."

He starts to laugh. And if H. Bergman hears him, too bad. So what, he'll fight that asshole now, on this sidewalk. He'll take Casper then and there. Because tonight, his life is starting.

"Yeah, it does."

"I'm really glad we can be friends," she says.

"Me too."

Friends. Heh heh. Right.

He hears what's in her voice. It's a risk to hear it, but love is always a risk. Life is. You could step into the street and get hit by a car, but then again, you could step into the street and get to the other side.

Chapter Thirteen

Mads needs water, bad. Water, or something else to help her swallow her mixed emotions. Why did she call him? She had her chance for a tidy ending at the ferry dock, but she just couldn't let it be. There's something she needs to *see*. Needing to see is what gets humans into so much trouble. Then again, you might find out that you haven't sailed off the edge of the earth after all.

Billy sounded mad at first, and who could blame him? *So, you called.* No one likes, no one *deserves*, some push-you-away-pull-you-close kind of person. He especially doesn't deserve that.

Mads has to tell him. She can't tell him. The more she goes on like this, the worse she'll need to confess about his mother and her, and the more impossible it will be to confess. Secrets only grow larger over time, and don't let anyone tell you different.

It was such a great night—talking, sitting in that bed made

up with Harrison's race car sheets, wearing Claire's old draw-string shorts and Thomas's Grateful Dead T-shirt (she forgot to pack her pj's). Billy's so funny, too, way funnier than you'd think. Mads cracks up on the way to the kitchen, just remembering how he said a person didn't have to be afraid of home invasion when you had a dog like Ginger. She might be small and white, but she could take a squeaker out of a rubber steak in two seconds flat. If you were ever attacked by a fake steak, she had your back. And when he told that story about getting a crane fly out of his room by chasing it around with his T-shirt, whacking at the ceiling while he stood on his bed . . .

"Well, you're having fun," Claire says.

Mads puts her hand to her chest. All that talk about home invasions. "Jeez. You scared me."

"Who was that on the phone?"

Mads scowls. This isn't like Claire, not at all. Claire has warm hands, kind eyes, and, sure, maybe a firm word or two. She doesn't usually huff like this, shooting *we both know what I'm talking about* looks.

Well. They both *do* know what she's talking about.

"A friend, Claire! God! Can I not have friends? I'm sorry if I woke you." Mads sounds like a quote-unquote teenager.

"Of course you can have *friends*. But of all the millions of people in the world you might be friends with, this is who you choose?"

"I don't know what you're talking about."

"Who was on the phone?"

"A guy from class." Her mind hunts for a name. Come on. *Come on!* "Ryan. Ryan Plug."

"Ryan Plug."

"Can you imagine having a last name like Plug? You got to feel sorry for the guy! I mean, it could be worse, it could be Phlegm or something, but who wants to live your whole life being called Plug."

"Madison."

"I told him, you know, you can do something about that. Go to court, whatever. He's very sensitive about it, but we had this whole open discussion . . ." They're at the bottom of the stairs. The front door is right there. Mads could make a run for it, but probably wouldn't get far with no money and no phone, and no shoes even, for that matter. As it is, she has to bunch Claire's shorts around her waist as she walks, even with the drawstring. Fleeing in those would be a disaster.

"Madison, look at me."

Why do people always make you look at them when it's an Important Moment of Confrontation? Oh, yes. That's why. Claire's eyes send a message that begs for honesty. Holy hell. Now those eyes are having the midnight showing of the mess that will be Mads's future.

"Harrison said . . ."

"Harrison said what?" Righteous indignation is her only option.

"That boy. *Her* son."

"Her?"

"The woman who . . . Don't make me say it."

Even Claire—enlightened, tolerant, progressive Claire—avoids the word: *suicide.*

Depression, too, is a term she steps around and eyes carefully, like an unattended piece of luggage at the airport. Is it a harmless backpack or does it have a bomb inside? Certainly, the bag must be avoided, reported to authorities. The words feel dangerous because they are dangerous. Something might be tipped over, and then terrible things could happen. To lots of people, not just one.

"Harrison said he saw . . ."

"He saw what?"

"The two of you. You and her son. Together."

"How would he even know who he is?"

"He looks stuff up. He looks everything up. *Everyone* looks everything up! He saw some picture of him online." Mads knows the one. Two guys on a snowy hill. No, Harrison probably uncovered images she didn't even find.

"He's on the computer way too much, Claire."

"He said that same guy, the son, was out front. Here. At our house."

Claire hands her Harrison's phone. It's Thomas's old one, so it weighs a couple of pounds. Harrison's supposed to use it only for emergencies. But now it's flipped open (that's how old it is), and there's a tiny picture.

"It's a foot. It's just a foot and some sky. You can't even tell who that is. That could be Ned Chaplin." Ned's the neighbor with a bunch of cats.

"In a Converse? Ned Chaplin wears dress shoes with tassels, even when he goes to get the mail."

"It could be anyone's Converse! What, are those the shoes of guys with suicidal mothers or something? Come on. You know Harrison has an overactive imagination. He should be in a summer program or something, Claire. What are those pretend astronaut things? When you're an only child, you can get into trouble if you don't have lots to do." *Take it from me*, Mads should add.

"If I got this wrong, I'm sorry."

"You got this wrong."

They've migrated to the kitchen. Claire pulls out a stool from the center island and sits.

Mads folds her arms. She's really getting into the whole outrage and unfairness thing. She practically forgets she's lying. And then Claire sighs, and Mads remembers. She starts to feel bad. She waits for lightning to strike, but nothing happens. "Can you make him stop following me?"

"Of course. Yes. I'm so sorry, Mads. Sometimes, Harrison just weirdly *knows* things. . . . And I've been . . . *We've* been worrying about you. I mean, after the thing at the lake, and then all that research you were doing . . . I thought—I just saw you getting more and more wrapped up in this whole *idea* of her, and what she did. . . ."

The kindness strikes, worse than any lightning. Damn

it! She can deal with an angry person. Angry people only make you angry. Your own anger is power, and it's distance. Kindness, though. Softness, sadness, anything even remotely pathetic—those are the things that hunt Mads down and spear her heart.

Those are the things that make her feel *guilty*.

Guilt is like her own shadow. Even if she can't see it, it's always with her, ready to appear in the right light. Real wrong-doing is not nearly as awful as the permanent, hazy chaperone who pursues her everywhere. Has she said something wrong, done something wrong, or is she just, as a person, wrong? Here's how it looks: Her mother says something out of nowhere, something that comes like a sudden smack after they're getting along just fine. *You're awfully selfish* or *What a big shot* or *You brat.* The shadow steps out, points the ugly finger. It makes her so mad. Makes her feel awful. But right then, she shoves it away. She goes off with her own friends, has a great time with Jess or Stephie or Sarah, plans a new life away from that bitch. But when she gets home, there are missed messages and there's remorse and maybe even a gift, like that stuffed bear holding the heart. It's on her bed at home. Honestly, she can't stand to look at it. The heart says *I love you*, and the words in red script make her feel ashamed.

Shame is one of the ogres, of course. The fattest, meanest one, who laughs when you fall down.

"Madison? Honey?"

"I'm sorry."

Great. Super. Her face is all screwed up because she's about to cry. Claire's arms go around her. Mads's face is smushed up against Claire's robe. "Sweetie, I'm the one who's sorry. Really. I'm so sorry."

Mads loves Claire. Claire is a wonderful person. Claire does not want to grasp Mads to her forever, but Mads can't stand to be smushed up against a mother's bathrobe. This will likely never, ever be a comforting feeling. She gives Claire a little push.

"Okay," Claire says. "Okay." She moves around to the other side of the island, opens a few kitchen cupboards as if searching for answers, settles on a cup and the kettle, which she fills with water. "Tea?"

Mads wipes her eyes with the back of her hand. Pinches her nose, so she'll stop the tears. "Sure."

"I'm truly sorry. I messed that up big-time. Here I am, worrying about you being sad, and the first time you seem really happy, I make you cry."

Claire's face is so honest that Mads wants to tell her everything. It seems possible she might really hear. "Sometimes . . ."

Claire waits.

"It all feels too much." Even this is a huge confession. One of the ogres has a hand clamped over her mouth, and she has to yank and pull so she can even speak.

"What does *too much* look like?"

"I don't know. Just too much."

Mads studies the countertop.

"Here's the deal," Claire says finally.

"We've made a deal?"

"I hope we're going to. You made it clear how you feel about talking to a therapist, but I want you to go see a doctor-doctor at least. We can't just ignore what's been going on, Mads. I think you know that, too."

"You think I'm really depressed."

"Do *you* think you're really depressed?"

"I think the word *depressed* makes me feel depressed. If there was a cheerier word, people might feel better right there."

"True enough."

"A watched pot never boils, Claire," Mads says.

"Come on, damn you." Claire shakes the kettle. "My mom always thought tea solved everything."

"I like that idea."

"Me too." Just before the kettle whistles, Claire takes it off the heat. Steam lifts as she pours, and there's a calm little hiss. It's late. Thomas and Harrison and Jinx the cat are off in dreamland. Harrison probably has a cape and a sword and there's likely a dragon with the face of his fourth-grade teacher.

"I'd go to the doctor for you, Claire."

"Well, I kind of hoped you'd go for you, but I'll take it. Monday?"

"You mean business."

"Better believe it."

"Suzanne'll be pissed if I cancel on such short notice." Secretly, this thrills her.

"To hell with Suzanne." This thrills her more.

"The tea tastes like grass clippings."

"I'm convinced it's healthy."

"Oh my God, it is! Look." Mads flexes both arms like a strongman.

"Impressive. It's a green tea miracle. And one more thing . . . When you're ready? I'd love to hear about Ryan Plug. Any guy who can make you laugh like that is a friend of mine."

It's going to be one of those mostly talking appointments and not a prodding-your-body appointment, so Mads gets to skip the gown that ties in the back. Still, she shifts around and crinkles the paper on the exam table. The clock ticks loudly. She's been in there forever, long enough to think about snooping in the cupboards. There's a blue paper sheet on the counter with only the innocent instruments laid out on it—a triangular rubber mallet, a scope with a light. There are no silver speculums that look like fancy salad tongs you'd give someone for a wedding present.

Dr. Kate Bailey has calm eyes and a round, maternal hum. This is how Mads imagines maternal, anyway. Dr. Bailey is the visual equivalent of a warm cookie. Her own mother isn't this. Catherine Murray veers between thin and too thin, and she's prone to illness and accident. There is not a warm hum around her, but more the high-pitched frequency only animals can hear.

Dr. Bailey shakes Mads's hand with her solid one. She

feels Mads's lymph glands and taps her knees and looks into her eyes, all the while asking about that day in the water, and what's been going on at school, and what important stuff has happened in the last year, and how she's eating, and if she spends time with her friends.

Finally, Dr. Bailey sits on her stool and rolls right up to Mads. "An event like that—it's understandable you'd be feeling this way. It's traumatic. It could trigger depression, or all kinds of other feelings. When did you start having trouble sleeping? Right after that? Before?"

Mads thinks. "Before. Maybe last year?"

"Last year?"

"Yeah, sometime in the spring."

"You said your mom's attorney drew up some papers around then?"

"Oh, yeah. Right." She shouldn't have admitted that, Mads thinks. She watches for raised eyebrows, or a squint of disapproval, something confirming Mads's betrayal, but Dr. Bailey only gazes at her steadily.

"And when everything started tasting bad, as you said? Feeling too heavy after you ate, around then, too?"

"Probably."

"Were you able to talk to anyone about what was going on? Your friends?"

"I don't know. Not really. I mean, we're, we were, in different life places."

"Okay. Well, we're going to take some blood, make sure

that sluggish feeling isn't an iron deficiency, and we're going to schedule a follow-up. I'm also going to give you a name of someone who might be helpful to chat with."

"What about that medicine that makes the black-and-white cartoon woman turn to color in the ads?"

The doctor smiles. She rolls away, writes on a pad. "I think we should try the other things we discussed first. Exercise. Eating. Routines at bedtime. And this."

Mads takes the piece of paper. Dr. Who-Knows-Whatever-She-Doesn't-Care-She's-Not-Going, and his phone number. Catherine Jaynes Murray has seen plenty of people over the years, people who she talked about for a few months like they were God. Dr. Goldblume, Janet Frey, Dr. Tamley, and the rest—the problem is, even God counts on you to do most of the heavy lifting.

"Can't you just tell me what he would say?"

"He wouldn't say, exactly. *You* would say. He'd help you learn about yourself. Why you might be having the struggles you are. How things might look different. It might take a while."

"What would *you* say if you *had* to say?"

"I'd say you'd been feeling like this for a long time, before the trauma even, and that you're probably ready for it to look different."

"Maybe I'll run away and join a rock band."

"Hmm," the doctor says. "That might be a pretty good idea."

"Or the circus."

The doctor shakes Mads's hand again. "*You* get to choose."

• • •

With no school and no babysitting, the whole day is hers. The doctor's appointment has left Mads feeling weirdly free. Some internal bass player is flipping off the media, and they're hopping on the tour bus for the next gig in Chicago. She even gets the window seat. When she arrives at Thomas and Claire's, Harrison is on the sidewalk, sticking playing cards to the spokes of his bike tires with masking tape.

"Kids still do that?" Mads calls.

"Dad taught me. It's going to sound like a motorcycle." He looks up. "What's in that white bag? Did the doctor give you Viagra?"

"God, Harrison, you have got to stay off the Internet. What do you know about Viagra?"

"It's what nervous ladies take when they go on airplanes."

"In here?" Mads shakes the bag, which contains a Butterfinger she bought on the way home. "Pills to slip in your chocolate milk if you spy on me anymore."

"Mom doesn't let me have chocolate milk. *Soy* milk."

"We need to fix that."

That's how buoyant she feels. She's generous enough to forgive the little FBI agent who almost got her busted.

Inside, Claire pops her head around the kitchen door. "Well?"

Mads rushes past her, heads up the stairs. "Exercise. Eat more. See some doctor, which I'm not going to do. Run away. Join a rock band." She doesn't mention *follow-up appointment*.

Dr. So-and-So exists, should she need him. It's practically enough to know he's out there somewhere. She feels better already.

"Join a rock band? That might be a pretty good idea."

Mads threw away the blue and green bathing suit she wore the day she found the body. Now she only has her old red one-piece from lifeguarding. She puts it on, tosses a pair of shorts and a T-shirt over the top. It's amazing how great she feels, just being cut loose from Otto Hermann and Suzanne. She can do whatever she wants. *She* chooses. It's a big, fat present. Look, freedom is the best drug, and yours for the taking.

Downstairs, Mads snatches up her backpack. Claire spots the red straps of her swimsuit. "Mads?"

"I'm not going to the lake. Don't worry. I could never do that anyway. I found a pool, though. An outdoor one, near that place where we went to the book sale?"

"Magnuson. I should have told you. You want company? A lumpy woman in a tankini and a little guy with a shark on his shorts?"

"Nah."

"Just phone first if you're going to leave forever with the drummer."

"Will do."

Before Mads starts Thomas's truck, she checks her phone. She's checked it so many times since Friday night that it's a twitch, a reflex. No, he hasn't called. He didn't call on Saturday or Sunday. Now it's Monday, and nothing. God, love drives you crazy. This isn't love, but whatever! Pre-love, maybe-love, sorta-love, it all makes you insane. And Mads has made one of those deals you make with yourself that allow you to do something bad, but only under certain conditions. As long as she doesn't call Billy, as long as she isn't the one to pursue, it's okay to see him. The discussions she had with herself about it were as complicated as some Middle East peace negotiations, and just as useless.

The current plan is a recipe for disaster: She won't tell Billy about his mom just yet. For now, keeping the secret is less of a mess all around. *Of course* keeping a secret is less of a mess all around! That's the whole great point of them! Never mind that secrets are like booze or drugs or gambling or other things that are a fabulous joyride until the crash. Poor, messed-up souls, poor humans, always grabbing at the *solution* part of *temporary solution*.

Mads arrives at the pool, checks her phone again. Still no call. *Whatever! It's for the best!*

Mads stands in line with the packs of kids clutching blow-up toys and fins and goggles and the crotches of their own saggy swimsuits. Inside the gate, the pool is a mash of wiggly bodies and splashing and screaming. It's bigger than the pool at home, with enough room in the deep end for Mads to swim laps cross-ways, avoiding the throngs. Two lifeguards are on duty, a guy on one end, a girl on the other. They look bored in their sunglasses. It *is* boring, yet you have to stay alert to every dunked head and minor struggle.

She drops her stuff on the grass under a tree. There's a line of drippy kids waiting to jump off the diving board. The girl in front of Mads yells, "Watch! Watch, Mom, are you watching?" Mom waves her hand to confirm, and then the girl steps to the end, wrestles with second thoughts, and finally leaps, popping up to applause.

Mads's turn. She hears the *wacka wacka wacka* of the board as she's midair, the second before she hits water. Then comes the familiar, bubbly quiet, with the muted fun of laughing and yelling in the world above.

She doesn't get far. She begins to stroke to the end of the pool, and then she opens her eyes. There are limbs, kicking legs, floating arms, flashes of color and swoops of hair. Mads starts to feel funny. She manages to find a spot to kick-turn back, but just before she reaches the end, the inevitable happens. She bumps a body. It's a girl, maybe fourteen, wearing a two-piece with stars on it, and she's only back-floating, gazing at the sky and the tree branches above, flapping her arms by her side and fluttering her feet, but it's enough. There's flesh against her flesh.

Mads panics. Flurries upright. She tries to walk. The water pushes against her, an impossible force. This was a wrong move, a bad decision. The water had belonged to Mads for years, swimming had, it was hers, but she's not the same person anymore. The moment she collided with Anna Youngwolf Floyd, she became someone else.

So, you're feeling better already, are you? the ogres chuckle.

169

Um, no. *They* are the bosses here. They will allow or not allow. Mads reaches the stairs. Only kids and middle-aged ladies and old men use the stairs, but she grips the railing, stumbles to the lawn. She sets her forehead against the trunk of the tree where her things are. She tries to breathe. She can't breathe. There's this crushing, stabbing. The red-suited female lifeguard is beside her. She is the former Mads, looking at who Mads is now and wondering what's gone wrong.

"You okay?"

"Just a cramp."

"Okay. Stretch it out."

Cold flesh, bloated body, battered by the fall. Blank eyes. Eyes that are forever gone. This is how desperate you might get, if you couldn't release yourself from the things that could drown you.

Something is pressing hard on her chest. She fights for air. In her bag, her phone begins to ring. Just as she is thinking so hard about his mother, there is Billy Youngwolf Floyd himself, as if he can read her mind.

"Were you *ever* going to call me?" he asks.

I did, she wants to say. *I just did, and you answered.*

Chapter Fourteen

Mads sounds strange. She's out of breath or something. He told himself he wasn't going to be some weird stalker, but, Jesus, the whole weekend passed, and now it's Monday, and he thought he'd never hear from her again. Not that he just sat there all weekend checking his phone or anything. He saw Casper both days, and on Saturday, there was this bonfire at the beach at Golden Gardens, and Sunday was his mother's birthday. He and Gran walked around sad all day until he wanted to run away and join a fucking rock band or something.

Still. Every time he looked at his phone and there was no call, no text, nothing, he wondered if he'd gotten it wrong. That Friday-night call—it seemed like something important had happened between them. He just feels this *pull* toward her. Maybe it's only his pull and not her pull, but that's not usually how it works with pulls like that. Not that he has a lot of experience, but it seems like a pull is fate and fate is mutual.

"Are you all right? I can barely hear you."

"I said, I didn't want to give the wrong idea. By calling."

"We're friends, right? That means you can call anytime."

"I don't know, Billy." She sounds like she might cry.

"Is this okay? I mean, I don't want to be pushing you into something you don't want."

He remembers the time Leigh broke up with Alex. Quentin brought over this stupid book about dating and knowing when to move on. He thought he was doing some intervention. He read parts out loud until Alex got pissed, and then they just played Night Worlds, and Alex used Barbarian Rage to wipe Quentin out. But Billy never forgot what that book said about girls who don't make any moves back. Man, love drives you crazy.

She says something he can't quite make out. The barking dogs in Heartland aren't helping. He heads outside. "What was that again?"

"I said, I just need you to be the one to call."

He tries to make sense of this. He sits down at the curb in front of the Rescue Center. He watches a garbage truck pass; a couple of guys swing off and bang some cans around. One of them shouts something bossy. "You need me to call so it's kind of like my idea and not yours?"

"Mmm-hmm."

"I can do that!" He sounds way too eager. He needs to bring it down a notch. "You know, whatever." On her end of the phone, he hears a bunch of kids screaming and running around. She's probably at the park with Ivy. Her voice still seems different, though. Like she's bent over, upset. "You sure you're all right?"

"Better now. A lot."

Amy's at the window, watching him. She looks mad, probably because of the big smile on his face. The *Better now* makes him feel pretty damn great. It isn't just any old *Better now*. It means better now because of him, and this plus Amy's pissed-off look . . . Well, you can't blame him if he's suddenly shot full of confidence. "You were just waiting for me, huh? Admit it. You were counting the minutes till I called." He doesn't tease like this with many people. Mom, Gran, Alex, and not even always him.

"You think so?"

"You're practically crying tears of joy now that you heard from me."

"Maybe I am."

That sits there between them for one beautiful second. One beautiful freckle-nose, tan-arm, leather-bracelet, goodhearted, bad-eyesighted second.

"Hotshot," she says.

He doesn't mind being the one to call, are you kidding? He calls, and meets her and Ivy for a stroller walk around Green Lake. He calls, and they go to see *Rio Rialto* at the Grand Illusion. He calls, and they get dinner at Uneeda Burger. He calls, and they talk and talk and talk on the phone until it's late. He calls, and on that Saturday, they meet in Fremont and drop her car off, because he has a surprise.

He can't wait—she's going to love this. It's a great idea because of the map. He drives them downtown in his mother's truck. It's strange, Mads being inside it. He's with a person his mother never met, in a place where he still smells his mother's hand lotion if he concentrates hard. He's maybe in love with a person his mother never met and never will meet. It makes him sad for himself, but even sadder for his mom. Right now, Mads holds the little beaded doll that his mother kept in her ashtray. Mads doesn't ask about it, and she doesn't comment on the seventies music blaring from the radio, either. She just turns the doll in her palm and puts it back. The lotion smell, the doll, the music—it makes Billy feel like his mom and Mads are together in some way.

He heads down the big hill by the waterfront, crosses the downtown streets full of tourists and shoppers. He makes her shut her eyes until they get there.

"Open," he says.

She does. "Really?" She stares up at the tall glass building with its bold sign, SEATTLE ART MUSEUM, and at the iron man statue with his slowly swinging hammer.

He just grins like crazy.

"This is so sweet."

She gets it. She understands. It isn't *the* museum, but it's as close as he can get. He doesn't know shit about art. He even shaved and dressed up a little, put on one of his good shirts and his good shoes, because he doesn't know what people wear to places like this.

The floors are really shiny. His dress shoes tap against the wood. He pulls at his cuffs, since this is the only nice shirt he has besides the funeral one, and he got it a few years ago for a holiday thing at school. People sit on benches and look at the paintings like they understand what they mean, though they're probably faking it. Mads seems giddy. He catches her running her fingertips along a velvet rope. She jokes about where he could hide his violin case.

"Perfect!" She points to a large sixteenth-century Chinese vase. "How about here?" Inside a Tlingit canoe.

"I like this place, but we need the real thing," Billy says.

"Definitely," Mads says.

Mads doesn't know it, but he's leading her to Decorative Arts. He looked it up online. There are no giant beds in the museum, mostly just chairs and cabinets and settees, so he decided to bring her to the Italian Room instead. He'd never even heard the word *settee* before, but now he knows it's just a fancy name for a little couch.

"Wow," she says.

It's all warm, glowing wood, ceiling to floor. They're surrounded by it, just like in the picture. No one's in there but them. The room is mostly empty—it's just chiseled wood columns and swirled wood arches and an ornate wood ceiling. There's a huge, carved mantel and frosted windows made of circles of glass that look like the bottoms of old Coke bottles.

He has not touched her since he kissed her that day at Agua Verde. Except for a hug good-bye after the movie, they're friends, and friends don't kiss the way he wants to. But now, in the Italian Room, he takes her fingers in his. He pulls her toward him.

"You know what?" he asks.

"What?"

"Don't get that look."

"What look?"

"That rolling eyes look. I'm being serious."

"Exactly. That's why you're getting the rolling eyes look."

"I think it's time." He yanks her hand. Sometimes you need to be serious. Especially when you're going to kiss someone again.

"Time for what?"

"To stop being friends."

He leans in, and she turns her head. Their chins bump, and it gets awkward with his mouth suddenly next to her face. He goes to Plan B, hugs her instead. He can feel the warmth of her. It's driving him crazy. Her heart beats against his chest. *It's enough*, he thinks. *Better than nothing.*

A guard wanders past. They step away from each other.

"This is where I'd put that cool bed," Billy says.

"Yeah. It's perfect."

"We need to see the real thing," he says again.

It's like his mind has a plan. *Like?* Ha. He has a plan, and he knows it.

He's got to tell her about his mom. The longer he waits, the weirder it's getting. He's been keeping this secret, and he doesn't want it between them anymore. He doesn't want anything between them. She should know who he really is.

It could ruin everything. If he tells, if he doesn't tell—either way he's screwed. It's a confession. The minute he says it, she'll see the stain on him. You aren't supposed to think like that, but you can't help how it feels. She'll hear the story, and she'll feel sorry for him, but maybe she'll want to step back, too. His own mother destroyed herself and he wasn't able to stop it, and he wasn't enough to stay for. What then? You just offer your broken self to someone else and say, *Here?*

It's a weight, and like all weights, you get tired of carrying it, if you're lucky. Billy and Mads walk down by the waterfront. They pass the docks with the shops, and even the aquarium near the spot where the big cruise ships come in.

"Why don't we ever meet at your house?" he asks her.

"Why don't we ever meet at *yours?*"

"My gran can't mind her own business."

"Same with my aunt."

"I don't want to be some secret."

"You're not."

"No?"

They stop talking, just walk and walk, and she looks out toward the sound like she has things on her mind, too. They're all the way down at the sculpture garden. They collapse by the statue of the enormous typewriter eraser.

"I can't move," she says. She's flat out on the grass, her body an X. He wants to lie right down on top of her, kiss her, feel every bit of her, make babies and marry her and be with her forever. A kiss would be good to start. He looks down into her flushed face and she sits up.

"Billy."

"I have something I have to tell you."

"Me too," she says.

"It's about my mom."

"I know."

"You know?" Well, he's been hinting. He tried a million times to tell her without telling her. "I didn't want to say it. She's only been gone for a few months. Jesus."

His throat gets all tight. He drops his head across his folded arms. He feels her small hand on his back.

"I know she . . ."

"Yeah, she . . ." He talks into his sleeve. In some ways, he hopes she can't hear him, even though he doesn't want to repeat this story ever again. He just keeps his head bent, lets the words sink toward the ground.

"You can tell me. It's okay."

"She . . . I was at work. A few months ago." He could be sick, just remembering it. "I was in the dayroom with all the dogs, and they were running around, and I was tossing a ball, like nothing. And then Jane shows up, and she says, 'Billy. Sweetheart.'"

He's not sure he can finish. His voice starts to wobble, just thinking of Jane standing there. You do what you can to keep it all away so that this very thing doesn't happen, this rushing in, this tsunami wave. (First, the ocean appears to drain, then comes the hundred-foot swell, he saw it on a nature show.) Billy doesn't realize—grief is every person's natural disaster.

"As soon as I saw Jane, I knew. I knew it was terrible. Only, I didn't know how terrible."

"Oh, Billy."

Fuck. Fuck! He's crying. He's sobbing, and this is why he didn't want to say anything. He's all crushed wreckage now. "Jane says, 'Sweetheart? It's your mom.' And we'd been through this so many times, but I could tell it was different. She, you know, she was depressed for years. Years, before me, even."

"I'm so sorry."

"She . . ." He's blubbering. His voice is high, strangled, and he sounds like a big damn baby. "They just laid her off, and I guess we were having more money problems than she ever said, but I could've helped! I have a job. I just bought shit with that money."

"It's not your fault."

"And I was . . ."

"It's okay."

"I was . . ."

"Billy, it's okay."

"Gonna move out. Gonna move out."

"I'm so sorry."

His grief rips through and howls and lifts up the seawater and smashes down. "I was gonna leave her, and I don't think she thought there was much left, you know?" He wipes his eyes with the back of his hand. Fuck! People in the park are staring. "They're looking at me."

"Who cares?" Mads says. "I don't care about those people."

"I guess she just left the house early that morning and started walking. I was still asleep! Can you believe I was *asleep*? I got up and she wasn't there, but I didn't think anything of it. Why would I? I just ate some breakfast and went to work. There was no note, no nothing." No good-bye. Not even a fucking good-bye or a reason. A written-down reason, or an apology, how about that?

He doesn't know if he can say what comes next. "She went over . . ." That's all he can get out. It's enough. He looks at Mads. He almost forgot for a minute that she was there. He forgot they're sitting in a park in the summer and that he's with a girl he might love. What his mom did—it feels like years and also five minutes ago. It feels like always.

"This bridge. That big bridge, Aurora? I mean, how could no one see her? It was the fucking morning, but still! No one saw her? Someone saw her! Someone had to, or else, she waited in the bushes like an animal until no one was around. Jesus. Someone should have stopped her! Someone should have saved her."

He's flattened and empty. But his body shakes with after-shocks. He's what's left after the tragedy. He's a toppled building with half a wall and no roof and his insides exposed.

"I'm so sorry," Mads says. "That's so awful."

"I can't believe it, you know? She was here, and now she

isn't here. The night before, I was going out, meeting Alex. I just said, 'See ya,' and she said, 'Come here.' And I said, 'Mom, I gotta go.' And she said, 'Love ya, Billy.' And I said, 'Love ya, Mom.' And that was it. That was the last thing she said and the last thing I said, and I never would have left if I saw any sign! I actually thought she was doing better! She seemed real cheerful, even with the job thing. . . . I know she had a disease. I know why it happened. But I don't know *why*. I don't know *how could she*."

Mads's arms are around him. She's rocking him back and forth like the big, stupid, public crying baby he is. She must be crying, too; his T-shirt is damp where her cheek rests. It's weird, but the rocking and her arms quiet him after a while. They just sit there like that, until it gets too hot to be stuck together.

Billy clears his throat. It's tight from so much upset, and his eyes are all puffy. He probably looks like an opossum. Like a creature who lives underground. He can barely get his voice out. "Do you know how far we have to walk now to get back to the car?"

"I don't care," Mads says. "We can walk to New York, for all it matters."

He leans his face right next to hers. She looks at him the way she looked at Rocko, as if pouring every bit of love right into him. Her eyes have gone a little punk rock from smudged mascara, but they are beautiful. Her breath is warm on his face. Her mouth is so close to his.

"This is a weird time to do this," he whispers.

"A really weird time."

"I don't give a fuck," he says.

And then his mouth is on hers, and he's kissing her so hard and she's kissing back, and they're down on the grass, and he pulls her head toward him, and her hands are all over his shirt, and—honestly, he could rip her clothes off right there, he could. God, he wants to. It's pent-up emotion, and being so close to her without touching for so long, and just some need to feel life and a person's breath and a person's beating heart, *her* breath and *her* beating heart, her desire and his desire right there on green grass on a summer day.

This, he thinks. This is why his mom should have kept fighting, no matter how desperate she felt. Because a moment like this is always possible, and you never know when it might arrive. You aren't supposed to think that kind of thing, because you can't truly know a person's struggle, but he does think it. *Here*, he says to her. *See? See this? This is beautiful enough to fight for, see?*

Right here. Love, passion, breath and breath, and a heart so full it could burst. A heart that's remarkably, and against all odds, grateful.

"What is that?" Gran says.

What's new? It's a Gaze Attack of the highest order. The funny thing is, he's barely played Night Worlds in weeks. He's barely even *thought* about Night Worlds in weeks. The controllers sit in a forgotten heap in front of the TV, the cords in a tangle, former lifelines, the yanked IV of a patient allowed to go home. In spite of missing his mom like hell, in spite of Casper and all the cruel assholes in the world, in spite of Gran looking at him like she is right then, this is the world he wants to be in.

"Christ Almighty. Is that what I think it is?"

There's a pot of beans on the table, and some tortillas, and some red, spicy chicken, shredded in a pile. He's starving. "No idea what you're talking about."

She points. "Right there."

He puts his hand up to his neck.

"Other side."

Oh, no. He shoves his chair back. He loves Gran, he does. It's DNA love, irrevocable, but she can make you feel so small and guilty. And furious. It's crazy, but you know what it seems like? His mom is gone, and so he's the one getting Gran's shit now. He's not her good, perfect grandson anymore, just someone being a burden, causing her trouble. He cranes his neck in the mirror hanging by the front door.

"This?" he says. "Is this what you're talking about?" He stomps back into the kitchen, flings himself into his chair. "It's not what you think."

"That girl. Who appeared out of nowhere on your street."

"No!"

"A different girl?"

"No girl!"

You know how he got that bruise? It happened late one night, when a memory shook him awake. *That* memory. *I'm thinking about getting my own place*, he said, and his mother looked up from her old computer, the blue glow turning her skin ghostly. *Oh*, she said. But there were a thousand words behind the *Oh*. They marched across her face. She didn't say anything more, but he saw the words and the waves of feeling— disappointment, loss. He wanted to take it right back, but what, was he supposed to live with her forever? *Quentin found us a house*, he said. His voice was flip. The *Oh* had ticked him off. Come on! For God's sake.

Lying awake in bed that night at Gran's, the memory drilled, filling him with shame, filling him with hatred. *Quentin found us a house. Oh. Quentin found us a house. Oh.* He hated her! He hated himself more. He was a loser; he was ungrateful, a lowlife, a bad son. He took the side of his neck between his thumb and forefinger and pinched and pinched as hard as he could.

"You better be careful, is all I have to say," Gran says. "You better know who a person is, and where they come from. I told your mother that a hundred times. Not that she listened."

Billy pushes his plate away. There are *always* so many words behind words. "Yeah, I know you did. More than a hundred, probably." He's never taken this tone with her before. You don't criticize her, that's the rule. She looks shocked. She can be a bully and bullies are always shocked when someone fights back. They're shocked for a second, anyway, before the lid of their true rage is lifted off.

"What are you saying to me?" She stares at him with dark steel eyes. He's never taken that tone with her, and she's never given him those eyes.

"Nothing."

"Are you blaming me?"

"I'm out of here."

"That's what you're doing. You're blaming me."

He isn't hungry anymore. He knocks over his chair as he gets the hell away from there—he hears the slip and bang. He snatches up his keys and his wallet and his phone, and he slams the front door of the houseboat so hard that the house rocks.

He screeches out of the parking lot. Flies down Westlake. You should see how fast that truck can go. By the time he's around the lake, he's calmed down some. He parks over by the Fremont Bridge, right at the spot where he first talked to Mads. He gets out, stands at the bank with his arms shoved in his pockets. Cars whoosh across the bridge. A sailboat passes underneath.

He's between the bridges, large and small, new and old. The old calls to him and tugs and fills him with longing. Old is deep and powerful. Sometimes it's a good powerful, and sometimes it's the thing you'll have to fight your whole life long. The way it pulls and presses will make it an epic battle. For a long time, Billy just stands there, thinking about the ways people destroy the best things, waging their virtual wars.

Chapter Fifteen

When she gets home after the park, Mads runs upstairs before Harrison can take a picture or something. She has grass stains on the back of her shorts and shirt. Her cheeks still blaze hot.

She wants to call Billy Youngwolf Floyd right then. She wants to spill everything; she wants to let him see her, the real her. She should phone him twenty times or more, for all the times he's called her. He deserves that, and God, his mouth felt so good, and she wanted him so bad, and his narrow shoulders were so much stronger than she'd have ever guessed. *He* was so much stronger, that's for sure, that boy with his wrinkled white shirt and defiant hair.

She almost told him her secret right there in the Italian Room and then again on the lawn. But she didn't. Now she's soaring so high, she almost forgets how much it's going to hurt to crash.

"Mads? Dinner!"

"Be right down!"

She tosses on a sundress. The backs of her elbows are green. They feel raw. They throb a rug-burned beat. She lathers them with a pump of hand soap, hurries to dry off the evidence.

"Look at you," Claire says. "You look beautiful. You look so . . ."

"You look happy, Mads," Thomas says, setting plates on the table, silverware politely beside. "What's up with the happy? I love it."

"It's a suck-face face," Harrison says.

"Harrison." Claire narrows her eyes.

"Your lips are big."

Thomas hands him the napkins to pass around. "Hare, sucking face is a great thing. One day you'll see."

"Don't make me barf."

"Well, you've got to invite Ryan over for dinner," Claire says. "We're dying to meet him."

"Who's Ryan?" Harrison says.

"You guys want soy milk, or just water?"

"Chocolate milk," Harrison says. "Ryan who?"

"A friend of mine?" Mads should lock the kid in his room.

"Ryan Plug, the young man Mads has been seeing."

Harrison snorts. "Pppplug." He makes his lips flubber. "Yeah, right."

Mads wants to squeeze the flesh on the underside of his arm, where it would really hurt. Everyone sits down, the way Claudia and Jamie's family would in The Book. They're having spaghetti and meatballs, made from lean turkey. Back home, people still ate Cheetos, and even that bean dip that comes in a can. Right now, Mads could eat every bit of that spaghetti and finish it off with apple pie. She's starving. She's so hungry, it turns to a big metaphor. She wants so much, all, everything. Her face feels sunburned from where Billy's chin rubbed against her face.

Mads's phone buzzes in her pocket, and she thinks, *Billy*. Thomas scowls at the sound. He doesn't like phones at the dinner table, so Mads ignores it. Harder to ignore is her own warm buzz at the thought of him. Oh, she's in deep. She is way, way over her head.

"Dog boy," Harrison says. Mads kicks him under the table.

"We showed the Wilkens couple the plans today, and—"

Her phone interrupts Thomas again. "Mads," he says. "Can you turn that off?"

"I'll just . . ." She takes it out of her pocket. Maybe she can shoot him a quick text, Thomas be damned.

"Please. How much uninterrupted time do we get in our lives, huh?"

She looks down. Mads is almost shocked—not at who's calling, but that she's practically forgotten all about her.

"It's Mom."

"She can wait," Thomas says.

The phone buzzes and buzzes in her hand.

"I've got to get it."

"She can *wait*."

"What if it's an emergency?"

"She's a grown woman. She can handle her own emergency."

Claire tries a softer approach. "This just happens too much, Mads, you know?" Harrison balances his spaghetti on his fork with the fixed gaze of a scientist formulating the laws of gravitation.

Buzz. Buzz, buzz. Mads can feel the urgency screaming through the phone. It vibrates, angry and ignored. Maybe Thomas has a great invisible shield against people who need him, but she doesn't. Maybe Claire can coolly remove herself from someone's disappointment and fury and need, but not Mads. The membrane between Mads and what people expect of her is thin as the translucent wall of a soap bubble.

"Excuse me." Mads shoves her chair back.

She interrupts the ring as she's halfway up the stairs. "Maddie? Thank God I got you." There's the half-sob exhale. Mads shuts the door of Thomas's office/her room.

"What's wrong, Mom?" She hopes they can't hear. If they do, she'll only prove them right about herself and her mom. This is what's called *being caught between a rock and a hard place.* She's so used to the rock and the hard place that calluses have practically formed on her elbows and knees, but not on the places she could really use them.

"It wasn't a date. None of the dates were *dates!*"

"It's all right. What happened?"

Her mother starts to cry. "James. I thought he really liked me. From that first time I met him. And he kept calling. Who calls like that? He took me out for drinks. A lot of drinks, too.

He drank like a fish. He took me out to dinner! Who takes a person to dinner that many times just to weasel their way into a person's business? He wanted to partner up, all right. With my *listings*. What an *asshole*!"

"Oh, I'm sorry."

"This is, like, more than *sorry*. He walked me right up to the door. I thought he was finally going to kiss me. I leaned in, and he put his hand on my chest, like *No*. Like I was some . . . He couldn't even stand to *touch* me. Who is he not to want me?"

"He's a jerk, Mom. He's not even worth your time."

"A jerk? He's a fucking psycho. You know what I should do? I should call every one of his clients. Every single one, and tell them that a man who drinks like that has no place handling the biggest investment of their lives."

She would do it, too. It's not just a thing a person says. Mads remembers red scratch marks up her father's arm, and those family photos in shreds. Mads paces. She doesn't know how to manage all this from here. She paces a circle—toe, heel, toe, heel—around the room, and starts again. "You should call Paula. Go have a girls' night."

"I can't stand Paula. I could never be friends with Paula. I wish you were here."

"I wish I was, too."

The lie is molten; it blisters as it pours through her. Mads does not want to be there. *There* is the last place she wants to be.

"If you were here, you could help me call. He's got a website. I can see every single person he deals with. Jim Beam. Talk about perfect."

"He's not even worth a second more."

"I don't know what I'd do without you. What would I do? God, I wish your class was finished so you could be home."

"I'll be home soon."

"If you were here now, we could binge on thrillers, like we did when you and Cole broke up."

"Maybe you can call that woman, Julie. The one you went for drinks with that time."

"All she did was talk about her son. In a weird way, too, if you ask me. Something was going on there. God, I can't *believe* that fucking *Jim Beam*."

There's the crickle of static and that's all. Downstairs, voices murmur and silverware clinks against plates. Mads stops pacing, sits on the floor with her back to the bed. She feels old, and suddenly tired. Exhausted.

"I better go. I should do some homework." It's a lie. She's barely glanced at her homework in weeks.

"You know what else? He had small hands. You know what they say about a man with small hands and what's below the belt."

Mads is silent.

"I'm better off alone. Why do I even want a man?"

"Forget about him."

"I have you, that's the important thing. You're my family. You're the only family I have. I love you so much."

"I love you, too."

After they finally hang up, Mads's suck-face face is gone. Some strange, bad feeling gusts in. She is a small, awful someone who lets people down. *Alone* makes her think of their too-big house with its jammed gutters and peeling paint, the sound of the TV on in an empty room, a single chicken breast. Mads's father lives in a beautifully furnished two-bedroom apartment with views of a canal, and meets friends for drinks in the historic district.

On the desk is *Mastering Real Estate Principles*, 7th Edition, and on the bed is *From the Mixed-up Files*. Her old life, her new—she sits between them. But *new* doesn't seem actually possible. *New* never does when *old* grips you so hard. Any stupid dream she played around with in her head vanishes in a flash. Thomas and Claire and Harrison stare down at her from the photo on the desk. What is she doing here, really, sleeping in Thomas's office, using Thomas's truck, pretending that this is her real life? This won't end well, because she is lying to them, to Billy, to everyone, and when you lie like that, it's usually in the service of one big, insurmountable lie you are telling yourself.

What *is* true? She can't stay here. She has to leave these people—Claire, and Thomas, and Harrison, and Billy, Billy, Billy—and the sooner, the better, because she will only become more attached, and her secret will only become more destructive. Nothing and no one will ride in to save Ivy, either—she'll have Suzanne and Carl as parents her whole life long. Mads curls her body into a comma on the floor. Actually, as far as punctuation marks go, she feels more like *dot dot dot*. An endless ellipsis, pointlessly waiting for something that will never come. The day she just had with Billy is gone like smoke.

Well, well, well, the ogres chuckle. It's so much fun for them to sit back and watch everyone else do their heavy lifting. Self-loathing, that obese ogre with the fat fingers, he points and laughs and spills gross stuff on the front of his shirt. He's been waiting around, so patient, through the kissy-kissy-happy drivel, but now, finally, he's back in the game.

There's a soft knock at the door.

"Mads? You okay?"

"Yeah."

"Can I come in?"

"I guess."

Claire sits down on the floor next to Mads. "You were talking to yourself in here."

"I was?"

"Yep. What were you saying?"

"I was saying I need to go home."

"You don't, though."

"I do. I want to."

"Really?"

Mads studies her fingernails. White crescent moons, pink lunar landscapes. "I'm just struggling to be here, Claire."

"You know what I think? You aren't struggling to be here. You're struggling to be away from there."

"I could do my licensing in Wenatchee. So what if it takes longer. It's pointless to be away."

"No."

"What do you mean, 'no'?"

"I mean, 'no.' Thomas and I won't allow it."

"You won't allow it. Are you forgetting that I'm eighteen?"

"I haven't forgotten that. Thomas hasn't. But we won't allow it. You need to at least finish the class. Here. Then we'll figure out what happens next."

"Claire. This is ridiculous. You can't allow or not allow."

"The decision is out of your hands."

They stare at each other there on the floor. Mads feels some bizarre relief.

"Fine," she says.

"Good." Claire stands. She actually brushes her hands together, as if some important business has been concluded. When she shuts the door behind her, it's another punctuation mark. A period.

That night, Mads can't sleep. She hears Thomas downstairs, arguing on the phone. It's awful. Getting mad at her mother won't help anything.

She folds the pillow over her head. She wishes she could stay forever in a feather-dark bed cave where no one could come in. A thought drifts in—that missed follow-up appointment with Dr. Bailey—and drifts out again. She should roll over, press the pillow to her face. Can a person smother herself? Or would you just fight and thrash, in spite of your wishes? She forces herself not to listen to Thomas's loud voice downstairs. She grasps the handle of her own violin case, but an ogre has his meaty grip on it, too. They yank it back and forth. Inside, there's the rattle of a credit card and a phone, all you really need if you leave home.

"What was I thinking, buttercup? How could I forget your Binky? A girl needs her Binky. Let's make that rule number two. The road is rough; take comfort where you can. Cute little giraffe or baby elephant? How about elephant?" Mads snatches it off the hook, drops it into the basket on her free arm.

It's an old Bartell Drugs—no swooping automatic doors here, just the regular kind that *bing-bong* in case the clerk is somewhere in the back. At the sound, Ivy suddenly leans backward like an Olympic gymnast. It's an alarming new trick, and Mads worries she'll flop right out of her arms.

"Give a girl some warning," Mads says. She supports Ivy's silly neck so she can see the upside-down diaper packages and upside-down lotions. She walks down the aisle, showing her upside-down shampoos and shaving lotions, upside-down toothbrushes and dental floss.

Mads helps Ivy right herself in the medicine aisle, just past the cough syrups. Ivy's cheeks are red. Her face is sticky when Mads kisses it.

"Gee gow." Ivy points. It's possible she's fluent in Chinese. "Almost done."

Almost, but not quite. Because there is Ivy's missing pacifier, but there is this, too. Mads's eyes slip past the Tylenol and ibuprofen and settle—*there*—on the sleep aids. It sounds so soft and comforting, *sleep aids*. So reassuring and help-ful. Twelve count, twenty-four, thirty-six. The boxes are all primary-color efficiency. How many would it take? Two boxes? Three? The ogres say: *Lots*. They say: *Easy*. They croon gentle words like *slip away*. They keep quiet about the violent ones like *stomach pump* and *destroy*. It's all soft-rescue-lies. It's peaceful-dream-violence.

"Mads?"

It's funny, really, because, before now, Mads has always been the lifeguard.

"What are you doing here?" She flinches, nearly drops the boxes like she's been caught.

"What do you mean, what am I doing here? What are *you* doing here?"

"Are you following me?"

"Why would I be following you? No, I wasn't following you! This is the only drugstore around. I came to get some—"

Billy waves his arms around a little. He blushes. The bag of Cheetos in his hand crinkles in the gesture.

"Cheetos? People eat those in Seattle? I thought they only ate dried kale rounds or something. Yam chips. You've prob-ably never even heard of bean dip in a can."

"I've heard of bean dip in a can." He's mad. He's staring at her hard, and he's spitting his words, and she's never seen him like this. "I *like* bean dip in a can. What are you doing, Mads?"

"Gog," Ivy says.

"Dog! Did you hear that? She said it again. Good one, Ives."

"Stop this bullshit, Mads."

"What are you talking about?"

"I can see your face."

"This face?" She pulls her mouth down, makes big eyes, tries to look silly, but the timing's all wrong. It's beginning to dawn on her. He's not just mad. He's furious.

"Stop it."

Billy's jaw is clenched. There's only one reason he'd be this mad. She feels suddenly sick.

He's found out.

"Do you folks need some help?" It's the Bartells man in the red vest. He grips his price checker like a pistol.

"We're fine," Mads lies.

"Ching gow," Ivy says.

Billy grabs Mads's arm. His grip is firm. The basket bangs between them, and then he yanks it from her. He tosses the pacifier on the counter. "Just this," he says, and throws down a ten. The Cheetos bag has been ditched somewhere.

"What are you doing?" she asks.

"We're getting out of here."

The cheery bell sings wrongly. Outside, Billy's mother's truck is parked right next to Thomas's.

Billy's steering her out of there. He holds her arm so tight, it almost hurts. "We need to talk."

"No stern voices around Ivy." She shakes him off, puts Ivy in her seat. She gives Ivy a little tub of her favorite fish crackers.

All the windows are down so she won't get too hot, and now Mads leaves the door open, too.

Billy looks like he's pacing while standing still. He's breathing hard.

"I can't believe it. God*damn* it."

Mads has no idea how to explain, or where to even start. He's found out, and he's so angry, his eyes blaze.

"Don't let her hear!" It's all she can think to say. She's trying not to throw herself at his feet and weep. She wants to beg for forgiveness. Ivy watches, like there's a crisis on Sesame Street. She pounds those crackers like movie popcorn.

"Fine! I'll be quiet!" Billy whispers. "But just so you know. I saw what you were thinking in there."

"What?"

"I know what you were thinking."

"What are you talking about?"

"I could see it on your face. Those sleeping pills. Don't tell me otherwise."

She's stunned. This isn't what she expected, not at all.

"Promise me. Don't *ever* . . . If you even *think* it, you need to tell—"

"I wasn't thinking—"

She was, though. Billy nails Mads to the ground with his eyes. They take her in, and they see. They really *see*. She's struck. Maybe no one has seen her like that, ever.

He takes her face in his hands.

"*Promise* me," he says.

Chapter Sixteen

"I promise," she whispers back. Her face is red, and her eyes fill like she might cry.

"A person . . ."

Jesus. He can't believe how the day's turned. He went over to Bartells to get—he feels like an idiot admitting this now—condoms. Yes, condoms! No glove, no love! What a fool. In spite of Gran, he was high with the thought of Mads and where they were heading. That kiss in the park *spoke*. That kiss told the future. If that kiss could talk, it would say, *Tomorrow*, and the next day and the next. He wanted to be ready, because all he had was a leftover pack from when he and Zoe were together. So he goes to Bartells after work, and when he sees her truck in the lot, he can't believe his luck. It's like everything is going his way. He thinks she's there to buy, he doesn't know . . . lip gloss, whatever a girl buys in a drugstore, and he jogs on in and grabs the Cheetos because he sure as hell isn't telling her the real reason he's there.

And then he finds her in the aisle. He sees where she's standing, and which boxes she has in her hand. He knows that face. He knows exactly what she's thinking. He can't explain this, other than, when you know, you know. Maybe he was wrong when he saw her at the bridge and at the train tracks, but he wasn't wrong in general.

He was high on hope, just trying to decide whether he should get ribbed ones! The day was all about fantastic ribbed condoms or not-ribbed condoms! Now he's so fucking angry. And scared. And upset. But mostly angry. It's hard to whisper when you're that angry, but he respects the fact of Ivy's baby ears.

"You have to promise, Mads. You have to. A person doesn't just kill themself. They kill a lot of other people. *A lot.*"

The doctor in his head folds his arms and *tsk-tsk*s. This is not the right approach! Getting pissed at someone for how they feel does no good. You shouldn't blame a person. You shouldn't add more bad shit to the bad shit. But how can he make her *hear*? She doesn't get this. Not from where he stands. "I don't want to make you feel bad. Worse. But that's no solution. That's no fucking solution."

Fucking sounds like a breeze over a river when you whisper it. He doesn't know how to say all of this strong enough. He knows, better than anyone, that people in that place can't always listen, but they need to! They need to, because look what happens! He closes his eyes and hears *Love ya, Billy.* He closes his eyes and hears *Mom, I gotta go.* He drives past that place where they'd have breakfast, or the flower stand where he got the flowers for Mother's Day, or a construction site where there's a new building that wasn't there a couple of months ago, and he hears *Love ya, Billy* and *Mom, I gotta go. Mom, I gotta go. Mom, I gotta go.* Every holiday, every birthday, every season, every triumph every tragedy every everything his whole life long, it'll be *Love ya, Billy* and *Mom, I gotta go.* She jumped from the bridge that day, and he will fall and fall and fall from that bridge every day after.

And it's not just that—not just the effect it has on other people, in his case, on him and Gran and everyone who knew her or even didn't know her but just heard about her that day. It's more than the responsibility a person has to other people, like it or not. There's the responsibility you have to yourself, like that or not, too. To life, yeah, fuck, whether you like *that* or not!

"Mads, don't ever lose hope, do you hear me? Because you don't know what your life will bring. It's going to look different. And every day, there's something, Mads. Something to fight for. I mean, look around. There's . . ." He points. Bartells has a rolling shelf of annuals, four for five dollars. "Look at those!"

"Pansies?"

Okay, they're a little sad-looking, and someone needs to come out and water them, but still! A flower is a great thing. "There!" A bird. A bird is a miracle.

"That crow pecking a candy wrapper?"

So, these aren't the best examples, but he can think of hundreds: a cloud, a leaf, snow falling, a baby in a car seat, packs of Starbucks coffee on sale two-for-one in the Bartells window, all the love that a person had in their heart for another person. Love, and a good day, and a shining moment, but not even just the corny shit. Not even babies and love and winter. But traffic. Yeah, hell yeah! Bad mistakes, flooded basements, heartache, loss, all of it. It all means you're in the struggle. It means you feel, and that you're part of the throbbing, beautiful fucking pulse of life. You're in the broken glass, metal shards, bleeding and aching, soaring soulness of it. It means you are a warrior in Night Worlds, with your glowing scimitar and amulets, with danger around every corner, but with the light of the prize, too.

Yes. This is too simple. The doctor in his head is shaking his head and sighing right now, because the *You gotta have hope* song is naïve. He knows that, okay? He knows depression can be a monster only felled by the most epic weapons. It's a bully that winches your arm behind your back when no one is looking, that wears you out, and shouts stuff that sounds romantic but is never, ever romantic. *But please*, he wants to beg. *Look at me!* Look at all the destroyed people left behind. None of it is simple, but he needs to get this whole big, impossible story across to her, because there's been too much wreckage already.

"This. There could be this." He leans forward and kisses

her so long and hard that she drops the Bartells bag with the pacifier in it. Her mouth is warm and he can taste salt from her near-tears. He makes that kiss full of planets and stars and storms and twilight and every single thing that is offered among every other thing.

He pulls away. She looks shocked. Her lips are wet.

He isn't stupid. He knows a kiss doesn't solve anything, but he needs her to *see*.

"Billy." She wipes her mouth. He wants to hold that narrow wrist with the bracelet on it.

"Talk to me. Tell me what's going on."

Sad people are good at hiding stuff. She said she didn't want to sell real estate, but it's more than that. The look on her face in the drugstore aisle means she thinks she's out of options.

"I can't talk about this now."

She's right. They're in the parking lot, and an old Honda pulls up next to them, and a big Coke truck maneuvers to make a delivery. A woman is poking around the pansies now, probably listening to their every word. Ivy squirms and gritches in her seat.

Billy pops his head in the car to check on Ivy. He's thinking he might hand her a toy or something, though what does he know about babies? Dogs, you can distract them with a rubber ball, and maybe it's the same idea.

That's when he sees the bags in Mads's truck. This is more than just ordinary baby stuff. There are a couple of brown grocery sacks and a few of those reusable kind, jammed full. There's the small sleeve of a coat drooping from one, and it's the middle of summer. An entire package of diapers sits on the floor.

Mads's eyes are guilty. Billy knows guilty eyes when he sees them—he sees plenty, working with Rocko and Bodhi and Runt. Dogs have a delicate conscience.

It is dawning on him (*dawning*, he realizes where the word comes from—the slow rising sun) that Mads is more complicated than she looks. Way more. Every person is. That's what you love, though, Billy thinks, the whole complicated person. Not some pretty, perfect idea. He wonders if Mads even gets that. A person needs to realize that their whole imperfect self can be loved, goddamn it.

"What is all this stuff?"

Did she have these bags with her before? Did he not notice? He sees exactly what this is. All at once, he does.

She just stands there, her eyes blinking. She told him about Suzanne and Carl, but now he feels bad, because maybe he didn't really hear her. There's the listening, but then there's the listening behind the listening.

"I was just—"

"I know what you were 'just.'" He does know, because of Jasper, and Olive, and Casper, still behind that fence. He knows it like he knows his own breathing self. "You want to take her."

"I could never do that," she says.

"Of course you couldn't. But you want to."

She just keeps blinking. "I never heard it said right out like that. But I could never really do it."

"No. But you would if you could. You'd run away with her. You'd take her from here. Because she's screwed where she is."

"I never even *thought* it right out like that."

He suddenly understands something else. "In the truck. Out by the ferry. How many times?"

"I don't know."

How many times has it been for him? How many dogs? He's lost count. "You better get her back. It must take a while to put this stuff away."

She doesn't say anything more. She just reaches inside the pocket of her shorts for the keys. "Well."

"Oh, I'm not saying good-bye. I'm going to wait for you. Until work is over."

"You can't. You can't wait on my street. My aunt . . . I already told you."

"I'll wait down the block."

"You don't need to. I'm fine. I am. It was a passing thought, Billy. I can't even believe you noticed. I feel bad. Especially with your mom and all—"

"A passing thought."

"Just an idea that came and left."

"Yeah, until it comes again and comes again unless you do something to stop it. I'll be behind you in the truck. We're going to meet after work, and you can talk your head off.

You can talk for years." You should hear how in-command he sounds. Like you can solve this by deciding.

"I don't want to talk."

"I want to show you something, then."

The doctor in his head is pissed. The real-life ones don't really get pissed from what he's seen, but the one in his head does. He's tossing off dire warnings like flares. What is Billy thinking, getting involved with this kind of girl? It's a big damn Freud picnic, falling for a girl that's sad as ol' Mom. *What a cliché*, the doctor spits. *Running in to save the day.* The doctor rolls his eyes, even though they'd never roll their eyes in real life, either.

But he's wrong. Yeah, Billy is parked a street away right now, watching videos on his phone to stay amused until seven o'clock when she's off work, but he won't save this girl, either. *You know why, Doc?* Billy says as the doctor cleans his glasses with one of the Kleenexes from the box in his office. *Because she'll save herself.* He can tell by all those bags. It's a desperate, pointless move, but it's a move that says something. She's trying to take action. Even if it's the kind of action that's pointless, it's a strike back. Action equals hope.

And you know what else, Doc? Here's what else. She's not like his mom as much as she's like Billy himself. Who'd have thought it, a girl that pretty with a house that nice, a girl with freckles, a girl who reads books and who's so smart, and whose dad is some big-shot journalist in Amsterdam, and not a drunk who installed cable whenever he even had a job. But it's true. They're so much alike, they could be siblings, Claudia and Jamie, only without the sibling part. Only without the perfect childhood and the hot fudge sundaes. And with some fabulous, fantastic, futuristic kiss. Two people who need the same things and see with the same eyes, only you'd never think that at first. They could be a team, Billy realizes. A great team. She might not know that yet, but he does.

His phone's losing juice, so he stops watching videos he's not really watching anyway. Those people, Suzanne and Carl, one of them will be driving up any minute. He should call Gran and tell her he's going to be really late, but he's still pissed at her, and bugged about the ugly shit weirdly growing between them. He tosses his phone on the seat beside him. Stares out the window. Looks around at the yards and living room windows, making sure everyone, every dog everyone, is okay.

Two kids ride up the street on their bikes. One is Mads's cousin, the kid who took his picture. Harrison. Harrison, right? He thinks he has that right. He's mad at himself—he should have at least listened well enough to remember her cousin's name. There's a smaller guy, too. His hair is so blond, it's almost white, and his matchstick legs pedal like crazy. They both have playing cards in the spokes of their bikes. Kids still do that, who knew.

They hit their brakes hard in front of his mom's truck. That kid, the cousin, his tires make a sweet black track. Nice one, boys. They drop their bikes on the ground, run around the truck like they're cops surrounding it in a sting.

Billy sticks his head out the window. "Hey. What're you kids doing?"

"What're *you* doing, more like it. Are you Pluuggg?"

"Huh?"

"Told you," Harrison says to the second little dude. He takes out a small notebook from his sock. He takes a pen out of the other sock.

"Jesus, kid. You shouldn't put a pen in there like that. What if you fall? That pen'll jab a hole through your leg."

"You got more to worry about than my leg, mister," the kid says. He flips open the notebook like he's writing up a ticket.

"Yeah, mister," the other little guy says. He has big bug eyes with those glasses, which makes you feel sorry for him. It's good he has at least one friend, because he looks like a paste eater who never gets a valentine unless the teacher makes sure he does.

"I've got more to worry about? Like you, tough guy?"

"We have a few questions for you," Harrison says.

"Does your mother know you're out here?"

"I can go as far as that stop sign."

The thing about kids, you have to be careful not to encourage them, or they'll never go away. You'll be sitting in your booth at Red Mill, and some kid'll pop his head over the seat, making a face, and if you make one back, it's over. The parents, hell, they never seem to notice, or care. They're just glad the kid isn't opening sugar packets and playing with the hot sauce bottle.

"I'll give you a buck if you show me how fast you can ride home."

"I want a buck," the paste eater says.

"We're not dumb. Nothing less than a ten."

"Talk about a business-minded little dude." Ah, excellent. It looks like a car is pulling up to the Bellarose house. He'll do the kid's interview to make him happy and then they can get out of here. He's Mads's cousin. Even if he's giving Billy a Gaze Attack, Billy wants the kid to like him.

"Name?"

"Billy Youngwolf Floyd. Need help spelling that?" It takes Harrison like five years and two pages to write it out.

"Mind if we get a picture?"

"Honestly, kid?"

Harrison takes his phone out of his sock. "You got a sandwich in there?" Billy says. "I'm starving."

"Smile," Harrison says.

Billy leans on the window frame, tries to give him a casual, confident-guy-in-a-booze-ad-without-the-booze look.

"Nuts," Harrison says.

"Not working? No surprise. That phone is a hundred years old, my friend."

Harrison holds it up, tries again. "Ughhh!"

"You probably dropped it in the toilet," the other kid says.

He starts cracking up, and then he accidentally farts, which sends him into hysterics.

"Gross," Harrison says.

"Bathroom humor won't get you anywhere, okay?" Billy says. The little man seriously needs lessons in how to be socially acceptable.

A woman gets out of the car in the Bellarose driveway. Must be Suzanne. She rests her back against the car door, talking on the phone.

"You need some help?" Billy says to Harrison. "Lemme see."

Harrison hands him the phone. It's all hot and slick from his small, sweaty hand.

"This thing weighs a ton." Billy examines the old screen. It's funny about devices—what seemed so great back then is now mostly lame.

"We can conduct the interview, regardless," Harrison says.

"Fire away."

"Do you know a Miss Madison Murray?"

Billy looks up for a sec from the blocky green letters on the screen. Suzanne's heading inside.

"Yep, I do."

"Where did you meet Miss Madison Murray?"

"I first saw her outside my old house." Wow. Technology sure has improved. The graphics alone. The icons on the screen look like cartoonish fuzz blobs.

"Your old house."

"Uh-huh."

"Do you know what she was doing there?"

"Yeah, I think—"

"*I* do."

"*I* do," the other kid mimics.

"I think it's working now," Billy says.

"Give it," Harrison says.

"*Please.* Buddy, you've got to remember your manners. Give it, please."

"Give it, please."

The front door of the house opens. Mads is out on the porch, and he can see Suzanne, blab, blab, blabbing at her.

"You want to try that again?" No harm letting him take his picture.

"Yeah."

"And you can tell me all about why Mads was on my street." He shouldn't use the kid like this. Mads never said much about J.T. and her. He kind of likes that. You don't want someone to go on and on about another guy, but he does want to know what she ever saw in someone like that. He and J.T. are pretty different people.

"Smile." Harrison lifts the phone, steps back.

And then, right at that second, Mads flies down the street, and he means *flies.* Things are practically jumping out of her purse, and her sandals slap the street hard and she's out of breath. She yells Harrison's name, and it throws the kid off, because he's not looking at what he's doing, and he takes another step back and falls over his bike. His ass lands right on the handlebars, and that's got to hurt. The second kid starts laughing. He's cracking up and holding his crotch like he might wet his pants. Billy forgot how much boys that age are all about poop and farting and peeing and other people's bad luck.

"Harrison," Mads breathes. Man, she's fuming right then. She grabs his arm and twists. It's kind of harsh. He's just being a kid, and falling over that bike seems punishment enough. Still, when you're in the dark corners of Night Worlds like Mads is, everything's out of proportion. He's had years of that kind of stuff with his mom. She'd drop an egg or burn a pot of rice and she'd be *pissed*. Even in her car, her *capsule of freedom* where she was usually happy, she'd honk or hit the accelerator with fury because someone took her parking spot or cut her off. She'd zoom past the person, just so she could give the *I've got to see how stupid you look* look.

"I. Will. Kill. You," Mads says.

"I'm not doing anything!" Harrison cries.

"If you so much as say another word to a single person, if you so much as look at me or follow me or use that stupid phone or notebook—I will. Kill. You. Understand?"

"Ow." He yanks his arm back.

"Do you hear me, Harrison? You, too, Avery. This is not funny."

"Come on, Mads," Billy says. "It's no big deal."

Mads gets in his truck. She's still puffing and panting. She closes the door, jabs her finger out the window in warning. The kid is trying to get his bike up, and the other one's examining his own elbow, like he fell, too. Ten-year-olds are always banged up. For a few years in there, you always have holes in the knees of your jeans.

"Let's get out of here," Mads says.

"So you don't want to go somewhere to talk."

"I'll go somewhere. I don't want to have some big, deep conversation, though."

"I'm not gonna let this go."

He's been driving around the lake, thinking of places they could stop. Somewhere nearby, where he doesn't have to look at that freaking bridge, or any bridge or any lake or body of water. Where is that around here? Maybe some parking garage at U-Village or something. You start to realize how much water is in Seattle as soon as you don't want to see water.

"I'm fine! I went to a doctor. I'm not planning anything. I'm just, I don't know. I'm in my own head all the time and I hate my own head and I don't see how to get *out*."

"There're options. Ones you haven't seen yet."

"I don't want to do the life I'm supposed to."

"Then do a different one."

God! He gets how wrong it sounds, how stupidly simple, even if it's right.

"I thought you had something you wanted to show me."

"I do."

"Well, then let's move on to the showing part of this evening's program."

"Okay. I've got to get something first."

He stops his aimless driving around. He heads for the red, lit cowboy hat in the sky.

"Arby's?"

"Action, a plan, a map. Doing something about something."

A little smile plays at the corner of her mouth. He leans over and kisses it as he waits for the voice to come over the drive-through intercom. It's another reason he believes in her. She'll rescue herself because she kisses back, she lets love in, and love is one of the only weapons that has half a chance in the dark.

Chapter Seventeen

"That is one heck of a lot of roast beef sandwiches in shiny orange foil," Mads says.

"You'd do the same for a friend." Billy closes the top of the bag so the steam won't escape. "You practically have. Or, at least, you've wanted to."

"Given a friend an enormous amount of roast beef?"

"Tried to save them."

The sun has gone down. Billy's profile is serious in the passing light of streetlamps. Some clouds have moved in. The night looks and smells like it might rain. The truck is a snug vessel. Mads wishes they'd take all that roast beef and ditch this place.

Earlier, Mads sent a text to Claire saying she'd be out tonight with Ryan, the mysterious Ryan, who now has a complicated story line. Ryan is a little of Billy, a little of Cole, and a little of this romantic comedy she watched a while back. All those lies—they looked like a possible escape, magic beans that might grow into a stalk she could climb to flee the ogres and her mother and Anna Youngwolf Floyd. But now the lies have grown and grown and grown so high, there will be no way down without falling. Did she say Ryan's favorite food was pizza or burritos? Were his parents accountants or artists or did his father have an auto repair shop? Private school (that was from the film), or small-town high (Cole)? Sister getting married (also from the movie), or an only child, save for a half brother he'd only met once (Billy)? *Have fun!* Claire texted back. *Bring him over after!*

Mads is *building* a fall. Constructing it on purpose, unable to stop. The fall might destroy her, but the only problem is, it might destroy the boy next to her, too.

She has a guess where they're going—to visit that white dog, only she can't admit she knows about him. See how precarious it's gotten? Two hours ago, the tipping structure of secrets could have crashed, thanks to Harrison and his big, fat mouth.

The air-conditioning is broken, and so the windows are rolled down. Billy takes Mads's hand, gives it a little shake like she's the champion. She can see his chest muscles under his T-shirt, the dark hair on his arms that likely came from his mother. Desire fights its way up over the sadness, offers itself like a small boat on a lonely island. Billy looks over at Mads, and the car swerves a bit. Is there such a thing as half a bomb? Can she blow up everything in her life except this odd boy with his sunken cheeks?

Of course, when she tells him the truth, this will all be over. The way he pulls over to the side of the street right then and turns off his engine. The way his dark eyes look shiny as sabers in the streetlight. The way he takes her bracelet in his hand and turns it in a circle.

The way he grabs the bag of sandwiches and pulls her across the seat and says, "Come on." She has to climb over the armrest, but it's okay, because the gesture says *now*.

She feels the tiny tip-tap of promise. No, it's more of a baby flutter. You shouldn't look to another person to save you, but maybe she and Billy could save themselves, together.

"Shh," he says, though Mads has not said a word. She steps like a thief, hush-hush. There's a sliver of a moon, and the smell of damp cardboard and dewy evergreen boughs. Down the street, a couple of car doors slam. Mads hears dinner party voices. A few porch lights are on. Mads sees the house a block away. It's small and white, with a cyclone fence. Two-bedroom, max. Maybe 1,700 square feet. Good neighborhood, but the price of the house would come way down because it has zero curb appeal. The yard is all sad scrub and one overgrown tree that casts a deep shadow. The windows are dark, except for the blue-red flicker of a television.

Now Mads hears the slink of chain against cement as the dog stands and walks toward Billy as far as he can. He starts to whine and whimper.

"Hey, buddy," Billy whispers. "Mads? This is Casper. Casper, Mads."

He doesn't need to say it—Casper is his Ivy. He sets the bag on the ground, opens it quietly. "It's not just that he doesn't feed him," he whispers some more. "He's chained up day and night. He practically has to sleep in his own shit."

They need to climb that fence right now, Mads thinks, but she also immediately understands the impossibility of it. You could get *in* that way, but how to get the dog *out*? Billy tosses the sandwiches one by one over the fence, this time lobbing them neatly. The dog gulps them down.

Billy throws the last sandwich, wipes his hands on his pants. Mads and Billy stand beside each other and look at Casper like the worried parents of a sick newborn. A fat drop of rain hits Mads's head, and then her cheek, and then her foot in her sandals. Billy sets one hand out, palm up, as if inviting a drop to land in it.

"Rain," he says.

"Rain," she says.

"You're a good dog, Casper. You're a good boy," Billy says, and then he takes Mads's hand.

"Nice to meet you," Mads says over her shoulder as they run.

They slam into the truck. Rain splatters against the windshield now. She wants to get that dog and run away so bad she can barely stand it. "He'll be out there in this."

"Better than no water. I worry about that. I think a lot about water."

He doesn't just mean the kind in Casper's empty bowl.

"Billy," Mads says. The words gather up. They wait to order

themselves. Once they do, she will open her mouth and they will come out, finally.

"I can't help him," Billy says. He scrunches up the empty bag, throws it to the floor.

"You are, though."

"I can't get him out."

"There's got to be a way."

"Do you see why I brought you?"

"I think so."

"You and me. We're pretty much the same."

"You want to kidnap him."

"Better believe it."

"You know he's screwed where he is."

"Yep."

"But you can't do it."

"Hell, no, I would. I'd do it in a second."

"I mean, you can't because of that *fence*."

"Right."

"You and me," Mads says. Who'd have thought it? A guy whose parents destroyed themselves; a guy who works at a dog rescue center, and who plays Night Worlds. Who only read one book for fun in his life, but who carries a piece of that book wherever he goes. It's true. They are so much alike they could be siblings, Claudia and Jamie, only without the sibling part. Only without the perfect childhood and the hot fudge sundaes.

"No wonder we're sitting here together, is what I'm saying."

"We can't get him over that fence?"

"How? I've thought about it a million times."

"What if we cut our way in? Wire cutters." *We*. A plan. The rising feeling of *act*.

"I don't want to get arrested. I've been looking at videos, you know, online? How to open a padlock? All you need is a couple of paper clips and some time. But that asshole, H. Bergman. He barely ever leaves. He goes to the Quik Mart for, like, five seconds. And every two weeks, he goes to Fred Meyer. I followed him, to see where he goes. But he's barely in there twenty minutes."

"That's the key. Keep him there longer."

"Yeah? How? Mess up his car, or something? I mean, as much as I might want to, I can't take a chance I'd hurt the guy. And I don't know shit about cars."

"We've got to do something."

"*We*. You said, 'we,' Mads. I knew you'd say 'we.'" He spins her bracelet again. He grins, even though his eyes are serious. "Maybe we can't rescue a baby, but maybe we can rescue a dog. It's *something*."

"Padlock, fence, car." She thinks through the problems again.

"Let's go. I feel like that asshole is looking at me from here."

This time, he heads straight to the garage of the U-Village shopping center. It's a funny place to park, but Mads doesn't even care. They face a cement wall. There's a sign on it that reads LOAD, UNLOAD ONLY. Personally, she'd rather unload. You can hear the screech of tires as they circle around the cement pillars, heading to MORE PARKING, UPPER LEVEL. In the side mirror, Mads sees a shopper with lots of bags, hunting for her car.

"I hate this thing," Billy says. He jiggles the armrest. "Maybe there's a lever." He searches around down by his seat and accidentally pops the hood. After getting out and slamming it shut, he's back. "Hell," he says. "Whatever."

He leans over and presses his mouth to hers, and dear God, Mads forgets about everything: her need to confess, her settled future, the ticking clock on her and Billy. All she can think—no, she's not thinking anymore. Thoughts turn liquid. They just kiss like crazy, and she grabs his hair and he grabs hers, and things get a little out of control.

Someone pulls into the spot next to them, and Billy mutters, "Jesus," and sits back in his seat, and Mads twists her shirt back down from where it's hiked up.

"We've got to . . . ," Mads says, but she doesn't know what they've got to do.

"This."

"What?"

He reaches in his back pocket. He takes out his wallet, and then the map. He lays it on her leg as the driver next to them locks his car with the *beep beep* of his key fob. "We steal Casper. And then we head out of town."

"You're crazy."

"We won't hide in the toilets or anything, but we can *go*."

"Go."

"Yeah. A different life, right?"

"You're nuts."

"Why?"

"I can't go. You know that. I've got, like, a month before I have to go back home."

"It's not what you want." He looks pissed. Like he could punch something.

"There are legal papers waiting for me. I have to go."

"Fuck papers. You don't even want papers. Papers are only causing you misery, from what I can see."

"I want papers more than I want the guilt of not having papers."

"I'll go there, then."

She's got no good answer for this. Just, the thought of him there, him and her mom, her friends from her past life, the whole picture—it's so wrong that it makes no sense. "God, Billy, do you know how late it is? We've been kissing here for hours."

"Not long enough," he says. "I could kiss you all life."

Mads creeps up to her room. Her sandals hang from her fingertips, so her bare feet soften her step. It's a guilty hour. That hour says things.

"Mads?" Claire calls softly. "You home?"

"I'm here." Damn that Claire. She always needs to make

sure everyone is in their place before her day is done. It's very motherly. Not Mads's sort of mother, or Billy's, but the kind of mother you imagine.

"It's after one. I was getting worried."

Mads doesn't want Claire to see her. The kissing, the entire night, has changed her once more. Claire will see that.

Claire waits there in the hall. Mads's politeness wins out as it always does. She cracks the door. Pops her head around it. "Sorry to worry you. We just . . . lost track of time."

"Did you have a fun night with Ryan?"

"Yeah. We . . . went to the movies."

"Mads." Claire smiles. "Are you in love?"

"Oh my God, no."

"I mean, it's okay if you are!"

"I'm not."

"All right. No need to bite my head off."

"Definitely not."

"It's just . . . You look in love."

Mads crosses her eyes, makes a scary jack-o'-lantern mouth.

"I mean, you could just *let* yourself, you know. See what happens."

"No, Claire. He's not really even my type."

"I don't want to talk you into the guy or anything, but sometimes not our type is exactly our type. You can be pretty similar inside, where it counts. You should have seen Thomas when we first met. He was in a band. You heard of KISS?"

"I think so."

"Heavy metal? Painted white faces? Garish clowns from your worst nightmare? That's who they were trying to be. And here I was, Miss Prissy, Miss Straight-A. I don't know how to explain it, but just I *recognized* him. Like, our essential selves were the same, if that doesn't sound too paranormaly."

"I couldn't feel that way about Ryan."

"Okay."

"This is just for . . . fun." *Fun* is definitely not the right word. Not after the body in the water, and all that's happened since. "Plus, you know, he'll have to go back to La Conner by the end of the summer."

"I thought you said his family was from Cape Cod."

"Cape Cod! Right. Why'd I say La Conner? I don't even know where La Conner is."

"Yeah. By the sound of his sister's wedding, I'm not thinking La Conner."

"Wow, I'm tired. No wonder I'm not thinking straight."

"Well, I'll let you get to sleep. Good night, sweetie."

Mads gets into bed and shuts her eyes, and when she does, she sees Anna Youngwolf Floyd in the lake again. She feels the bump of the body against her. She wants to scream and rise from that bed and run, but a ghost needs to be seen and heard. Mads forces herself to imagine the alive Anna instead of that battered one, the Anna who cradled Billy as a baby, and washed his toddler face, and waited with him for the school bus. Anna once held Billy in her hands until she stood at the bridge and let him go. In a way, he's in Mads's hands now, because this is how it is with love. And she isn't holding carefully.

It's so, so late, but there's the curve of headlights turning into the Bellarose driveway. Suzanne or Carl likely drove off in anger, and is now returning. Mads thinks of the dear, sleeping lump of Ivy in her crib—her milky dreams and her satiny hair and her eyes that take in everything. She thinks of Casper. It's so scary, the way we rely on others to do right by us. She thinks about Billy again. *You and me.* That map, spread out. *We steal Casper. And then we head out of town.*

The body bumps her again. Ghosts just don't quit. She squeezes her eyes shut until she sees stars, clenches her fingernails into the palms of her fists.

Mess up his car, or something? I don't know shit about cars.

I don't know shit about cars.

But Mads does.

At least, Cole, who's worked at Rainier Auto Repair his whole life, does, and one day after school, Mads stood beside him in the garage of Rainier Auto Repair, as she did every now and then after school. They stared at an engine under a hood, and she felt like the student doctor during the open-heart surgery.

What's wrong with this one?

Nothing. Not a single thing. Someone swapped the spark plug wires. See here? This guy, and this guy, just like that. Just pull, then switch. Do you know how long it took us to figure it out? Long. Someone didn't want this car to go anywhere.

She opens her eyes, glances at the clock by the bed. Past

two now. She shouldn't call. A call at two a.m. says *I can't stop thinking about you*. It says *You* saw *me*, and *You waited for me all day to* hear *me*, and it says *We could be a* team, *me with my violin case, you with your map*.

But her phone is in her hand anyway, and she's dialing, and he picks up on one ring.

"I was lying here thinking about you," he says.

She feels a warm rush. It's all gold lights, a sunrise.

"Get over here," he says.

"I'm not calling for *that*. I'm calling for a perfectly practical reason."

"Too bad."

"Quit it. This is important. It's about Casper. It's about two spark plugs."

"I've looked at the videos, Mads. I'm afraid I'd kill the guy. I don't know a spark plug from a . . . from whatever else is in there."

"I do."

"You do?"

"Yes."

"You're kidding me."

"No. It just hit me."

"Okay, Claude, when do we bust out of here? And how?"

Of course she knows the line. Jamie says it just after Claudia chooses him to accompany her on the greatest adventure of their lives. She knows what comes next, too.

"Here's the plan. Listen carefully," she says.

Chapter Eighteen

"Don't tell me. You're *in love*." Gran pours some food into Ginger's dish. At the sound, the dog runs in like she's got the winning lottery ticket. Billy feels sorry that brown crunchy stuff is as exciting as things get for Ginger. If he could, he'd give her a hundred dog butts to sniff, or a steak a day. He swirls the last of his morning coffee in his cup.

"Why do you make that sound like a bad thing?"

"You look like a goon, is all, the way you're smiling."

He hears it—the jab of the dagger, the vial of poison, the *accusation*. Still, he makes a face. His mother would have been drawn right into this fight. But Billy won't. No way. He only crosses his eyes and sticks out his tongue. Here you go, old woman, love looks like this, and this, and this. He rams his fingers in his armpits and gives an apelike scratch, *ooh-ooh-ooh*s like a stupid goon, because he'd rather be the biggest and most hopeful fool than a bitter, hardened person too scared to risk passion. He has his mother's face and his father's lean build, but he'll tell you something right now. He's his own self. His mom and dad dropped an egg on the earth, and it cracked open, and out he came, made from them but different from them. He has to be. He *will* be.

"Well, as you prance around, just remember all the good love did *her*," Gran says.

She means Mom, in that blue-gray urn on the mantel. Billy's last swallow of coffee suddenly tastes like ass water. Why, why does Gran do this every time he feels okay? The dagger slices now, and he feels his guts about to spill. He could cry, but he also feels fury rise up his throat. He wants to push Gran down, smother her with the couch cushion so he never has to hear another word from her pinched, mean mouth.

And look at that. In spite of his good intentions, she got him. No contest. She's a master. In the past, he only watched this from the stands. All these years, he thought he could do better, just like most spectators.

He was wrong. He gets it now. He's sorry, so sorry, he didn't get it before. And you know what? His mom shouldn't have to stay here, locked in battle with Gran forever. Neither should he. The thing is, if you try and try to drive people away, you shouldn't be surprised when they finally go.

"I thought you told me I should live my life."

"What are you saying?" Gran looks up from the cupboard where she's fetching a pan to fry up some eggs. He can't believe how indignant she looks. It's funny what happens when you call people on their bullshit. The worst offenders always feel the most wronged.

"I'm saying, you always tell me to live my life, but then you remind me I'm living my life."

"Oh, come on."

"It's true."

"You little shit," she says. But it's all disbelief, not anger. She looks like she might cry. Bullies always crumple.

The weakness kills him, though. Give him meanness and the blade anytime. Right then, her old eyes fill with tears and for one second, one split second, he understands feeling like such a disappointment, such a worthless ghost-child, that you could walk to the rail of that bridge and fling your legs over. "Gran, I'm sorry. But, come on. You keep . . ." He doesn't even know how to sum up what she keeps doing. It's all strange stuff he can't even describe in regular words. "I'm seeing a girl, so? So, yeah, I like her a lot. So what?"

"I'm asking questions, is all. Who is she? Where'd she come from all of a sudden? You don't even know her. She just *showed up* and now you're all off in your own world."

"Maybe it's fate, Gran. Maybe God. Maybe Mom."

She snorts. He should never have said it. Still, none of those things—not fate, not God, not Mom—should be snorted at.

"You think being paranoid about everyone is gonna keep you safe?"

"*You* safe."

Now *he* snorts. "I gotta go to work."

"I'm just asking a question. I'm only looking out for you. I don't get why she never comes around here. You never bring her around."

"Look at you! You gotta ask? My mother is in a fucking *vase*. . . ." Jesus, why did he say that? Why, why, why? He wants to take it back. It makes him hate himself. He wants to slice his arms and gouge his eyes for being so horrible.

He's *got* to get out of here. He can't stand it anymore. At first, he had nowhere to go. Gran needed him. They only had each other. But lately, with her, he can feel the real-life Night Worlds around him, the dark chambers of loathing. Shame and rage duel, and the blood of that ancient pair soaks through the layers of his skin and sinks into his spirit. The creature who emerged from the cracked shell—he has to start walking if he wants to survive.

"You never even told me her *name*."

He can't say *Mads* here. It'd be like opening his cupped hands and letting a butterfly loose, only to see it smacked dead with a shoe. "Amy," he says. "Her name is Amy."

"Sounds like a cheerleader name."

"She was never a cheerleader." He's not even sure about that, but he'll find out. When you love someone this much, you should know everything.

"I'm just saying you better watch out."

"I better watch out, huh?" He puts his cup in the sink. Now he's late for work.

"Yeah."

"I'm just going to end up hurt, right? Something like that?"

"People always have motivations, Billy. And any girl who lets herself be hidden has something to hide."

"One, I don't care. Two, you don't know what you're talking about."

Poor Billy.

He doesn't know it yet, but he will soon: Even bitter old ladies are sometimes right.

It's not the best part of the job, but someone has to do it. Jack and Lisa have the dogs in the dayroom, so Billy cleans out the pens. Everyone takes turns. It's a shitty job, heh heh, but he tries to look at it this way: He's making a better home for them. He's giving them the kindness and respect they deserve.

He hoses everything down. And then he fills water bowls and carts the puffy dog beds back from the big dryer. After that, he heads over to the indoor playroom. The dogs are inside, because Jane Grace is getting the outdoor enrichment ready. *Enrichment* includes fun and challenging stuff like hidden treats, puzzle balls, and blocks with food tucked in them. It's the same with dogs as it is with people—if you aren't doing what you're capable of, you're probably going to get yourself into trouble.

Halfway down the hall, he smiles. You should hear those dogs in there—they're having a blast. Every now and then a couple of them get into it, but flare-ups are fast and forgotten. Dogs know how to work stuff out. They tell each other what they'll take and won't take, and that's that. He respects that about them. You might even say it's a personal life goal of his.

He's surprised when he sees Amy there, not Lisa. He's barely seen Amy at all, thanks to Jane Grace. But now she bops over in those shorts and that T-shirt with the shooting star on it. Bodhi follows her as if she's a vision in beef.

"Hey, stranger. Stranger McWolfie."

"Hey."

"Where've you been? Alex said he hasn't seen much of you, either."

"Just busy."

"Yeah, busy with a *girl*. A girl who's not me." She flicks his chest with her finger.

"Yeah, well."

Jasper spots him. He runs over, bumps into Billy's legs, and circles him in greeting. "Jas boy. Way to be a great dog." Billy scratches him a good one on his neck, right where Jas likes it.

"Did you hear about Lulu? Getting adopted?"

"Really?" Billy says. Amy seems honestly happy about it.

"Really. Two kids. Fenced yard. The jackpot."

"That's awesome."

Jack whistles, using two fingers. Bodhi's just made a big puddle, and now he's jumping on Rocko's back, and Jack's supposed to head outside to the yard now. Rocko is already looking better. Sometimes Billy's sure that Rocko smiles back at him.

Amy punches Billy's arm. "You better get the mop."

His phone buzzes in his pocket as he slops the floor. Jane Grace doesn't mind cell phones as long as you don't look at them every minute. He's hoping maybe Mads sent him a text. Probably it's Gran saying she broke her hip or something, just so he can really feel like shit.

He gives it a quick glance. It's not Mads or Gran. Amy's sent him a picture from across the room, a close-up of Jasper's nose and black lips. She grins at him from over there, and he gives her a thumbs-up. Maybe ten minutes later, his phone buzzes again. Another picture, this one of Bodhi in the time-out box, looking like a hockey player who just wants back in the game. Amy grins again, and Billy shakes his head to say *Can you believe that guy?* She sends a couple more. Lulu scratching at the floor with her paw; Runt barking his damn head off.

The pictures make him happy. He's even having fun with Amy. That's the thing. Sometimes you can actually like the people who annoy you the most.

Jane Grace is at the front desk, and Billy's in the adjacent storage room, unpacking a shipment of supplies. Food, treats, toys, medicine, cleaning stuff, laundry detergent, it's a mess back there, and Jane Grace wants it tidied up. Jane Grace is an organized person, but not one of those organized people who drive you crazy because of how organized they are.

"I heard about Lulu," he calls to her as he hauls and stacks bags of kibble.

"Great news, huh?"

"Yeah. The best." He doesn't even have to ask if that ass-hole Mr. Woods ever came by to look for her.

"You'll love the people. They're coming on Friday to get her, after the background check comes through."

"Awesome." He slings another fifty-pound bag of food.

"Hey, Billy?" Jane Grace is in the doorway now. She folds her arms. Her eyebrows bend into a serious V. "I had a young couple . . ." She stops. "This is hard."

"What?"

"I had a young couple who were interested in Jasper."

It's a sock in the gut. A blow. Jasper is his boy. *His*, ever since he first spotted the dog in that yard with all the junk—old refrigerators and car parts and tricycles, massive televisions and ditched stereo speakers, stuff people had bought with pride, now discarded and forgotten. Jasper lay in front of a stack of tires, the chain (always some chain) hooked around the Y of a trailer hitch. Right away, Billy saw the patches of bare skin that let him know the dog had been locked up there a long time. It killed him, the way Jasper was curled up. A body did what it could to shelter itself. He looked right at Billy, though. Sometimes the dogs won't even dare. They duck their heads, getting ready for what your hand or foot might do. But Jasper met his eyes. And those eyes spoke to him, swear to God.

"I told you," Billy says to Jane Grace. "I was going to get my own place. . . ." Yeah, well, that plan got derailed, didn't it? *Oh*, his mother said. In his head, she said it again and again and again. *Oh, oh, oh.*

"I know. I know you were. What should we do, huh? I mean, we can't keep him here forever. It's not fair to him. He needs a home."

"I was going to get a place with a yard."

"Man, with what I pay you?" She rolls her eyes, laughs a little. Heartland is mostly run on donations, and she's right; he barely makes anything. Jack, who helps run the place, doesn't get paid at all. He's got a dot-com past, so he doesn't even need to work. He's just there because he cares. It's not a job you even do for the money.

"Yeah, well."

"And . . . you, either," Jane says. "You don't want to stay here forever. We've got to think about what's next. We need to get some ideas going for both you and Jasper. I was talking to Dave. He said he could get you a good construction job with Stein Reynolds. You could do really well."

"Construction?" He stares at Jane Grace and she stares back and they both know that him working construction is as likely as him becoming president. Those guys are built like trucks. Worse, though—they stand up on high girders and look down.

"Maybe not out in the field? Maybe the office."

"I was going to call my uncle," Billy says. He didn't even realize he'd been thinking that, but it seems to be true. "My half brother works for him. He tests games and stuff."

"You'd be great at that." He loves Jane Grace, that's all there is to it. This talk—it's mostly about him, not Jasper. He sees what she's doing. She wants him to have a future beyond no-money-an-hour and Gran and bridges and loss.

"If I worked with my uncle, I could maybe do this on the side."

"Exactly right, because this place would not be the same without your face in it."

"I wouldn't be the same without my face in this place."

"I get that. Do I ever."

"Jasper's mine."

"Okay."

"I got a plan."

"Okay, Billy." She holds one hand up, as if it's been decided.

"I need a little time."

"Sure. And you know what else might be good?"

"Don't say college. I've got to get a place to live first."

"Something I've told you before. Something you should do before you settle in to make the big bucks. It involves a certain piece of paper in your back pocket."

"Oh." He laughs. "Road trip."

Jane Grace nods. "Can't think of anything better for the spirit than making a dream come true."

Two weeks ago, they were ready. Billy had his small but powerful weapons—two paper clips, a little knowledge; and Mads had hers—a little knowledge, her glasses. The idea was simple: Mads would follow H. Bergman to Fred Meyer, switch the spark plug wires, while back in H. Bergman's yard, Billy freed

Casper from his cell. Billy had been practicing, using a padlock from his old high school locker. He was nervous.

They held hands in Billy's mom's truck, their eyes glued to H. Bergman's garage door. Mads's palm was sweaty, or maybe Billy's was. A half hour passed, an hour. Something was wrong. That asshole wasn't coming out. Mads had skipped class for this, and Billy felt bad.

"Let's hope he's dead," Mads said. "Let's hope his heart got sick and tired of being so evil."

The house just sat there, closed up. The windows looked like sleeping eyes, and the door like a yawning mouth. Casper heard Billy's truck coming, and he stood there, waiting. The sound of that particular truck meant *food*, but Billy believed it meant *him*, too. He could feel their connection, and anyone who says dogs only care about food is wrong and narrow-minded besides. He was glad he had that ham he picked up from the deli counter at QFC, though. He was going to give it to Casper once they'd gotten to the truck, but now it was another care package lobbed over the fence.

"I hope H. Bergman pissed himself in his last moments," Mads said.

"We'll come back in two weeks, is all. Same place, same time."

"We're not giving up," Mads said.

See? Right there. That's where the doctor in his head is wrong, wrong, wrong about her and him. That flash of fire and anger, the kind of fire and anger you'd never expect with those freckles—the girl has fight.

237

And H. Bergman isn't dead. Three days later, Billy spots him hauling his garbage cans to the curb, honking into a handkerchief. Who even has those disgusting things anymore?

Until they can try again, he and Mads see each other every night. Right after Mads gets off work, they meet, and they practically have a whole weekend together, except for the few hours Mads has to help out with yard chores.

Yard chores! It's so awesome. Afterward, Mads smells like grass, and she has an arc of sweet suburban-like dirt under her fingernails, and it all makes his heart fucking sing. Chores and order and grass stains are so different than brown splotches of forgotten, rented lawn.

The love, the grass, the mission—it all becomes part of a secret he has now. A plan. Since Billy spoke those words to Jane Grace, *I got a plan*, it's become true. He has one. The plan feels like a fragile living thing with feather wings, emphasis on *living*. Jesus, love makes clichés true, because he wants whitefence grass stains with that girl, and a kitchen. He can maybe cook three things, but they could have their own stove and a refrigerator with their own food in it, and a bed, God yeah, he wants their own bed most of all.

This is *Plan A*, even if Mads keeps talking about going home after her licensing test. That's a hurdle. So what? The doctor in his head should shut up about it, too, because Billy thinks she's stopped going to class. He's afraid to ask. The plan is a baby bird, and those guys drop out of trees and crash into windows and get eaten by hawks. All he knows is, she used to spend some of their time together doing homework. Studying. Wearing those cute glasses. But lately? Nada. So there, Doc. How high is the hurdle, huh?

There've been no textbooks at Gas Works Park, or Green Lake, or the University of Washington campus, all the places they go, anywhere with grass, anywhere he can lay an old blanket on the lawn and wrap them up in it. Goddamn, no wonder he's so fond of grass stains lately. Even the words get him hard. Jesus. Mouths on mouths, hands shoved down pants, if he doesn't get them a bed soon, he'll go crazy. Being at Gran's anymore makes him feel twelve years old, and worthless, too. Plus, he needs his own bed, not just one at Alex's place. It sounds stupid, but he wants to be a man about it. He wants to take his time, and then maybe she'll stop talking for good about going home.

Baby bird, hell—the plan is airborne, yeah, but powerfully airborne, all burning gases and interplanetary thrust. He *believes* a bed and so much more is in their future. See, Mads hasn't run off with Ivy even once since that day at Bartells. And she doesn't have that look in her eyes, either. Instead, you should see the way she checks him out. She does, all the time! She's crazy about him, and he knows it. He's not an idiot. He knows he can't cure her or fix her (and that she can't cure him or fix him). He knows that even love (the biggest weapon, atomic and forever) isn't enough by itself. But maybe the love plus her own fire plus grass-stain hope, saving-Casper hope, hope in general, no matter where they find it—maybe that has a chance against despair.

And now, H. Bergman, watch out. Sometimes you have to try and try and try again to conquer bad shit. Mads and Billy are ready once again. Billy—naïve and doomed, optimistic beyond reason—sits in his mother's truck a block away from H. Bergman's house, trying not to puke from nerves. He waits for Mads. He has another package of ham, and he has his paper clips. It doesn't seem like much, but he's also got something you can't see. He's got burning desire, which can shoot to the sky, flash like a comet, and make the stars step backward in awe.

Chapter Nineteen

"I think he's coming." Mads grips Billy's arm.

H. Bergman's garage door rises. It's a one-car garage, which lowers the value of the home. Everyone wants two or three now, but it has an electric opener, at least. Her mind still pretends to care, even though she hasn't been to class in two weeks, ever since Thomas's truck refused to go on the freeway at all. Otto Hermann sent a letter. Mads told Claire it was an invitation to a class party. A class party! Can you imagine? Standing around and talking about open floor plans with Ryan Plug (she has no idea what his real last name is), and the scowling Mrs. Chang, who smells like oversteamed vegetables? Linda Erickson could bring her three-layer dip. Mads hopes Linda has moved on to a new friend.

In the two weeks they wait to steal Casper, Mads calls her mom every morning, same as usual. Then she walks Harrison to the bus stop, gathers her backpack and books, and pretends to go to school. At the library, she looks at college catalogs with images of stately, ivy-covered buildings and brick squares, fall leaves, and serious students. After that, she reads. *Madame Bovary*, with Emma, who eats a fistful of arsenic. *The House of Mirth*, with Lily Bart drifting toward suicide as the man of her dreams prepares to ask her to marry him. The reading lulls the ogres to sleep.

Then, at her regular time, Mads babysits Ivy. She does not drive her to a ferry dock or to the county line, though. Instead, she practice-walks Ivy around the garden, holding her little hands while telling her things she needs to know. After rule number three, *The only thing that should curl up on the bathroom floor is a dirty towel. You are not a dirty towel*, she lost count. *Screw it all up, so you can see how the world loves you anyway. Wear the lipstick called Passion Flower Pink. Turn down everyone else's voice, but turn the music up.* Mads stashes the wad of cash Suzanne gives her, same as Jamie with his card game earnings.

And she sees Billy. As soon as she's off work, they meet, and he grabs her so hard that their teeth clack together when they kiss. Kissing him makes her want to be alive. This is not the early-imagined Billy with a dead mother she pulled to the shore. This is the real him, with his own Arms and Armor, with Great Halls filled with what she thinks are masterpieces. Small, regular, daily masterpieces—thoughtfulness, heart, valor.

All of it—it can make a person forget that it has to end. Sooner than she even imagines.

"Here we go," Billy says. H. Bergman's Ford Escort backs

out of the garage. Mads knows she will likely devastate Billy, and her mother, and Claire and Thomas, and even herself. She will likely disappoint Cole, and her friends at home, and Otto Hermann, and Linda Erickson. But she will save this dog if it kills her.

Mads's head is in Billy's lap. This would be the perfect time for a joke, but Billy's concentrating. He's slunk down and peeking over the steering wheel. She can tell he's nervous, which is making her nervous. He's talking fast, like he's had a double shot at Java Jive.

"Backing up, backing up . . . Garage door is coming down. Okay, it's down. Pulling forward . . ."

"I'm out of here, then," Mads says. She kisses him quick. He tastes like pancake syrup. She runs to Thomas's truck, which, bless its little automotive heart, starts up like a dream. She practiced this route with an online map, but just to be sure, she gets the GPS woman talking. Thankfully, the woman (with her robotic patience) is right there this time. Mads's hands shake. She can practically hear her heart. It sounds like the dryer when she puts her tennis shoes in.

Driving down Forty-Fifth, she has to stop at every light. She swerves around bikes and parallel parkers. The traffic isn't helping anything. She's lost sight of H. Bergman. Every time Billy's followed him, though, he's ended up at the same place. Too late, she realizes it's pitiful information to base criminal activity on. H. Bergman could be anywhere. Fred Meyer, sure, but a million other places. A million other places closer to his house, where he might show up right as Billy is picking that lock.

Mads prays. It's a prayer involving the words *Please* and *Fred Meyer*, not likely a combo God hears very often. The GPS woman is the only calm one here.

Your destination is on the left, she says. The lot is huge. Mads scans—Ford Escort, Ford Escort—but only sees shopping carts and children; large SUVs with their back doors opened; cars reversing from spots. MINI Coopers, VWs, Hondas, Hondas, Hondas . . . The place is a madhouse.

But wait.

There he is! What a relief—H. Bergman is heading to the automatic doors, wearing his green old-man pants and gray shirt, with his slicked-back hair, and his cigarettes-and-booze face. It's a clichéd dog abuser face, hardened by meanness, but what are you going to do. Mads can tell he smells bad. Alcohol fumes and long-ago smoke and shut-up rooms. She knows that if she brushed up against him accidentally she would get the creeps.

Where is his car, though? He'll only be in the store twenty minutes or less. Enough time to pick up a few groceries, and that's it.

Mads drives down the aisle he seems to have come from. No Ford Escort. She starts to sweat; drops actually roll down her sides, like rain on a window. She is going the wrong way, and a Jeep driver glares. Nothing. Up another aisle, and then down another, more nothing. She's about to cry. She's afraid to check how much time has already passed. If Billy gets caught and Casper remains a captive, it will be her fault.

Back down the aisles again. And there, right where the Jeep driver scowled, she sees it. Ford, beautiful Ford. She whispers thanks, pulls into the closest spot.

"Please help me," she says aloud, to God or maybe a dog saint or to anyone who might care. Before she made that fateful swim that started hundreds of lies, her list of wrongdoings included parking in load zones and snitching bunches of jam packets at IHOP because Mom only bought the diet kind she liked. Now Mads is about to break the law for real. She has no idea which law, but definitely a law.

She tries to breathe through her nose to keep the throw-up feeling at bay. She gets out of the truck, which means she's really doing this. She looks both ways, like an inept bank robber, and approaches the Ford Escort. She doesn't want to touch it—even the car gives her the shivers. In the back, there's a green Windbreaker, and a black pop-up umbrella, splayed out and looking like the ribbed wings of a bat.

An engine starts up nearby; the doors of the store swish open and closed. A woman wheels a cart with a large potted palm in it. Another has more paper towels than you'd ever need in your life. The potted palm sways, heads Mads's way. A clock starts ticking in her head.

She pops the hood. That was easy. The engine gapes. Now what? She hunts around in there. She pats her pockets, looks for her glasses. Once they're on, everything is sharper than sharp and dirtier than dirty.

This guy, and this guy, she remembers Cole saying, but the engine's a maze.

The large palm in the cart clatters and bumps and finally stops next to her. A woman with rainbow-shaped eyebrows opens the back door of her wagon.

"Car trouble!" Mads says. She smiles the way she imagines the innocent driver of a Ford Escort would smile. Her armpits are drenched. She sneaks glances at the store, hoping H. Bergman doesn't walk out right then.

"Oh," the woman says.

"It's the darn spark plugs!"

"Well, good luck."

"You, too! Good luck with your new tree! Ugh, car trouble's the worst!"

The woman lifts the plant into the back and slams the door. Another vehicle has its turn signal on while it waits for the spot. Mads needs to get out of there, fast.

There. She sees them! The wires. *Just pull, then switch.*

"Pull, then switch," she says.

It's easy! She feels almost giddy. It's thrillingly simple to break whatever law she's breaking! The first one comes out with a satisfying *pop*. She is so pleased with herself, she can barely stand it. The wagon leaves, and another car veers in. A short guy gets out. He has thinning dark hair and is sporting sunglasses and one of those untucked Hawaiian shirts men over forty always wear. It's a shirt that says *I was a stud in 1981*.

"Need a jump?" he says.

"Oh, no. Nah. Got it handled."

"Those are the spark plug wires."

"Yeah, I know. I'm . . . replacing. Replacing one. Them. All of them."

"You sure it's the plugs? Maybe it's just the battery."

"I'm sure."

"Engine been surging?" Mads has no idea how to answer this. She has a fifty-fifty chance. Her shirt is now stuck to her back with sweat. The sun is beating down. She could swear it's moved. That's how much time has gone by.

"Yeah."

"Rough idle?"

Jesus!

"Yeah."

"Probably the spark plugs, all right. Need a ratchet? I got tools in the car. I once had a Ford that made it to two hundred thousand, but they're prone to cylinder box problems, so you've got to watch that."

"Thank you, mister, but I *have this handled*."

"Hey, you don't need to bite my head off. Fine. Just trying to be helpful." He takes off, gives one of those loud exhales of disbelief that are actually fury.

Jerk. Thinks a girl can't know about cars! *Pop!* There! Second one, off! See, Mr. Sexist Luau Man?

The doors of the store open. A woman and two kids walk

out. Hurry, hurry! He'll be coming any minute. Mads shoves a wire in the now-empty hole, does the same with the second. She slams down the hood, just as the doors open again.

There he is! He's coming out, all right, carrying one brown grocery sack, one small white pharmacy bag, and a four-pack of toilet paper.

He's seen her. She's sure of it. She strolls to Thomas's truck. This might be what it feels like to have a heart attack. She's listening for the yell, the *Hey, you!* She's expecting him to grab her arm from behind. But none of that happens. She gets in the truck. Her chest is squeezing. It's been too long since she's taken a breath. She risks a glance toward H. Bergman. He's whistling! She sees his creepy, pursed lips. He's smiling away with his new TP. *Get out of here!* she screams to herself.

Thomas's truck gives a little skip to keep things exciting, and then, *thankyouthankyouthankyou*, starts. She is sure H. Bergman's eyes are burning into her, sure the silky-shirted man is running back outside with his finger pointing, sure that she's switched some wrong wires, or maybe hasn't switched them at all. What if she just put them back in the same place? What if the car blows up, like in one of those movies Cole likes? There's a siren far off, and she's sure the silky-shirted man has called the police. She'll be arrested for spark plug swapping and jam packet theft.

According to their plan, she is now supposed to park on the side of the road and watch the lot. Should H. Bergman's car start up, she'll need to alert Billy. Mads's hands shake. Her legs shake. Her whole body is doing the same trembling dance it did after she'd hauled Anna Youngwolf Floyd from the water. That seems like so long ago. She can almost convince herself it didn't happen.

H. Bergman is in his car. He buckles his seat belt. He adjusts his rearview mirror. He sets his hands at ten o'clock and two. Then he leans forward a bit, reaches for the key now in the ignition.

Rrr.

Rrr, rrr.

He tries again. More *rrr*s, but nothing else. And again. More nothing! Again and again, and nothing, nothing, nothing! Dear sweet God, dear beautiful life, nothing! She's done it! Mads does a little panicked yet joy-filled car dance. H. Bergman gets out. One thing's for sure—he won't be smiling for a long while.

Soon enough, though, neither will she.

Chapter Twenty

"I'm outta here, then," Mads says. She kisses Billy quick, and she tastes like toast and peanut butter. He wants to watch her drive off. That's the thing—he thinks she's so beautiful that he just wants to watch and watch every little thing she does, but he has no time for that. He can't take chances, even if he's gotten pretty good with the lock. You should see him now, compared to when he was first learning. If he wasn't such a law-abiding type, he could be like a guy in one of those movies with a safe and millions of dollars and a boat speeding down a Venice canal.

He tosses a glance up and down the street like he's in a jillion-dollar suit, about to pull off the heist of his life. All clear. No guys in ultracool sunglasses, no zipping Vespas in sight. He does the high-stakes saunter. Damn Converse is untied, though. After he rises from his knees and brushes the pebbles from his burning hands, he has to search around for the second paper clip. You need a pick and a tension wrench to open the lock, that's how all the videos show it, but his paper clip tension wrench just skidded across the sidewalk and jumped off the curb, landing too close for comfort near the sewer grate.

All right. Try again. And look at that, just look at that! Casper. He's standing, wagging his damn tail. He thought that dog had lost his wag, because he hasn't seen him do it all this time. But look. There it is, a sweet, half-speed swish, as if he thinks his life's about to change but he's afraid to believe it.

"This is it, boy," Billy says.

So far, so good. Billy shakes his shoulders, tells himself to relax. He's both the trainer and the boxer in the *Rocky* movie. He has plenty of time. There's no one in sight.

The sun is out, and it's warm, and Billy begins to sweat. The glaciers are melting and lakes are forming right in his underarms, but the padlock is cool in his palm. It's harder to do it like this, with the padlock hanging. At home, he always practiced with it in his lap, sitting on his bed.

He sticks paper clip number one into the hole of the lock. Why, why, didn't he just buy a real pick and tension wrench? A store-bought tension wrench wouldn't have bent like this homemade one. Why did it somehow seem more wrong to go out and purchase his breaking-in tools? Now this makes absolutely no fucking sense to him. Either way, breaking in is breaking in. Failing will be much worse than taking his stupid conscience over to Ace Hardware and plunking down a few bucks. He gets it finally—that whole idea they read about senior year. Machiavelli—he's surprised he remembers the dude's name. The ends justify the means. He didn't even do well on that test, but now it makes sense to him. Hell, yeah. Machiavelli would have gone to Ace Hardware.

He straightens the paper clip tension wrench with his thumbs, tries again. He jabs around in there. It's like he's a blind dentist, ha ha. Casper starts to whine. Billy's got to find the pin that will click open the lock. But it's just nothing and more nothing. *Concentrate*, he tells himself. *Special Ability: Blindsight. Operating effectively without vision. Such sense may include sensitivity to vibrations, acute scent, keen hearing.*

He wipes his sweaty palms on his jeans and checks up and down the street again. No one, just a crow watching him from a telephone wire, his marble eyes staring and his beak half open like he's a nosy neighbor about to tattle.

Tension wrench in, pick in. Feel around. Stay calm.

And then . . . there it is. There it fucking is! The lock clicks, and the safe door pops open and the bars of gold are all stacked and shiny inside. Look at that, H. Bergman. You are now nothing over no one! Billy wants to whoop with victory. He slips the lock off and edges the gate open. It hasn't budged in so long, weeds and dirt and shit have grown all around it and he has to really shove his weight against it. Casper gives a half-yelp of excitement. No more prison visiting, no more barriers. Casper's at the farthest end of his chain, trying to come to him.

"Casper, boy," Billy says. He could cry, goddamn it. He could. He has his arms around Casper, and the dog doesn't mind, and this just chokes him up. Casper doesn't flinch or whine; he only leans in. "Good boy. Good big boy." Billy's voice is high and tight with tears. The dog is smashed up against his legs, and Billy has to feel around down by his big neck for the clasp to that chain.

The crow caws. To Billy, it sounds mean and threatening, but when he looks back at this day he will wonder if it was something else, a warning maybe. Because what happens next needs a warning: two *whoop-whoop*s, two ear-shattering shrieks of authority.

There is no mistaking that sound. No! No, no, no! He wants to fall to his knees. He wants to weep. He's failed. He's failed himself and Mads and Casper most of all, and now he is also in one big shitload of trouble.

Really, God? Really? He deserves this?

He dares to look up from the ground, which he's been hoping will swallow him. The blue light of the police car is not spinning. The cop has his window rolled down, and he leans on one arm, all arrogant-casual. He's got his cop sunglasses on, the mirrored kind, where you can't see his eyes. Billy recognizes him, though. He's seen him around there sometimes, cruising, sitting at that busy street by the school, pointing his speed radar at traffic. The radio in the police car bleats stuff that sounds important but apparently isn't as important as Billy himself at that moment.

Billy's frozen. He may need CPR.

"Son," the cop says. "You stealing that dog?"

253

Billy might throw up right then and there. It'll be the grossest arrest the guy ever made. Billy faces a choice. Confess now, or come up with some story when he's clearly been caught redhanded. Don't they go easier on you when you confess? No one ever gets caught stealing the painting from the art museum or the money in the safe or the computer chip with the data that will take down the major corporation with government ties, so he has no idea what to do.

"Yes, sir," he says.

The cop drums his nails on the window ledge of his patrol car. He gazes for a while at Billy and that dog.

"Carry on," the cop says. "I didn't see a thing."

It's so hard to drive, but who cares. Billy's heart is soaring. Soaring! When he gets to Green Lake, the post-kidnapping meeting spot, she's already there. His Mads, his very own partner in crime and adventure, his own Claudia, but without the sibling part. He can barely reach the brake, but he manages. She lets herself in, because it's too hard to do anything with such a big dog on your lap.

"Billy!" she breathes. "Casper!" She has big sweat stains on her shirt. Billy never knew before that sweat stains could be so fantastic.

"We did it!"

She gets right in there, next to him and Casper, who doesn't seem to mind. She kisses Billy, and it's the three of them, him and her and Casper, and Casper's hot breath smells like ham, and the rest of him doesn't smell that great, either, but who cares. Billy can feel the big beast's chest going up and down right next to him and the dog is panting loud in their faces and there are her soft lips, and the three of them are squished and smushed together, but they are *here*.

"I have never been so happy," he says, practically into her mouth. He wedges one arm out from around Casper and grabs her and pulls her closer.

"Oh my God, I was terrified! I almost didn't make it! I couldn't find his car at first, and—"

"I love you, Mads," he said. "I fucking love you."

"Oh, Billy."

"I do."

"I've got to tell you what happened!"

"So tell me, but know that I love you when you're telling me."

She tells him her story, and he tells her about the cop. He loves cops so much right then, too, he wants to sloppy kiss every one of them. And crows, even. Crows are awesome. He wouldn't kiss them, because it'd give him nightmares, but anyway! And sure, she didn't say she loved him back, but so what! It's a hurdle, that's all. When they're done talking, they start making out again. Casper hasn't budged. Billy's leg is falling asleep. Casper's big breath steams up the window, and so does theirs.

They pull apart. Mads holds his face in her hands, and then he can feel her lips in his hair. Those lips are saying something.

Not out loud, but still. Her mouth forms the *o* of *love*, and the *oo* of *you*. Heh heh, he's a lip-reader! He knows exactly what those lips just said! Add hurdles to the things he loves. They can seem so cold and mean, you know, but then you're on the other side of them, and you see what a thing of beauty they are. In the distance, those hurdles stand for everything you've learned and everything you now are and everything you had the balls to overcome.

It's kind of a special moment. Not just walking into Heartland Rescue with Casper, but standing at the counter with Mads. Mads and Jane Grace, there in the same room, meeting. Two of his most important people and one of his most important dogs.

"Mads, Jane Grace. Jane Grace, Mads." He sounds like an idiot.

"It's so good to meet you." Mads puts out her hand, and Jane Grace takes it in both of hers. It's more of a hand-hug than a shake.

"And who is this?" Jane asks.

"No collar," Billy says.

"Hmm."

"I think he looks like a Casper."

"Casper," Jane Grace says. The dog's ear twitches.

"We just found him wandering around."

"I'll bet."

"Lost," Mads says.

"Well, not anymore," Jane Grace says.

• • •

One thing's for sure—he's sick of kissing in his mom's truck. Right then, Mads says, "Ow ow ow," as he leans down and catches her hair on the armrest. Now, trying to right the situation, his elbow clanks on the window, but hell. They kiss some more. Who cares about pain when you want someone that bad?

They shift. The windows are all steamed up again, and the light outside is dusky perfect.

"We should drive by his house. I'm dying to know what happened next," Mads says, just before his mouth is back on hers again.

Billy pulls away briefly. "I can tell you what happened next." Billy's voice is husky from kissing and want. "He towed the car someplace. Got a ride home. Probably didn't even shut the gate. That's the thing—you wish they'd hurt a little, but they don't."

"Okay," Mads says. Actually, she just says the *O* part before his mouth takes the rest of the word and makes it his. Her fingers are on the buttons of his shirt. This is flowers and fireworks, yeah, like the movies, but it's also majestic ice caps and surging seas and protons and neutrons and the everlasting meaning of the everlasting universe. If he weren't in that car, if there weren't a roof over the top of them, he'd zoom right into the air. He'd hold her hand, and up they'd both go.

Jesus, he needs his secret Plan A. He needs it *now*. But he doesn't have his own house and his own bed yet, and they've *got* to get out of this car. It's crazy and heated here, and even

257

though they've gone to the farthermost spot in the Gas Works parking lot, people are walking past.

"Let's go." He doesn't even button the top of his pants back up; he just rises off her and shifts in the driver's seat and starts the truck.

"Where?" Mads's cheeks are big circles of red.

"Just trust me." It sounds good. But what he's thinking makes him nervous as hell. Gran, well, she doesn't exactly go out with friends or go to movies or anything like that. She doesn't *have* friends. But for the last three Fridays, there's been this thing at Swedish Hospital, some bereavement group, some suicide thing. She's there now. It's dangerous. Still, if he doesn't do something quick, their first time is going to be in the front seat of a car, and that would just be wrong.

Of course, it's pretty damn wrong to bring Mads home to have sex when his grandmother is at a *bereavement group*. Billy can barely stand what an awful, fucked-up picture that is. Sex, death, rightness, wrongness—it's one big buzzing, stinging hive. *Will I ever just plain be happy?* he thinks. The answer is no. *Happy* is never a *just*. It's not a destination you reach, a place to finally set down your bags. There are large happys and a million small ones and a bunch of awfuls and daily smashups and successes and droughts and rainfalls and perfect, dewy spiderwebs on a sunny morning and creepy, sticky spiderwebs in your hair in a dark attic. Life is always everything, all at once.

Prepare for the all at once, two lovers in a car.

• • •

He's driving like a maniac. Mads even squeals a little, and so do his tires as he takes that corner. He gets there in all of five minutes. Gran probably left a good half hour ago; he's going screaming fast because he wants them to have as much time as they can.

Billy yanks the brake next to the big China Harbor restaurant. Good news—he can't see Gran's Torino anywhere. It's hard to miss, because it's red with a black hood. It used to be Billy's dad's car, but his mom would never drive it and neither would Billy. It might have looked awesome, but it was unreliable, same as Daniel Floyd. It also smelled disgusting, but that was another story, involving his dad and a deer and a gun; a story that's an animal lover like Billy's worst nightmare. Forget it. It's Gran's now because she never really goes anywhere. It can be trusted for about ten minutes, which was also true for Daniel Floyd.

"Here?" Mads asks.

"Come on," he says.

Billy takes Mads's hand. He runs her down the steps to the dock. He speeds past Glenn and Craig's big sailboat, practically trips over the neighbor's cat. He's hurrying like there's a fire, because it's true; he's all heat.

Ginger is barking her head off. "Shut up, okay?" Billy says through the door. He pats his pockets for his keys. *Oh, Christ, don't tell me.* He may have just locked them in the truck back there. No matter. He upends various pots of flowers until he finds the hidden key. It's black from dirt and kind of rusty, but he jiggles it into the lock.

Mads looks around, taking it all in, as Ginger jumps on her legs. Billy worries it might smell a little like frying burgers in there. Still, he knows that even with Gran's ancient plaid couch and that painting of a leaping whale, people always like the place. There is water right outside the windows, and boats, and little lights blinking on, and shimmery sunset colors reflected from the sky.

They kiss. He walks them backward. They fall onto the couch. His hands are everywhere. Mads seems to have distanced herself a little, cooled down in this new location. The more they kiss, though, the more she returns. He undoes buttons, his, hers. But then he has to hop up for a second. He grabs a nearby pillow, yanks off its case. The case is decorated with a seagull, who's suddenly gone limp. Billy tosses the pillowcase over the urn on the fireplace. They should go to his bed, but he can't stand the thought of changing places for what feels like the hundredth time.

"There," he says.

He lies on top of Mads again. Her face is so beautiful, and he leans back down and puts his mouth on her neck and starts to reach into her shirt.

"Billy."

Her skin is so soft.

"You know, earlier? When you said . . ."

"I love you," he says into her neck and then into her shoulder. "When I said I love you."

"Billy. Before we do this . . ." Her hand is on his chest.

"I have something, don't worry. We're fine."

"I need to tell you something."

Her skin smells like sweat and almonds and brown sugar. "You smell so good."

"I need to tell you something."

"Jesus, Mads. I can't think about talking—"

"Billy."

"I want you so bad."

She shoves him hard, because Ginger is barking again. Mads's whole body has gone rigid and she tries to sit up, and he can hear it now, too, footsteps, the rattle of the door handle. Oh, shit! Shit!

"Oh my God," Mads says. His shirt is off, somewhere in there he's taken it off, and now he can't find it. Mads's own shirt is half undone, and one sleeve is hanging and she's trying to get it back on. Her hands are shaking too hard to get the buttons.

The door opens. Ginger has it all wrong, with the joy and excitement. The dog quickly realizes her error when Gran says *What the hell* in that tone. Ginger speeds off to hide in Billy's room.

"What. The. Hell."

"I'm sorry, I'm so sorry." Mads's face is red, and red blotches break out along her chest. She's managed a few buttons, but they're done up funny.

"Bereavement group?" Billy manages to say. He's in a panic, but he's also suddenly pissed.

"I had enough of it! And now look. Came home not a minute too soon, if you ask me."

"Come on, Gran."

"I think you and Amy need to leave."

"Amy?"

Shit. *Shit!*

"What, you're not Amy? If you're not Amy, who are you?"

Why did he say her name was Amy? How can he ever explain this now? No matter how he explains it, it's going to sound bad. Mads looks like she might cry. She's hunting around for her purse, which has half-spilled into the couch cushions in their hurry to get to each other.

"Who are you, I asked." Gran sounds like a hissing snake, a viper. Fuck. It's all ruined now; it'll be like Jacob and the weed, he's sure of it. A person doesn't forget that kind of venom. You can't explain to other people how Gran is lots of different things. How, sure, she's a paranoid bitch, but how she's loving in her own way, too. How behind all that hardness she's someone who'll do anything for the people that love her.

"I'm sorry," Mads says again. "I'm sorry, I'm so sorry."

"This is rich, Billy. This is really rich. First your uncle calls to say he's *returning your message*, and now look. I mean, get a room, for Christ's sake."

Mads jams the stuff back into her purse. She heads to the door.

"Mads," he says. "Mads, wait! Let me give you a ride home."

"Mads?" Gran says. "Who the hell is Mads?"

Everything is fucked up. It was going to be a perfect day,

the stealing Casper day. But now Mads is running out of there, and he runs after her, feet pounding the dock.

She stops. Turns to face him. He reaches out, grabs her wrist. "I need to be alone, Billy. I need to *be alone*."

Her car is still at Green Lake, for one. It's getting dark, for two. She's this upset, for three, four, five. He can see she means it, though. He stands there helpless and stupid and he watches her go.

Her bracelet has come off. It's lying in a broken circle on the dock. The sight of it makes his heart break, too. He's scared. He's scared of all of the things broken, breaking. Back inside, Gran is in her room with the door shut. There's a lip gloss still in the crack of the couch. He twists off the lid and smells it—peach. It's possible that these are the things he'll have left of her. He holds the bracelet and the lip gloss up against his face. And then he takes the map out of his back pocket and he folds the bracelet inside.

Chapter Twenty-One

Her phone begins to ring somewhere after Fifteenth Street. Billy and Billy and Billy again. Mads runs all the way home before she remembers that Thomas's truck is still parked at Green Lake. As if she doesn't have enough to feel bad about, there's the thought of it—that loyal pile of metal sitting abandoned in the lot. She imagines it shining faithfully underneath a streetlight, its round headlight eyes ever open and unwavering.

She tries to sneak into Claire and Thomas's house without being seen. It smells like popcorn in there. It must be a sleepover, because Thomas and Claire are still up, watching some scary movie with Harrison and Avery. Mads hears ominous noises like door creaks and suspenseful music, and Harrison says, "Don't do it, don't do it!" and Avery says, "They always do it, stupid," and Thomas says, "Avery. Don't call Harrison stupid." It's dark in the family room, but the TV shoots bolts of colors.

Mads needs to get to her room, because things are falling in on her, and she needs to take cover.

Just tell me you're okay, Billy texts.

I'm okay, she replies, just so he doesn't think she's on a bridge somewhere. The idea of a bridge seems almost comforting. The ogres shove and huff. Their putrid breath blows on her cheeks. She hates herself. She is such a horrible person that she understands why they want to snuff her out. She turns the sound off on her phone and shoves it under her pillow.

There's a rap at the door.

God! Why does Claire persist so? Just because Mads needs her to persist, it doesn't mean she has to persist every single second! Why do the people who love you keep on loving you even when you don't deserve it?

"Mads? You home? I didn't hear the truck."

"I . . . I left it . . ."

"Are you all right? Can I come in?"

"No, Claire. No."

"Did you and Ryan have a fight?"

"Yes."

"Oh, damn, honey. Are you okay?"

"I'm okay."

"All right. Well, we'll figure out the truck tomorrow."

"I'm sorry."

"One time I left Thomas at a Wendy's drive-through. Walked right out of the car. It wasn't even because of the chili."

Mads feels too awful to laugh. She pushes her palms against

her eyes so she doesn't cry. She wants to go home. She wants to go home so bad she'd leave immediately if Thomas's truck weren't stuck in the Green Lake parking lot. She needs her mother. What she doesn't have right then (and never had at all, really) makes her feel so lost.

"We're right here, got it? I love you, sweetie."

"Love you, too," she says, because she does. Oh, hers is a failed love, a flawed love, a complete-disregard-for-their-trust-in-her love, but it's love nonetheless. And theirs is a stumbling love, a tumbling love, a trying-hard-and-getting-it-wrong-anyway love, but, look, it's there, too. Love isn't always beautiful, but the beauty isn't what matters anyway. The steadiness is.

"I wish you'd come join us. It's me against the boys out there."

"Thanks, Claire. But I'm okay here."

She is okay if being terrified is okay; she is okay if being a coward is okay; she is okay if being a liar is okay; she is okay if making mistake upon mistake is okay.

Mads thinks about her hand around Anna Youngwolf Floyd's arm, an arm that was hard and slick and cold as a seal. She thinks about Anna's eyes, the ones in her yearbook photo that are so similar to Billy's own eyes. The flashback slaps her. She might throw up at the memory. The ogres—they are mean, mean, mean, with the way they twist the truth. Because instead of remembering Anna's own struggles and failings, instead of remembering that most people in the world are compassionate and that the rest can go fuck themselves, Mads can only think about how disappointed Anna must be in her now.

• • •

Mads finally gets to sleep just as the sun comes up. In the weighty blur of a dream, she hears the doorbell. She thinks it's Avery's dad come to pick him up. The glowing numbers of the clock, though, read 6:02. Six? In the morning? Her sleepy head can still calculate: Saturday plus sleepover plus six a.m. does not equal Avery's dad. Bad night plus Saturday plus six a.m. can only mean Billy.

Billy, *here*.

Mads flings off the covers, hoping to reach the door before Claire does. Claire can be woken by a soundless fever or the sense of someone missing. The doorbell will be a siren.

She flies down the stairs. She hasn't brushed her teeth, and she's wearing only her underwear and Thomas's Grateful Dead shirt, which barely reaches her thighs. She pitches open the door.

He isn't on the front porch. No. Instead, Billy stands on the lawn. He looks like hell. Clearly, he hasn't slept, either, and he's in the same clothes as yesterday, and he has dark stubble cheeks from not shaving. One Converse is untied. Inexplicably, he holds an old record player on his shoulder. The cord hangs down. Its arm swoops back and forth as the turntable wobbles up there.

"Billy?"

Nothing. He just stands there, staring at her intently.

"What are you doing with that turntable?"

"Honestly?"

He hauls it down from his shoulder. Holds it in his arms. He looks sad. So does the turntable. "You don't get it? *Say Anything*? You don't know that old movie? Where the guy has the boom box on his shoulder and he's out on the girl's lawn and he's showing how crazy he is for her, and playing their song . . ."

"We don't have a song."

"And I don't have a boom box. This is Gran's old record player. She's going to kill me."

"I never saw that movie."

"Oh, hell. Just erase this from your memory, then. Pretend you don't see this record player, okay? I thought . . . Never mind. Mads, come here."

"You stay there, and I'm staying here. Don't come any closer. *Amy?*"

"Mads, I'm sorry. I want to explain. About Gran, Amy, the whole fucked-up mess . . . Come over here."

"I can't. I haven't brushed my teeth."

"We need a song, Mads."

"You've got to keep it down. You're going to wake the whole neighborhood."

"Mads? Wait a second. What are you wearing?"

She yanks the shirt down. Tries to cover more of herself than it's covering.

"Don't look."

"No, I mean it! Come here! What is that? Is that what I think it is? Is that Grateful Dead Summer Tour, 1987?"

She gazes at that upside-down skull. "Yeah. I guess so."

"I have that shirt," he says.

"It's Thomas's."

"It was my *dad*'s. Jesus! Don't you see? Don't you see what this is?"

"Not exactly."

"A book, a T-shirt, objects through the *ages*? Bridges are meant to be *crossed*, Mads! Maps are meant to be *followed*!" His voice is hoarse, cracking. He's been up too late, and the lack of sleep is getting to him, likely. But so is all that he's lost, and all that he's sure he's found.

This is not how she has ever imagined telling him, right there on Thomas and Claire's own dewy front lawn, Billy with his grandmother's record player at his feet. But this cannot go on a minute more. He needs to know the truth. Mads can only hope she'll be forgiven.

"Ryan?"

No.

Please, no.

"Ryan Plug?"

"Ryan?" Billy asks.

Claire's hand is out. "It's so great to finally meet you!"

Claire is heading toward him. She steps across that wet morning lawn. She's thrown on some clothes, but her feet are bare, and she looks down to see where she's walking.

She looks down, and then she catches sight of his shoes.

His Converse.

She stops right where she is. She *freezes*.

"I don't know any Ryan," Billy says. His face is all questions. He can tell something large is happening, only he doesn't know what.

Harrison and Avery are also awake now, and they push past Claire and spin out onto the lawn, rays of a zip gun, fueled up by the lawlessness of a sleepover. Avery lets out a war cry and Harrison in his spaceship pajamas chases Avery in his alien ones. Avery stops abruptly, lifts up one bare foot to examine the bottom.

"Eyuw," he says. Ned Chaplin's cats, probably.

Harrison stops, too, long enough to see who's there.

"Hey, Billy," he says.

And then it is over.

Chapter Twenty-Two

"Billy! Wait! Come back!" Mads runs down the front walk in her/his-Thomas's/his dad's Grateful Dead shirt with the skull on it. She makes a grab for Billy's own shirt, the stealing Casper shirt, the joy and triumph shirt, the passion and blue balls shirt, the loss and leaving and staying up all night shirt, and now the betrayal shirt. He knows it's betrayal by the look on Mads's face, only he doesn't exactly get what the betrayal is. How one T-shirt could live through all of this is beyond him. It should disintegrate on the spot, like an attack by a Breath Weapon.

He's exhausted. Energy Drain, level: red. He wants to cry. Something else is happening—Slimy Doom Attack. Where the victim turns into infectious goo from the inside out. This can cause permanent Ability Drain. Yes. Every bit of him is useless. He's deep into Night Worlds, lost in the maze, and if he ever finds his way out, it'll be a miracle.

"I need to be alone, Mads. I need to *be alone.*"

She looks shocked. Shocked he's this angry, shocked he's taking that tone with her. As shocked as if he just lit his underwear on fire or started speaking in Latin. Well, hell. What does she expect? Who the hell is Ryan Plug? Is this an actual guy she's also with right now, another J.T. Jones, or is she hiding Billy? Is *he* Ryan Plug? The thought makes him sick.

Hypocrite, the doctor in his head says. *What about* Amy? He tells the doctor in his head to shut the fuck up. Still, the doctor folds his arms and gives a smug smile.

Billy clutches that record player like it's a baby. He turns away from Mads, that house, the street that's as close to a real-life suburban-ish dream as he'll ever get. He can feel her eyes on his back, and he can feel so much more, too. Dread. It's his Blindsense working. It's a lesser ability, lacking the precision of Blindsight, but it lets a creature notice things it can't actually see. *Ryan* means something much more than Ryan, and he knows it. He doesn't know what the more is, just that it's coming.

The tires of his mother's truck scream out of there. He feels bad about that, but not bad enough to slow down. Good thing that car's got speed. The record player rides along beside him like a slightly disapproving passenger who's keeping his mouth shut. No one is even outside yet. No one is up. Every sane person is still in bed, sleeping, or thinking about pancakes. At least no one will see his despair.

On the dock, though, someone *is* up. Billy smells coffee. He could drop right down there and weep, but the coffee draws him forward, like a spell. Blindsense has made his abilities keener—the chicory fumes are Gran's, coming from a just-brewed pot.

Whatever. He'll put on his Cloak of Disappearance and head straight to his room. Sullenness can be powerful. It says *back off.*

Ginger doesn't bark when he comes in. She's lying low. The energy in the house is like an actual sound she's wisely hiding from, same as she does when it starts to thunder.

Gran is in the kitchen. Billy sees the slump of her robe, her shoulders curved as an old gnome's. In the quiet house, the clink of her spoon against her cup is loud as a chunk of polar ice breaking off from the mainland. The slurp of java is the ocean spiraling down an earth drain.

His head hurts. It sucks that his father was an alcoholic, because he could sure use a drink right now. There are certain vows he won't break, though. No morning booze. No getting misery-wasted.

He flops on his bed. He's never been more tired in his life. And great. Terrific. Gran's been in there. It's her room, but still. She's used her big old computer and left it on. It hums and glows. The thing is huge. The mouse alone is as chubby as a dinner roll.

He hauls himself back up to shut it off so he can sleep. When he moves the mouse, though, an image appears. A giant, close-up image, made large, zoomed in, the way they zoom in on the critical piece of overlooked information, the footprint, the crowbar, the fiber—evidence—in the crime shows.

The image looks like a strand of DNA, viewed under a microscope. It's twisted like that, links linking more links. He can't figure out how to make the image smaller. His fingers have to remember old technology. He clicks the corner of the photo. Smaller. Clicks again. Smaller. Is it a road, maybe? No, that's an arm, he thinks. An arm and a wrist. It's a *bracelet*. *Shit, goddamn it to hell, Gran, what are you trying to do to me?*

How did Gran get a picture of Mads's bracelet? Fuck, man, what is going *on*?

Click. It's an arm, all right. The arm leads to a hand; her head is resting in that hand. You can't even see her whole body, because that's not even what the image is about. She's off to the side. He can't really see her all that well. The girl is not the point of this photo. Click. Click. The point of this photo is that ambulance and the park and the water's edge.

Of course, he's seen that photo, just before Gran ditched the paper into the bin. The article was so small, but at least it had a picture. After that, and after some two-second mention on the night's news on TV, there was nothing more.

He doesn't understand. He can't grasp why Mads's bracelet is on that girl who's sitting on the grass as his mother is wheeled away.

And then he does.

He crashes the computer to the floor. It takes some doing, too. It isn't some arm swipe, some neat cinematic swoop, no. He has to shove, especially with the Energy Drain he has already, and with the Demon Fever approaching. Then he storms out to face the wicked crone. The crashed computer with its cracked screen is nothing compared to the damage she's done.

Gran still just sits there at the kitchen table. "Are you trying to destroy me?" Billy screams at her. Her face has gone slack. It's a pile of sags, an old dress discarded off an old body, lying in folds on the ground.

"I'm trying to *save* you, Buzz. You want to leave here and go off with a girl like her—"

"You went *searching* for that!"

"I remembered! My mind knew something. I *felt* it."

"Because you're paranoid!"

"It's only paranoia when it's not true. Otherwise, it's good instincts."

She's a witch.

He has to get away. He slams the front door hard enough that the houseboat rocks. He's fighting through all of it: Demon Fever, spread by night hags, causing permanent Ability Drain. Devil Chills, almost impossible to recover from, since you must be saved and then saved again. The Red Ache, which makes your skin hot and bloated. The Shakes—involuntary twitches, tremors, and fits. They descend; they take over his body as he flies back to Mads's house in his mom's truck. He drives so fast, he's a blur of white fog, a manic apparition.

There's the smell of pancakes in the air when he gets out at Mads's house. He doesn't even turn the truck's engine off, just yanks the parking brake. His door is left flung open. The windshield wipers are wrongly on, ca-shunk, ca-shunking. His front tire is half up the curb.

His hand is just over the doorbell (aunt and uncle or no aunt and uncle, Ryan Plug or no Ryan Plug, none of it even matters) when Mads opens the front door. She's heard him pull up, and her face is open, expecting, what, another record player? Another burst of *innocent, trusting love?*

She takes in the scene—his face with its color long gone, his trembling hands, that suddenly ditched vehicle. He probably doesn't even need to say what he does next.

"I know who you are."

The words are a Breath Weapon. They instantly melt her. She starts to cry. He's so furious and confused that her tears are just meaningless raindrops he barely notices, a slight dip in barometric pressure.

"Why, why?" he cries. That stupid, endless why!

"Billy, I'm so sorry. I'm so sorry. I don't know. After what happened . . . I just got caught up . . ."

"Caught up? You just got caught up?" *Caught* plus *up*, the words don't make sense. He *loves* her! What does his love even mean, what is it even made of, if she's just a lie? Her mouth gapes. It opens and closes. There are more tears and gulps. She is shaking and wiping her face with the back of her hand. Thank God she is wearing shorts and a tank top now, and not his/her/their lucky shirt. How pathetic that this is all he can find to be glad of.

"I wanted to tell you. I tried—"

This is no good. The tears are meaningless and the words are meaningless, and he is made of vapor. He's disappearing. She's a stranger, and he's on some strange street, and the engine of his mom's truck is chugging a message: *out–out, out–out, out–out.*

"No," he says to the girl in front of him. And then he shouts it. "No!" It's a word that should be shouted more often, likely. His voice is so loud, the windows of the semi-suburban house rattle. The pancake smell runs off in fear. Mads claps her hands over her ears.

He is out of there, all right. *Out. Of. There.* Billy realizes he is barefoot only when he takes off across the lawn. He gets in the truck, slams the door. Just before he hits that accelerator hard, he sees the uncle appear in the doorway. He has his hand on Her shoulder. Who are they? Billy doesn't know these people. These are not his people. It's possible that as far as people go, he has very few left.

The worst is the Mind Fire. The stupor of it is paralyzing. It's like your brain is burning.

He is back in Night Worlds. For days, he's been there. Even with the dangers, even with hidden rooms and spells and weapons, that place feels safer than the real one.

After two nights at Alex's, he's back under Gran's roof. He hates her. He hates her, and he still loves her, of course, in some shrinking, withering way, with some desperate *need* keeping it alive. She's practically all the family he has left, except for the uncle he can't bear to call now. Billy ignores Uncle Nate's messages until he stops phoning. What's Billy going to do, cry and fall at his uncle's feet, because he just needs one fucking shred of kindness he can count on? Plan A is gone, and the rest of it is back: the not eating, the not sleeping, the fists and fury and self-hatred. He can't even *think* Her name. In place of it, he thinks only *Why?*

He goes to work, though. He would never, ever ditch the people and dogs who count on him. Every minute he's away from Casper, he misses him. He wants to bury his face in him and Jasper. Freeing Casper was a great thing, no matter what else came along with it.

In the darkness he swims in, in this putrid, prehistoric pool in a prehistoric cave, he can almost understand what his mother did. But then he thinks of Jane Grace and even Gran, and even, yes, even Her, and definitely Casper, and the *almost* stays an almost. In the middle of this black water of all he's lost, the almost is the life ring that keeps him from going under.

He blocks Her calls. Because, wow, she's sure calling him now, isn't she? He's so angry and confused that his thoughts spin out like faulty fireworks screaming and thrashing on a sidewalk. Her pleading and crying and semi-explanations sound similar to a black ripple, with the strange distance of liquid. It all turns to a submerged echo, the blub and whoosh of the underneath.

At work, Jane Grace gives him the hardest jobs. Physical labor. Cleaning, mowing the whole backyard. Replacing wood chips in the outdoor pens. Sanitizing playrooms. All the dog walking, multiple times a day. He walks every dog at least twice. She sends him out with Jasper and Casper three times in one shift.

It's good for Casper to have that exercise. He wouldn't come out of his cage for the first few days. He was scared, but he was also probably exhausted. All that trauma kicks a creature's ass. It's good for Casper to be with the others, too, especially a great guy like Jasper, who's not someone to get aggressive or make some surprise play for a ball Casper's been brave enough to sniff. Casper has to learn to trust again. He barely leaves Billy's or Jane Grace's side, so he needs to get out in the world, too. His cage, the hallways of Heartland that lead to rooms and other rooms—it's fine, but the real world waits. *Out in the world* is the last place Billy wants to be, but he'll do it for Casper.

"They need you in the yard," Jane Grace says. He barely has Jasper's and Casper's leashes off.

"Okay." Jasper's raring to go after a big, sloppy drink, but Casper is as stuck to Billy as his own soul.

"You all right without a break?"

"Yeah."

"Good." She actually claps twice. It's a get-going clap. It's a don't-stop-or-you-might-fall-into-a-pit clap. Yeah. He knows what she's up to. Jane Grace heard from Amy and Amy heard from Alex, though he'd only told Alex that Mads was seeing another guy, Ryan. Old Ryan. He almost starts to believe Ryan exists. He hates the dickwad. Plug. Slobbery, self-centered asshole. He can barely meet Jane Grace's eyes. If he looks straight at her and sees her kindness, he'll bust right up like a big baby.

He's never been more tired in his life.

"Get a move on," Jane Grace says.

"Come on, man, you're not even trying," Alex says.

The weird thing is, Billy can't tell if Alex is right or not. He feels like he's trying harder than he ever has in his life. Every single move, on the controller, in general, takes more effort and energy than he can describe. Lifting a spoon is raising a boulder. Walking to his car is plowing through earthquake rubble. The game takes the concentration of detonating a bomb. Still, it's true—he's playing like shit. They had to quit last night, because he was instantly slain due to his negative energy level. This meant he couldn't rise again for twenty-four hours. After twenty-four hours, depending on the creature that kills you, you might rise next as a monster, or you might rise as a wight. Of course, he's a wight. Wights are about the height and weight of a human and speak Common, but a wight's appearance is only a weird and twisted reflection of the form it once had.

"You can't let a girl destroy you," Alex says.

Yeah, he should talk. After Leigh, Alex barely got out of bed. Now they have this hot-cold thing going, and look at the four beers Alex has downed already. The bottles are spread out on the floor of his sister's place, next to the couch that's also

Alex's bed. Not to judge, but Jesus. It's a good way to end up drowned in a water-skiing accident.

"Whatever."

"Shit! I almost forgot. I found a place for us on Craigslist today. It's been on awhile, probably because it's by Highway Ninety-Nine. But at least that means we have a shot at it."

"Okay."

"One bedroom, but if a girl comes over, you can use it."

"Does it have a yard?"

"You didn't say anything about a yard! You said you just wanted a place, fast. I'm the one doing all the looking."

"Okay."

"Okay, you want it?"

"Whatever. It's fine."

"It's gotta be more than fine. It's gotta be 'write a check for half the deposit.'"

"I can't think about this now. My head is killing me."

"You wanted fast! Fast is fast, or it's slow."

Bam, bam, bam—there's knocking at the door, and Billy hears laughing. Girl laughing.

"Who's here?" He's in no state to see anyone. He hasn't even put on deodorant.

"I texted a few people. You think I want to spend the whole night with your depressed ass?"

"A few people?" More pounding. On the other side of the door, Quentin shouts, "Open up, ladies."

Alex sticks his hand down into his pocket and comes up

with an Altoid that's seen better days. He pops it in his mouth and lets them in. Leigh kisses Alex fat on the mouth and Billy looks away. Amy sets a case of beer on Alex's sister's table. His sister is a nurse's aide at a hospital and works late. Sometimes they have to be extra quiet while she sleeps behind her closed bedroom door.

"I told you there'd be no food," Jenna, a friend of Amy's, says after slapping shut the fridge door. She was in Billy's freshman PE class. He had to hold her feet once when they were doing sit-ups. "We should have stopped at Dick's. I'm starving."

"Wolf," Amy says. "Get up off the floor and hug me."

Billy stays where he is. Amy smacks the back of Billy's head, changes the channel of the TV, wiping out their game. She puts on some music station. Jenna scrolls through her phone, looking for a place that delivers.

"I don't want anything unless it's cheap," Alex says. "Billy and me are getting a place."

No one cares. No one even hears him. The doorbell rings. It's Drew, and Jenna's friend Shawntel, and some girl he's never seen before, whose name turns out to be Emma. Food arrives, the kind of discount pizzas that are mostly dough and sauce. Drew starts a game of beer pong with some plastic cups he finds in Alex's sister's cupboard and a Ping-Pong ball that appears out of nowhere. God, it's a weeknight. Don't these people work? "West Coast rules!" Drew shouts. He says it again, making it a song that comes with a dance. "It's hot in here! Someone open the door!" He'll be taking his shirt off any minute, watch.

Amy grabs two beer bottles by their necks, takes Billy's wrist and pulls him up. "I need to talk to you."

See? There goes Drew's shirt, up and over, tied around his head now like an Arabian knight, and there's his chest with its hard desert dunes. Alex has the door open, and Amy yanks Billy out. Fine. He doesn't mind. She tugs him down the steps of the tiny house and walks him in reverse until his back is against a big tree.

Somewhere in there, she twisted the caps off the beers, and she hands him his. He takes a few swallows.

"What?" he says. He doesn't want to look in her face, not really. He watches the leaves of the trees shush against the purple of the moonlit sky.

"*What?*" she teases. She sets her hips against his. "You tell me what."

"Why are we out here?"

"We're out here for an important conversation. One we've needed to have for a long, long time."

Her face is close, close to his. Whatever. More than whatever. Why not? She's giving herself right to him, and he doesn't know a single guy, not one, who'd do different. Her breath is warm. She smells like beer and girl shampoo. She's kissing him, and he isn't stopping it. Her tongue is in his mouth, and it's a quick creature of its own that he's supposed to catch.

Now his mind does it. It says her name. For the first time

since he found out, she isn't *Her* but *Mads*. Because this isn't Mads's mouth. And those aren't Mads's hips—they're wider and more square, and it suddenly feels all wrong, like getting into someone else's car, where the seats are adjusted too close to the windshield and the mirrors are off so you can't see what'll save your life.

Her tongue is darting, all Whac-A-Mole. He gives her a little shove away.

"Um, Amy."

"Seriously, Wolfie. Shut up."

There's the tongue again, and now all he can think about is the time he let Jasper lick the almost-empty cup of his McDonald's sundae.

His back and his ass are right up against that tree. So is what's in his pocket—his wallet, with that map, and the bracelet inside it. Yeah, so judge him for his foolish heart, go ahead—he steps away.

"Amy." He stands next to the tree, like he's just taken its side in an argument.

"You can't tell me you don't like this, Wolf. I mean, I can *feel* that you do."

So what. A hard-on isn't exactly choosy. A hard-on likes everyone. It doesn't mean anything.

"I'm just . . ."

"She was with another guy, come on."

She betrayed him worse than that. She was with his *mother* after her tortured decision, and *he* wasn't even with his mom then. Mads was inside his and his mother's most private moment, and then she lied about it. She sought him out, wanted him for her own dark reasons, wanted an *idea* of him. And here is Amy, and who cares, really. Why not, huh? Why not!

"I gotta go," he says.

"Ugh! You are impossible!"

He is! She's totally right. Even his own self agrees. Come on! Jesus! His heart is being firm with him, though. It might be broken, but it's still steady. Stupid hearts. It's a damn shame sometimes, that true love is so stubborn.

Chapter Twenty-Three

After Billy screeches around that corner, after the shouted *No!* the house is all stunned silence and the abandoned remnants of breakfast. Mads is shivering. Thomas takes his hand from her shoulder, grabs his keys off the table by the door, and says, "Let's get out of here. Go get your shoes."

"Where are we going?" She can barely speak.

"To pick up the truck? Hopefully, it didn't get towed."

As Mads passes the kitchen and heads up the stairs, she can tell that Thomas and Claire have already had some kind of important, shorthand conversation. Claire doesn't look at Mads. She only silently wipes up pancake batter dots and Harrison and Avery's maple syrup streaks. Even the back of Claire's head looks disappointed. Mads walks carefully past so nothing else breaks. The flip-flops Mads puts on in her room are guilt-ridden flip-flops, dirty and flat with wrongdoing. She has stopped crying and shaking, and has now moved into some strange disconnect. Her feet don't seem to belong to her. Her body doesn't. She creeps down the stairs and out the door, a devastated criminal trying to flee the scene of the crime.

The crime follows. She buckles her seat belt and flinches as Thomas snaps off the radio. Mads's toenail polish is peachy pink, cheerful, singing the mood of a day long gone. She can't bear to look at it. Her toes wear a party dress to a funeral, and they're naïve and embarrassing and should be ashamed of themselves.

Thomas's profile is stony as a cave wall as he drives. "I don't know where to start, Mads."

"I'm so sorry."

"This whole thing . . . Ryan? Jesus."

"I don't know what to say."

"So many lies, Mads. Right to our *faces* . . . And that boy . . ."

She can't think about Billy, and the way he looked, and the way he sounded, that *No!* Her throat gets tight, and her eyes begin to burn with tears again. She pinches her own arm to get herself to stop. It's not fair to cry anymore about her own losses. Claire and her loyalty deserve tears, not her.

Thomas glances at Mads, and she puts her head down. She doesn't want to see him, because his face has softened, which is just awful. Thomas has a way of talking to you like you're two buddies in a bar having a cold one. Like you're *friends*.

"I know you've just been through a lot back there, but we've got to talk about this. The woman, her son, this whole spiral down into their lives . . ."

"Spiral?" He's right, though. It was a spiral.

"*Fixation*. I mean . . ." Thomas exhales. Rubs his forehead. He isn't paying attention. He's following too close to the car in front of them. Mads doesn't say anything. She has no idea what to say.

"Claire and I . . . This is our fault. What happened at the lake—it was too much on top of everything else. A trauma like that? We should have *insisted* you get therapy. Your dad said we should follow your lead. So we were trying to follow your lead."

"He doesn't even know me." She is talking, but she's not sure how. It's odd, how her mouth opens and robot words come out.

"You're right. And you shouldn't *follow the lead* of someone who's had a shock like that. Who's already going through so much."

"I wasn't going through so much."

"Your mom? The Murray and Murray thing? I know about those legal papers waiting for you. No wonder you've been depressed."

"Lots of people don't get what they want."

"Do you hear yourself? God, I've got a million things I want to say to you right now. . . . At your age, the world is your oyster."

"I don't even like oysters."

"You should be going to college. You should spend some time being *young*."

"I can't go to college! Why does nobody understand this? Mom *needs me*."

"Who is the mother here, you or her? This is exactly why we should have insisted you get help. Your mom, you being depressed already, and then what happened at the lake? God, Mads. It was too much. Too freaking much. Too much for you, too much for Claire and me. We're over our heads. After this morning, Mads . . ." Thomas waits for a light to change as Mads stares out her window. "We need you to commit to therapy if you want to stay with us."

It's a hit after a hit. She feels it in her solar plexus, if that's what it's even called. The place where you breathe or don't breathe. Because it's an ultimatum. Thomas and Claire are making her choose. And *over our heads* is large. It means what she's done is so, so bad. It *is* bad. She knows that. Billy's face . . . She will never forget that face as long as she lives. She *did* that to him. The ogres poke and giggle. What a hilarious, victorious moment for them. A sob rises and escapes.

Thomas hears it. He leans over and takes her hand, steers funny for a second. "Don't misunderstand, Mads. Even with this Ryan shit. Even with the son, the guy in the Converse. Billy, right? Even with Billy. We are here for you. We will always, *always* be here for you."

It's quiet in the car. Thomas waits. He's asking her to choose, and so she does.

"I want to go home," Mads says.

They reach the parking lot at Green Lake. For the last mile, Thomas has only been shaking his head to himself. Now he says, "Come on, Mads, no. Think about this." He looks at her hard, asking one more time, giving her one more chance.

It seems like a million years have passed since she and Billy stole Casper. Time is strange: A day can bring endless, hollow hours of looking at shoes online, or else, a day can change your life. It can bring momentous events, or the same old twenty-four hours every other day has.

The sight of Thomas's truck chokes her up. The truck is just so friendly-looking, and it's still there after all, with its bright headlight eyes and chrome smile. It gets her, you know, the way some people and even some things have a goodness that can hold you in place. They hold you down and urge you to *stay*, even if you feel *go*. They are patient anchors, softly repeating what's most necessary. *You're not alone. This will pass. My chrome will always smile for you.*

It makes it even harder to turn to Thomas with her final answer.

"I'm done here."

She keeps calling and calling, but gets only the single ring that means Billy's shut off his phone. Mom picks right up, though. It's the third time they've talked that day.

"Are you sure you want to wait so long to come home? Because I can come right now. I can come right this minute. There's no need to wait two weeks."

Mads can't leave yet; she can't simply run, because she would never, ever just ditch the people who count on her. The *baby* who counts on her. Now that she's decided to go, every minute Mads is away from Ivy, she misses her. She wants to bury her face in Ivy's silky hair. She wants to watch every arms-up, hurtling-forward step that Ivy's been taking lately. "I need to give Suzanne some time to replace me," Mads says.

"You're probably dying over there."

Yes. That's exactly what this slow disappearing is. But she can't just leave Ivy chained up in that cage. Even if this is Ivy's chain and Ivy's cage and even if Ivy will likely spend her whole life feeling the weight of captivity, Mads must do *something* before she leaves, whether it's futile or not.

"I am so excited you're coming home! Your friends are going to be so happy! I saw Sarah in Macy's. She said you haven't called her in weeks. She has a new boyfriend. They'll be thrilled you're back. And I was thinking, you know, why wait? Why wait until you're done with the exam to sign the papers? Of course you'll pass. You'll have your license in no time. It's ridiculous that we've been waiting. Let's get this started! I moved up our appointment with Mr. Knightley for the Monday you arrive."

"Great."

Mads thinks this is what she says, anyway, because she can barely hear her own voice. It's like the smallest creak of a floorboard on a listing ship.

"Finally," her mom says. "Can you believe it? We've only been looking forward to this for years."

Mads remembers something silly, then. Something from

The Book: Claudia and Jamie, discussing their homesickness. Their lack of it. Since they ran away, Claudia says, she feels older. Even if she's already been the oldest child forever.

It's all back, the not eating, the not sleeping, the weighty dread, the endless search for online answers. *Are You Self-Destructive? Is a Real Estate Career Really for You? Goldberg Depression Screening, number twelve: I feel like a failure. Goldberg Depression Screening, number sixteen: I feel trapped or caught.*

Mads finds a picture of Anna Youngwolf Floyd she's never seen before. After typing in *Anna* and *La Conner*, she locates an image of *Anna, a volunteer, and a few of the hundreds who turned out for the annual Oyster Run. . . .* Anna is about her age, and the world is literally her oyster. At least, she holds one in each hand as she stands next to an outdoor grill, surrounded by a few guys in motorcycle gear.

Spiral, fixation, food that's gone tasteless, sleep that's the opposite of bland, all this and the beating heat of summer, too. Mads stops calling Billy, stops leaving messages with pleadings and apologies, because she has no real way of explaining herself, and she'll be gone in a week's time, anyway. Harrison is following her around again, and Claire yanks her out of bed one morning, shoves her into the car, and heads to Dr. Bailey's office. A small amber prescription bottle now sits on the desk in her room, watched over by the photograph of Claire and Thomas and Harrison. It's like a little beacon, from a lighthouse at the end of a rocky shore, something so the sailors don't crash. She won't open it until she's sure she should be saved. During the day, she click click clicks on the image of that bridge, to the place her own feet would be standing. At night, she dreams of diving into that water, again and again. The body, the cold flesh, bruises. The body is Anna's, the body is Billy's, the body is her mother's, the body belongs to Mads herself.

At work, she has a job to do. She has to hurry, too. There's not much time left.

She lets Ivy play with dirt and Play-Doh and frosting, because Ivy needs to know that she can make messes. She takes her to the playground so that she can see that there are bullies and brats, but people to trust, too. Mads takes her outside as much as possible, so Ivy can see that the real world awaits. *Out in the world* is the last place Mads wants to be, but she'll do it for Ivy.

She tells Ivy everything she knows so far. *Trust the boy who has eyes like old stars. Let the rain soak you. Kiss like it's the last time.* She sounds like the bad, annoying stuff printed on decorative pillows, but she doesn't care.

"I sorted through the resumes," Mads tells Suzanne.

"I can't believe there are so many," Suzanne says. "It's a *babysitting* job. That's the economy for you. Carl says I should be reading them all myself, but I told him it's the least you can do, leaving on such short notice."

No, Carl. Shut up, Carl. If Suzanne chooses her replacement, Ivy will get a younger version of Suzanne herself, or else another girl like Mads, helpless and hopeless in this con-demned situation, swimming too far out over her head.

"I really like this one," Mads says. She hands Suzanne the resume as Ivy lets a handful of Cheerios fly like confetti.

"Jesus, Ivy!" Suzanne peruses the paper as Mads picks up the cereal bits. If she does it quietly enough, if she barely moves, Suzanne won't notice how much she wants this. "God, the woman graduated back in 1980!"

Yes, and she lists her hobbies as *dogs and babies*. She sounds loving but firm. And she previously stayed with a family until their children were grown.

"She's old enough to be *my* mother, let alone Ivy's," Suzanne says.

Exactly.

"Guess what? I have the best news! Mr. Hermann talked with the people at WCC, and you can pop right into their program and finish up. He said he was amazed you did so well, given what happened with that woman. He said he had no idea."

"You don't exactly go around telling people you found a dead person in a lake."

On the phone with her mother, Mads feels the bump and soft give of the body all over again. That day is bigger and more present to her than ever. It's like a whining child, getting louder and louder the more it's ignored.

"Have you heard from Billy yet?"

"No."

"That's awful. That's the worst." This is another thing people will never understand. The way her mom can be there for her, too. In Mads's worst times, she's there with an almost eager loyalty. "I know you really like this guy, even if the way you met was . . ." She stops there. "Well, if it's meant to be, it's meant to be."

"Right."

"Either way, Knightley says he's got the notary ready for Monday."

One of the ogres squeezes her throat so no sound at all comes out, not even a squeak. It's so easy for the beast; he taps a foot at the same time, gazes out at the twittering summer day. She could thrash and bite, scratch and flail, but this seems like more energy than she has. The pulse of her own desire is faint. It has only the tiniest throb, like the heart of a mouse.

Thomas is barbecuing. Big columns of smoke roll across the yard and make a run for it over the fence. Harrison fills up his squirt gun with the garden hose, and Mads and Claire sit on those precarious outdoor chairs with woven plastic seats. Mads feels like her butt is hanging low. She probably couldn't get up if she wanted to, not without help anyway—it's a lawn chair message.

"Three more days." Claire sighs.

Mads has no answer for this. How do you answer a fact? "You know we're the first ones he's going to shoot after he fills that up," she says.

"Harrison, I'm warning you," Claire shouts.

"I'm getting *Dad*," he says, but Thomas doesn't hear. He's got some old transistor on and is busy wiping the tears from his eyes, caused by smoke and burning turkey dogs.

"Are you tired of having big talks?" Claire asks.

"Kind of."

"Same here."

Claire is so nice. They are all so nice. Mads, too, in spite of what she's done, and in spite of the fact that nice is the last thing she'd call herself. Try *selfish*. Try *cowardly*.

"I'm so sorry again." Lately, there is an abundance of regret. Mads has been handing out apologies right and left. No one even wants them. She's the woman in the grocery store, trying to get people to take her tiny biscuit-wrapped sausages.

"Enough sorrys! We're just sad, is all. We're going to miss you so much. If you can't tell, Thomas and I are pretty much crazy about you."

"Even though I lied my head off."

"Even though you lied your head off."

"How can that be?" Mads just doesn't get this. It's like all the things that don't even seem possibly possible: supernovas and winged dinosaurs and our own thin highways of nerves and vessels.

"Mads, that's *love*. It just *is*. We can love you even if you disappointed us. Plus, you're not exactly a terrible, scheming psychopath. You're one of the sweetest people I know."

"You're too understanding, Claire." Mads could cry again.

She hates to cry, but there it is once more, that squeezing in her rib cage. "Someone's going to steal your life savings."

"Not at all. The thing is, I get it. Thomas does, too. Speaking your own truth—sometimes it's one of the hardest things we have to do. It seems easy. Open your mouth, let the words come out. . . . But it can look so huge, even lying seems like a party in comparison."

"Lying isn't a party. I can tell you that much."

"Honestly? I'm kind of glad it wasn't that Ryan guy. That whole rich family on the East Coast thing—he sounded like a snob. I mean, that wedding was over the top. There were *doves*, Mads." Harrison squirts Thomas's knees, and Thomas lunges for a handful of his shirt. "Careful, Hare! Hot barbecue!" Claire shouts again.

"Too far with the doves?"

"I was starting to hate those people. I'm sure I'd like Billy much better."

The squeeze in Mads's chest turns to a horrible crushing. She presses her palms to her eyes. A tear escapes anyway, a single drop bent on survival; it rolls down her nose, heads out of there.

"Oh, honey. Now I'm the one who's sorry." Claire reaches in the pocket of her jeans but only finds a crumply old Kleenex. "Oh, this is gross. Never mind."

Stupid crying, there's nothing she can do. Mads is a wreck. "He's really an amazing person," she manages to say.

"A resilient one, for sure."

"He's not just the stuff that's happened to him." She says this into her hands. It deserves volume, but it's also just another thing she's lost.

"Of course not, Mads."

"He isn't."

"You really care about him."

Care? So much more than that. The truth of it shakes her shoulders with grief. Claire struggles out of her chair—Mads hears it tip. Claire's arms are around her. Thomas is no doubt watching nervously and burning more hot dogs, but Mads can't stop herself. All that's gone catches up, and she just misses Billy, too. She misses him bad, and now she'll have to miss him her whole life. She cries into Claire's soft shirt.

"I think I lmm hmm."

"What's that, sweetie? What's that?"

"I think I lumm hmm."

"Love him?"

"Yeah."

"Oh, honey."

"I don't know what to do. I don't know where to *go*."

"Who does, huh? Whoever does? It's okay, sweetheart. Everyone gets lost. Every single person. It'd be nice to have a map, or something, wouldn't it? How about a map, huh?"

A map.

Mads thinks about maps that night as she sits in her bed, knees up, book propped on top. Yellowed maps with dark ink letters, old maps, wrong maps, the maps before anyone even really knew where we were, when they thought the poles were seas they could sail to, or the earth was a land one might drop from. *Wouldn't it be terrifying*, Mads thinks, *to not even know what was beyond where you stood, or what was over that mountain range?* Except, little nomad, we do it every day.

The essential maps for the lost would say, *Out, this way.* They'd say, *Don't turn back, go only forward.* They'd say, *Courage, traveler.*

It's dark, and she reads by the small lamp near the bed. Claudia has just retrieved her violin case from the carved marble sarcophagus. Again. She retrieves it *again*, the third time for Mads, the zillionth time or more for Claudia. Who could even guess how many times, since E. L. Konigsburg first typed those words.

Mads opens to the middle of the book, her own purchased copy, since Harrison snitched the one from the library. She wonders how many kids are reading it right along with her—how many shiny bookmarks or bent-down pages are between its covers, how many hungry eyes pause on the thrilling word *sarcophagus*. Mads and Anna Youngwolf Floyd and millions of others might be entirely different people, but they all hid in that museum together.

Maps for the lost would have corridors like this, and rooms leading to rooms. They would spread large, because life has those places where old, old stuff is tucked away, and where arms and armor are collected after battle. Routes would wind around buried things and unearthed objects charred and damaged by war and floods and hard history. There would be twists and turns to exits. Dead ends. In the terrain of those maps, tragedy would be everywhere you looked, but so, too, would be the huge halls of treasure to be discovered.

Mads is not wearing her glasses, and the print on the page is tiny. It's hard to concentrate. She sets down her book. The window is open and it smells like night and cut grass and August, all of which are the scent of something finishing or finished. The moon is a crescent, a lunar hammock. It gives off a yellow glow, the world's night-light, same as the one in Ivy's room.

Fate can trump the ogres if you let it. Trouble wrecks stuff so a person has a shot at a second chance. Elsewhere, there's a swirl of heat and change rising. Right then, as Mads rests the book on her knees, Amy has Billy Youngwolf Floyd backed up against that tree. There he feels the lift of true love. It can't save or rescue all by itself, but it can stand by and urge you to save yourself.

So strange, but Mads hears a small voice: *Courage, traveler.* Weird. It's coming from inside her. *Hold your little map and shout to the darkness*, it says. *Shout this: You are nothing, darkness, against something as old as love. Shout: I walk right through you, darkness, because I am, and I will be.* This boldness—she's felt it before. In the truck, when she first saw Billy. No, before that, when she was brave, so brave, and brought Anna to shore. *This* is how you save yourself? *This* is what can defeat the ogres?

This small voice inside? This microscopic cell of belief, allowed to divide?

Yep. Uh-huh. The voice is your own personal sword and shield—remember that. Remember that every hard day.

Mads sticks her head out the window, gazes at the tilt of the moon, takes a long inhale of her approaching future. Hear that? *Future.* It's a decision. It's a *vow.* Across the street, she sees that the lamp in Ivy's room is on. She hopes—no, she prays—that Suzanne is holding Ivy close. Trying to rescue everyone else is so much easier than rescuing yourself.

She knows what she has to do.

Two things.

Number one: She sets her laptop on the desk and turns it on. She opens a new document. She begins to type.

To my lawyer, ~~Saxonberg~~ Knightley:

I can't say that I enjoyed your last visit. It was obvious that you had too much on your mind to pay any attention to what I was trying to say. . . .

When she's finished, she jogs the envelope out to the mailbox before she can change her mind. She's in bare feet, and she's wearing the Grateful Dead T-shirt, Summer Tour 1987. The mailbox door clangs shut. She's exhausted and exhilarated, totally terrified. Number one: done. Tomorrow, number two. Out in the driveway, she pats the hood of Thomas's truck, which shines like a gem under the lamppost.

"Be ready, pal," she says.

Chapter Twenty-Four

The doctor in his head thinks it's morbid, but fuck him. Sometimes lately, Billy just likes to take a little tour. It makes him feel closer to his mother. He misses her so much, he feels brittle as a dropped leaf. He could be crushed like that, right underneath the sole of a passing shoe.

He needs his mom. How much he needs her—it makes the gut-socking feeling come. His broken heart (broken and broken and broken heart) would be something that mattered to her. She'd be great about it, too. He knows her suicide makes her sound all pathetic all the time, but it wasn't like that! She wasn't, and their life together wasn't. Not at all. Sometimes, occasionally, but not always, okay? He even knows what she'd do now. She'd make him some apple cobbler and she'd put it in a bowl with a blop of melty vanilla ice cream on top. She'd tell him, *Some girl will love you like mad, a girl who deserves you.*

Do you see this? *See the whole picture,* he wants to scream, *not some single word like* pathetic *or* tragic. He doesn't know who he's talking to, or even why he wants it understood that his mother was more than what she did. What does it even matter? But it does. Yeah, on some days she might have stayed in bed, and the house would be so dark and dim he'd want to run away (he hopes she can't hear him think that). But, too, she once put together a wood swing set for him when he was a kid (he can still remember her squinting at the directions), and she treated every gift he ever gave her like treasure—calendars with pictures of garden gates, and fluffy pink socks, and even that huge eye shadow set with colors he now knows she wouldn't wear in a million years. She was a human being who loved him and he loved her, and now he's all nuclear ash and flatness, radioactive shit sinking into his earth.

He's lost, is what he is. He needs a map. Since he doesn't have one, he drives the known route that punishes and comforts. Seventies songs play on the radio. He thinks about the new dog they got at Heartland that morning. Harv. Harv's a rescue from a landslide in the north part of the state. Billy hopes—no, he prays—that Harv's owners are still alive and that they'll see his picture on the website, because Harv is beautiful and sweet and a true gentleman. It kills Billy to think Harv is wondering where his family went and why. What does a dog understand about tragedy? What if he thinks they left him on purpose?

His heart splits, and a sob escapes at that thought. He grips his steering wheel.

First stop: their old house. He passes the Fremont troll and heads down their street. Mr. Woods needs to mow his lawn, and J.T. Jones is actually in his driveway, messing around with his car, which is jacked up. He can only see J.T. Jones's Vans, sticking out from underneath, like the witch in *The Wizard of Oz*. He shoots a zap of hatred to the Vans but then realizes he doesn't have to defend Mads against J.T. Jones anymore. She didn't even know the guy, he realizes. Still, those self-important shoes, and the thumping hate-cops music that J.T. Jones apparently thinks the whole neighborhood needs to hear . . . He's still an asshole even if he didn't break Mads's heart.

The FOR RENT sign's long gone, but now there's a big RV parked in their driveway. Its license plate reads CAP'N ED, and it has a bumper sticker on the back that says HOME OF THE REDWOODS. The front door of their house is open, and Billy can see the big sheets of plastic that mean someone's painting inside. He rolls down his window to smell. Yeah. New paint. The clean, plasticky odor makes him want to cry. There's a large clay pot on the porch, planted with those red old-lady flowers that look like Afros.

He hopes the guy paints Billy's mom's room, too. And the ceilings. They have yellow splotches from water leaks. They deserve better.

He is so choked up about the way things go forward. Also, about the way things go forward in a way that might be nicer, only his mom will never see that. The plants look good.

He starts up his mom's SUV. Earth, Wind & Fire is blasting; it's the song about a shining star, with trumpets and one of the heaviest bass lines ever, and so he's not sure at first, but he thinks he hears something. The sound of a jet plane, the familiar deep rumble of Mads's truck. He looks around. His heart starts to beat hard. Is that Mads reversing out of there like the police are after her?

Probably not. He can't be sure. Just the thought of seeing Mads—there's a stampede of feeling, throbbing and thumping inside to the beat of the hate-cop music and "Shining Star" and some old love and fury song his body is making up right then. It's August. And while he's seen Mads in August, he's never seen her in September. He's never seen her in October or November. Even though he's so pissed at her, he wonders what her hands would feel like in mittens. He wonders how she'd look in a hat with a pom-pom on it, or with snowflakes falling in her hair.

If it was her truck, it's gone anyway.

The Tragedy Tour continues. Next up: the bridge. Dark, you think? Gruesome? Keep your opinions to yourself. This is between Billy and his mom, and anyone else should just shut up about it, because your grief belongs to you and you alone. Driving across, he smells exhaust, and fries from some restaurant, and cancer-smoke from a cigarette tipped out a car window. Note the important words here: driving across. *Across.* Bridges are not meant to be jumped from. Bridges are meant to get you to the other side. This is what he does now. He *can.* He's able. He's strong enough, and the bamp of his tires off the ramp proves it.

Finally, he drives around to the other side of Lake Union. It's a new piece of the ritual, added on after he saw that article again. The park is small, too small for a parking lot even, so he finds a spot on the street and gets out. This is weirdly the most peaceful stop on this circuit. Trees rustle like book pages, and the lake burbles like a lyric. See, he has nowhere to visit her. Mom is in that urn in his grandmother's living room, but that big blue-gray vase is all Gran and more Gran, and their endless struggle. Billy needs a place to think clear thoughts about his mom, *commune*, sort of, excuse the fake-Seattle-hippie-with-Pantene-washed-hair bullshit word. Before now, he never understood why people put flowers and creepy dead girl photos at the edge of a road, at the scene of an accident. Why not decorate where they *lived*? But now he gets it. It's about that person, but it's also about what happened. The before and the after. Where the two intersected.

There's a small, sloping lawn. This is where Mads sat in the photo, her head in her hand. The lawn leads to a dock, surrounded by weedy reeds and cattails. He walks to the end of that dock, sits on the edge of it with his legs hanging over. The soles of his Converse tap the surface. The water is smooth and still, and it's the same bright blue color of the sky, except for the patches of deep green where the fish prob-ably hang out.

He tells his mom, you know, private stuff. It's mostly about love, and it fills his chest the way smoke fills a room, and he's about to start coughing and blubbering because of it, and that's when he swears he hears it again. That rocket rumble.

He looks over his shoulder. Oh no, oh yes, oh shit, there's that chrome smile, those patches of primer. He's so happy to see her, he wants to run and grab her and bite her and eat her right up—that's gross, but so what. And he's so upset at seeing her, he could jump in that water to get away (there's nowhere else to go), into the water where his mother floated; he'd slap and flail and look like a moron, because he's a terrible swimmer, but he'd escape Mads.

His eyes prick with tears. His hands start to shake like a big baby. He can sit there and pretend to be as furious as he in many ways still is, or he can be the man he wants to be, a man like Jane Grace's husband, Dave, or like his uncle even, and go to her.

So he goes to her. Her shiny hair is in a red barrette, and she is stepping across that park like it's a dark house with ghosts hiding behind the curtains. Her arms are crossed over her body, as if to protect against the spirit-cold. It's taking everything she has to get to him, he can tell. And so he closes the distance, and he takes her in his arms and she starts to sob and he starts to sob and anyone watching is getting a big damn eyeful.

Her body is wracked. He realizes—why didn't he get this before?—that this place on the grass brings her different memories than his. He sees it now—he's also been an asshole. In this large lake, she and his mother found each other, and she held his mother and swam with her, and brought her to shore. Her heaving shoulders tell that story. They say she's been haunted by that.

They've both been haunted by that.

"I'm so sorry," she says.

"I am," he says.

"I can't believe we're here. I never wanted to come to this place again."

"You for sure followed me today. This one is no coincidence." Heh—she did.

"Okay, okay. Yes, I followed you. Sometimes you have to make your own coincidence."

His arms are happy to hold her, even with all his tumbling emotions. His eyes are about the happiest they've been in a long, long time, just setting themselves on her. She looks like hell, like pretty much the most beautiful hell he's ever seen. Yet, still, there's this hole, the spot where the bomb dropped.

"Why did you do this?"

"I asked myself that a million times! I had no idea why. I didn't. And then last night . . . I don't know, I just realized. It's like in the book," Mads says. "Claudia sees the angel, and she knows it holds the answer to a question. She doesn't even know what the question is exactly, but she's sure the answer is there. All she understands is that, no matter what, she has to find out what the angel means."

He takes this in. This is different than the crying explanations Mads left in her messages. He *gets* this. And he sees something else: They were a team even before they met.

"I have something to show you," she says next. Her eyes have deep raccoon circles and she finds a smashed Kleenex in her pocket and blows her nose.

"Okay," he says.

"I forgot it in the truck."

She races back over, and he watches her. If you could see how cute she is when she runs, you'd just die. She comes back, fast, with an envelope. She's out of breath.

"I am so out of shape," she gasps. "I was scared you'd be gone before I got here."

He hasn't moved, though. He takes the envelope from her and opens it.

"It's a copy," she says. "I sent the real one."

He reads. *To my lawyer, ~~Saxonberg~~ Knightley.*

When he sees the first lines of The Book, he smiles. God, he does, the biggest smile you've ever seen. He hopes his mom is looking down like some sort of angel right now. Because, yeah, he wants to prove her wrong about hope and life and love because he's still so damn pissed at what she did, but he also just wants her to *see*. To be a part of this.

Billy just grins and grins at Mads. "Complications," he says.

"There's going to be a lot of those."

"Have you talked to your mom yet?"

"I just put this in the mail last night. I figure I have until tomorrow morning to call her. I mean, I don't want her to hear this from the lawyer."

It's his turn now. He needs to give her something, too. It's how the exchange of forgiveness works. He reaches into his back pocket. He takes out the map. He opens it up. Her bracelet is inside. He repaired it with a piece of shoelace he'd cut from his pair of dress shoes. He holds the map in his teeth as he ties the bracelet back onto her wrist.

"There," he says. *Err*, with the map in his mouth.

Now he takes the map, opens it, and points. "Here."

Her face says he's crazy. She tilts her head and squinches her eyes. She makes a little *I wish* scoff in the back of her throat.

Scoff, nothing. This is one thing he's sure of. You've got to know that dreams are possible, like Jane Grace says. And, too, you've got to remember that people will be there for you, even when there are complications, even when there are big storms of dark and mess. She looks at him with her fucked-up red eyes, and he stares straight at her with his.

"This belonged to my mom."

"I remember."

"She kept this. It was her favorite book. It meant something to her."

"It means a lot to me now, too."

"We're going, Mads. All right?"

"Oh, Billy."

"Better pack your violin case."

Chapter Twenty-Five

It's a sweet summer morning when Mads opens her mouth and lets the whisper of her voice out. A garbage truck rattles down the street, and a bird tweets, and some blossom blooms on a tree.

"I can't," she says aloud.

She can almost feel her mother's breath on the other end of the phone, fiery and spewing like a dragon.

"I can't," Mads says again, and the dragon roars, and the ogres beat their drums and form a circle. Her tiny voice is jeweled armor against the heat and the noise.

"How could you do this to me?" her mother cries. "How could you be so selfish? I can't believe you'd betray me like this!"

Her mother yells and weeps. Mads is so, so disappointing. She is a bad daughter! She is an awful, disgusting person! It's just her and her little truth finally spoken, as the ogres stomp around and gorge themselves on all their favorite foods, greasy guilt and oily shame. It's a revelry.

"After all I've done for you? How *dare* you." The fury frightens Mads. Her soul shrinks. She feels like throwing up. Mads's apologies are meaningless; they go unheard. "I never thought you'd be just like everyone else," her mother rages. Mads is so small and so despicable.

When Mads finally hangs up, she's shaking. She's trembling, and her stomach is sick. She knew it would be horrible, and it was horrible.

But look.

Even with the flames and the blame and the beating drums, she is still alive. She has spoken and survived. Sure, there will be more of this. It's not over. Her mother is not done; it's not that easy. But see that? Mads's head is above water, and there is nothing muted or hidden anymore. The trembling will subside. The sick feeling will abate. Those drums? All that clatter is just Ned Chaplin's recycling. She's still here.

"You better not forget to turn that book in, Hare," Mads says. "I've already renewed it twice."

Harrison ignores her. He keeps eating his bowl of cereal, his eyes traveling across the words. He's on the last few pages. Mads is breaking one of the Reader Commandments: Thou shalt not interrupt at the end of a book. She loves that weird kid, even after the trouble he's caused.

Mads carries her cup of coffee upstairs, heads into the bathroom to finish getting ready. She dries her hair. It's Saturday, and she's leaving this place. *It'd be a great idea to get out of town for a while*, Claire said, after Mads and her mother talked.

Yes, yes it would. And now she's going.

In the mirror, she looks different to herself. She looks older than before, but younger, too.

She finishes packing. There's a polite tap on the door. She thinks it's going to be Claire, with some last words of advice or maybe an organic carrot muffin, so she's surprised to see Harrison standing there.

"It was really good." He holds the book to his chest. Yeah, that's how you feel when you finish a book like that.

"Wasn't it great?"

"I wish they could've stayed in the museum forever."

"Sure, but the adventure changed them. Plus, you've got to go home sometime."

"I'm going to learn to play cards and make some money."

"You'd be a shark, Hare."

"I can make way more than twenty-four dollars and forty-three cents."

"Especially if you play Avery." Mads winks.

"What's that?" He gestures toward the bed.

"It's your dad's old saxophone case. It was the only instrument they had in the house. You should have heard how excited your dad was when he finally found it behind all those boxes of your baby stuff."

Harrison is poking around in there. He finds the pill bottle, shakes it like a maraca.

"Hey, get out of there, snoop."

"Did you take one?"

"Yeah, I took one, if it's any of your business. It's not like a miracle cure. It's all going to take a while."

"If you have a boner for four hours, you have to go to the doctor."

"Noted."

"Is this all you're bringing? Pukey underwear and a couple of books and drugs? Don't you need clothes?"

"Just hauled my roller bag downstairs." Mads closes the lid of the saxophone case, shuts the clasps.

"Billy will really like this when he sees it, won't he?" Harrison flicks the case with his finger.

"Yep."

"Where are you gonna hide it? The sarcophagus?"

"I'm not going to actually hide it. We're just going to buy a ticket like everyone else."

"Bummer. You're coming back, right?" He sounds worried.

"Better believe it. We'll only be gone a few weeks. I told you. You can't stay on an adventure forever. You've got to come home."

"Home, here?"

"Home here, Mr. Professor."

Billy will be arriving soon, and so Mads makes a quick trip across the street. Mrs. March, the Bellaroses' new nanny, will be starting today, but she's not at Suzanne and Carl's yet. Mads rings the bell.

"You can come in," Suzanne says, "but this place is a mad-house. You-know-who has been screaming her head off all morning, and I can't find my keys."

Ivy's in her high chair, her face all blotchy from crying. She holds her arms out to Mads, and Mads lifts her up. She holds the baby close. This babysitting job is over, but it won't be the last time she sees Ivy. When she returns to start classes, real classes, at the community college, she can come by and visit her and Mrs. March. Mads sets her cheek against Ivy's satiny, meringue-poof hair.

"Scream and yell," Mads whispers. "Let them hear you."

She sets Ivy on the floor with her favorite toys—the stuffed frog and the ball that makes music. Ivy's up in a flash, ready to walk all around like a champ.

"Carl probably took my keys to the gym. Watch. I'll be stranded here. He probably won't even—" Suzanne is still talking as Mads shuts the door behind her.

"So, I made a few of each. Roasted vegetables, and tuna. Dolphin safe, right?"

"God, Claire. How much can we possibly eat?"

"It's a road trip. You've got to have food."

"It all looks amazing. Thank you."

"Thomas should be home any minute." Claire's shoving napkins and drinks and who knows what else into that already-stuffed bag.

"He didn't have to hurry through his errands for this."

"Are you kidding? He wants to see you off."

In the distant country of Mads's purse, there's the chirp-chirp of her phone ringing. She and Claire freeze, meet eyes. Of course, her mother's wrath is far from finished.

"Don't answer," Claire says.

"I have to." Yes, Mads still has to. She does. Stupid change. It's a verb way more often than it's a noun.

Mads locates the phone, answers in the living room away from Claire. Talking in front of her feels like a betrayal of her mom. See: *change*, above.

"I'm calling you from a Chevron in Ellensburg," Mads's mother says.

The happiness Mads has been feeling all morning is shot down, a direct hit. "Mom, why? What are you doing?"

"I'm coming over. I said I'd be there on Saturday, and this is Saturday. I'll be there in an hour."

"Mom, no."

"You can't mean any of this! What am I supposed to *do*?" She starts to cry again. She sobs and weeps. Mads hears trucks whooshing past, freeway sounds.

"Go home, Mom."

"I will not go home. We have to talk about this. I can't believe you're being so selfish. You know I can't manage all this by myself. Jesus! Do you know how upset I am?"

"Are you okay to drive?"

"Of course I'm not okay to drive! If I don't get in an accident, it'll be a miracle."

"I love you, Mom, but go home."

"You love me? I can sure tell."

"Mom, please . . ."

"It's those people. His brother. They've turned you against me."

"No, Mom."

"I'm coming, and we're going home. You can't do this to me."

"I don't—"

There's a click.

"Are you okay?" Claire asks in the kitchen.

No. She is definitely not okay. Mads feels worried and devastated. There's the burning curl of shame and its leftover debris. A cinder of fear glows orange. Every time she defies her mother for years to come, she'll feel the same way. Every time, she'll survive it. "She's in the car. Heading here."

"Looks like you and Billy better hurry it up, then."

"Claire . . ."

"She'll be fine."

"You don't understand what she can be like. She's furious. She's so upset. . . ."

"Thomas and I can handle it. Just get a move on."

Maps for the lost could lead to an angel. The angel might be small and beautiful, standing alone in a room, or she could be battered and fierce, seaweed wrapped around her ankles. Either way, she would hold mysteries. You would need to find out about her. Finding out could change your life.

Mads and Claire and Thomas wait outside. The roller bag is there, too, a short, patient traveler. Mads holds the saxophone case by its handle. Two shiny metallic flashes zip down the street and then spin out in front of them. Harrison and Avery wear capes made out of pillowcases and duct tape.

"First-prize skid mark," Avery says.

"Hey, here comes Billy," Harrison says.

Yep. Here he comes. Claire gives her a kiss on the cheek. Thomas squeezes her arm. *Come on, Mads*, says that weird voice in her head. *There's a final order of business. It's time. Do it.*

She does.

In her head, Mads sticks her middle finger up to the ogres.

Chapter Twenty-Six

"Take the ferry out to the Statue of Liberty while you're there," Jane Grace says. "You won't believe how huge she is in real life."

"Okay," Billy says.

"A few days extra to veer through Yellowstone won't kill you."

"Sure."

"It's beautiful. You'll love it."

"Sounds good."

"Here." She grabs Billy's hand. She tucks something into it, closes his fingers around it. "A little spending money. Look, dreams do come true."

Last thing he wants to do is cry like a big damn baby. She's making him feel all choked up and stuff. He hugs her hard.

"Thanks," he says. "You . . ." He doesn't know if he even has the right words. But Jane Grace, she always understands him.

"Never mind. Go on. Get yourselves out of here."

She's giving him a Gaze Attack. She's sprinkling Monster Blood and Insanity Mist and Spider Venom. She's only using her eyes and her crossed arms, but still. Ginger watches it all from up on the couch where she's not supposed to be.

No Gaze Attack, no Poisons, no Psionics, nor Rays, nor any weapon at all can touch him, though. His energy level is high, but even more importantly, he's taken on an alternate form. He's retained the type and subtype of his original self but seems to have gained the natural weapons, natural armor, and movement modes of his new creature.

"Stop with the mood, old woman."

"You're making a mistake."

"Oh, well, too bad if I am. Now, come here. I only have a minute. The dogs are in the car. Give me a hug and quit being bitter."

"I've never even been to New York."

"If you stop being such a mean old lady, I might take you next time."

"Mr. Made of Money already? You haven't even started your new job yet. How much did your uncle say he'd pay you?"

"None of your business. Anyway, I'll get you a computer, before anything. You're in the freaking Dark Ages."

"You're lucky they made things so sturdy then, unlike now."

"After that, I'll get Mom a real place to rest."

"What are you talking about? She's fine here."

Billy disagrees, but it's an argument for another day. Every time he defies Gran for years to come, they'll battle. But right now, he wants to be gentle, for his own sense of peace, if not for Gran herself. "Give me a hug."

"You know I love you," Gran says, putting her arms around him. It's a strange kind of love, a different version of the word he's not sure he'll ever understand. She leans in. Her body is always smaller than he thinks it'll be.

"I love you, too, even if you're a pain in my ass."

It's hard to drive with a dog on your lap. Billy has to sit tall so he can see around Casper's big white head. Casper pants, and his tongue lolls out of his mouth. "You guys are going to have to get in the back when Mads gets in. We've got a long drive." Jasper's pretty comfy in the passenger seat. His head is out the window, and his nose is up in the air, taking in all the great smells of what's passed and what's coming.

"Best behavior, got it?"

Casper shifts. Billy's leg is going to sleep already.

He drives fast. He'd break the land-speed record if he could. Finally, he reaches Mads's neighborhood. Now he's on her street. "Okay, look. We're here," he tells the dogs. "In the back, you guys. I mean it." There. That was easy. Two giant dog butts shove practically right past his face. The dogs move around back there in excitement.

He knows how they feel, because, damn, man, there she is. Her aunt and uncle are both waiting with her, too, and so is her cousin, Harrison, and that neighbor kid with the big owl eyes. Mads's hair is shiny in the sun. She's leaning against her uncle's truck, with her suitcase beside her. She wears her shorts and that Grateful Dead shirt and her bracelet, and she's so cute, and . . .

What? Oh my God, is she holding what he thinks she's holding?

It's a case. An instrument case! He's so happy, Jesus, he's flare-heat, star energy. He's force times distance, rocket propulsion; leader of the Rebel Alliance against the Galactic Empire. Billy yanks his parking brake.

"Don't go finding a cure for cancer or anything until I get back, okay, Hare?" he hears Mads say through his rolled-down window.

He loves her. He's bursting with it. And he loves her enough to be the guy she might need, so he's ready to get out and talk to Aunt Claire and Uncle Thomas and maybe do some hand-shaking or backslapping or whatever the hell you do in the semi-suburbs. Claire and Thomas seem to have other ideas, though. They're hugging Mads fast, and waving and blowing kisses and making *go, go* gestures like they're in a big hurry. Well, okay. Whatever. There will be other days for backslapping, for sure.

He's half out the door to help her with her bag, but she's already tossed it inside. She scoots into the front seat, settles the instrument case on her lap.

"Floor it," she says.

Whatever she wants. Anything. And hey, that he can do,

because the truck's got speed. He sticks an arm out, waves good-bye to Aunt Claire and Uncle Thomas, and hits the accelerator. In his rearview mirror, he sees Thomas's truck in their driveway, smiling like it's all pleased with itself. Its grin gets smaller in the distance.

"Mads. A violin case," Billy manages to say. He feels so much, he can barely talk.

"Well, saxophone. Do you love it?" She lifts it for a better view.

"I love it so much my heart is going to explode."

"I thought you would." She clicks open the clasps. Raises the top. She fishes through a bunch of underwear, the pretty kind that's the colors of Easter eggs. Somewhere in there, she finds her glasses. She puts them on.

"I love you in your glasses," he says.

"I love you in your plain face," she says.

Jesus, he doesn't know how he can take it. He can't wait to kiss her.

Now she looks over her shoulder. "Hi, guys." Jas and Casper *har har har* their greeting. She scruffs their silky heads, leans way over for dog kisses.

"You know what else I brought?" she asks, searching around in the saxophone case again. He's getting on the freeway, eastbound express lanes, but he sneaks a glance. Two pieces of paper, folded in half.

"What?"

"Museum tickets. You can buy them online ahead of time."

"See, Mads? That's why I chose you for the greatest adventure of our lives. You bring the organization, and I bring . . ." He reaches inside his pocket, no easy trick while he's merging. He tosses all the cash onto the seat beside them. "The cash."

"Also this." She waves two smaller sheets, taped together. He knows what it is. He can see the tiny print and the squares and rectangles of rooms and hallways. "From my own book."

"Two maps are good. Every person needs one. What are we going to see first, Mads, huh? That awesome bed?"

"I don't know. I think we should look for the angel first."

Yeah. That's exactly what they should do. "You got it."

His mom's station has God for a DJ, because look what's playing. Fate loves the right music at the right moment, doesn't it? Any new lover or brokenhearted one will tell you that. And here it is, a favorite song of Billy's, the Simon and Garfunkel one about the bridge and the troubled water and the rough times. The being weary and the being there. He always turns the radio up, like he does now, when he hears it.

More stuff will come, so much more. Good, bad, downright fantastic; sorry mistakes and shiny triumphs—all that, plus. But never mind the glorious mess that's the future. Right then, Billy is full of so much love and hope that even the doctor in his head has to shield his eyes from the brightness. Poor sucker, he's never seen such light.

"Hey, Mads," Billy says. "I was thinking we could stop and get married. Maybe somewhere in Montana."

Mads looks at him like he's crazy. She makes that little

scoff in the back of her throat. My God, she's adorable with that saxophone case on her lap. "It's way too soon for that, and you know it."

"On the way home, then."

Mads smiles and shakes her head like she just cannot believe him. She takes his hand.

It's a hurdle, but so what. So the hell what. He's crossed so many bigger ones.

ACKNOWLEDGMENTS

No book would be complete without thanks to my dear long-time agent, Ben Camardi. Special thanks, too, to my dual editors: Sara Sargent, whose talent and insight made this a better book, and Liesa Abrams, kindred spirit, whose support is invaluable. My books and I are lucky to have you.

Big thanks once again to my S&S clan. I appreciate every single one of you: Jon Anderson, Mara Anastas, Mary Marotta, Lucille Rettino, Carolyn Swerdloff, Jennifer Romanello, Michelle Leo, Anthony Parisi, Candace McManus and Betsy Bloom, Jessica Handelman, Regina Flath, Katherine Devendorf, Julie Doebler, Teresa Ronquillo, and Matt Pantoliano. Also double-hugs and gratitude to Christina Pecorale, Leah Hays, Victor Iannone, Christine Foye, and the rest of the sales team at S&S. Readers, these people are the best.

Love and thanks to my family, as ever: Paul Caletti, Evie Caletti, Jan Caletti, Sue Rath, Mitch Rath, and Tyler and Hunter Rath. And most especially Sam Bannon and Nick Bannon, who belong on the first page, the last page, and every page in between, and John Yurich, sweet husband, patient friend, love of my life.